Praise for *The Sound of Everything*

'Rebecca Henry is a rare precocious talent. She has an incredible ear for dialogue and I'm excited to read what she produces next.'   Alex Wheatle, author of *Crongton Knights*

'A stunning new voice. Outstanding, complex writing. So pleased this book is here!'

Patrice Lawrence, author of *Orangeboy*

'What a voice! I can't believe the author is so young and that this is her debut. The writing has such confidence... a remarkably accomplished debut from a truly talented author.'

Jenny Downham, author of *Furious Thing*

'Fizzing with energy and purpose, a vibrant new voice in UK YA'

Lisa Williamson, author of *The Art of Being Normal*

THE SOUND OF EVERYTHING

Rebecca Henry

Published in the UK by Everything with Words Limited
Fifth Floor, 30–31 Furnival Street, London, EC4A 1JQ

www.everythingwithwords.com

A catalogue record of this book is available
from the British Library.

ISBN   978–1–911427–15–5

This novel is entirely a work of fiction.
The names, characters, events are the work of the author's imagination.
Any resemblance to actual persons, living or dead
is entirely coincidental.

Printed and bound in Great Britain by
CPI Group (UK) Ltd, Croydon CRO 4YY

I live by the rules to protect myself – and everyone else.

It's simple:

1. Don't count on anyone.
2. Act. Always act.
3. Be prepared to lose everything.

Kadie

> I'm nobody! Who are you?
> Are you nobody too?
> Then there's a pair of us! – don't tell!
> They'd banish us, you know!
>
> How dreary to be somebody!
> How public, like a frog
> To tell your name the livelong day
> To an admiring Bog!
>
> Emily Dickinson

ONE

I can tell from the get-go when I'm not wanted. When you're just another foster kid, sometimes it seems like eventually everyone stops caring – except to get chatty patty about you before you've even walked in the door.

I'm one of those girls. People know about me before they meet me.

I'd like to think that Mr Tucker sat me at the front of his history class to make sure I'm doing okay. It's probably more like he was given a folder labelled *Kadie Hunte* which advised him to sit me under his nose where he could keep one eye trained on me.

At the moment I'm actually supposed to be a Lucas, but I've always kept my real name. I rock back in my chair and test it in my head. *Kadie Lucas*. It has a good ring. I could fit in. I've got standings. Aside from the whole rapper/singer thing, my fashion sense is on point and I live in the same house as Miss Popularity.

'Kadie!' An explosion on the desk in front of me jolts me back into perspective. I start, dropping my chair back into place, and ball my hands into tight fists. Mr Tucker has a thing with whacking wooden board rubbers on the desks to get people's attention. I'm pretty sure I felt some reverb in my bones.

'Remind me when the Suffragette movement was.' He taps the board rubber insistently on the desk. I've only been at this school three weeks but I know he won't stop until I've given him my attention.

I grit my teeth. 'Stop banging that stupid piece of wood!'

Mr Tucker's eyebrows shoot up. He stops banging the board rubber. 'Lose the earphones and pay attention. Next time I see them you're staying after school – and that's me being ridiculously lenient. Open your ears and listen to me.'

I manage to resist the urge to roll my eyes. Listening is effort, and for the most part, I don't do effort.

'Look at me when I'm talking to you!' Mr Tucker leans closer. 'Do I need to repeat myself?'

I reluctantly pull the ear bud out of my left ear. Background noise leaks into my brain, squeezing my thoughts into the corners of my head. Feet shuffling; a whirring somewhere; the road outside the open window. I can push the noise out if I want, but it's less effort to slouch here and listen to the bits of the world that nobody else seems to hear. Instead, my free hand spins my pen around my thumb repeatedly without stopping. It's the only adept thing I can do with my fingers.

'So. The Suffragette movement?' Mr Tucker prompts. His voice still dominates the battlefield of noises, but it could easily get lost like a generic face in a crowd.

I shrug. 'Beats me.'

'Think about it.'

'I'm thinking hard.'

'Think harder.'

I suck my teeth. 'Aren't there twenty other kids you can ask?' I twist around in my seat. 'Does anyone else know when the Suffragette movement was?'

There's a shifting of bodies, a few snickers, and some murmurs. I catch a glimpse of Shadavia – the totally snazzy, straight-A-grades, head of the school council, Miss Popularity. I'm kinda honoured to be her foster sister. I mean, if it weren't for her I'd already have dropped to the negatives on the social scale. She's right there acting like some goody-two-shoes but she's trying to keep a straight face. A row forward from her, her mate Eisha is hiding a smirk behind the ends of her cane rows.

I smile sweetly at Mr Tucker. 'Let's take that as a yes. You can carry on now. Ask someone else.'

He's red in the face. 'Excuse me? Who's the teacher here?'

I curl my lip at him. 'You are. So teach.'

His eye twitches. 'Go and stand outside. You're obviously not mature enough to be in here.'

'Let's not talk about maturity,' I sigh, rolling my eyes – but really I'm proper glad for a reason to get out. Usually I'd just leave when I feel like it, go for a walk (this has been a major cause for trouble in my behaviour history), but the way the desks are oriented, I can't get out without shoving past four other people.

I grab my bag and drop my pen in it. I never take out my whole pencil case, because I know I'll just spill everything everywhere.

Mr Tucker folds his arms. 'Kadie, if you walk out that's an automatic hour detention.'

'So? It's nearly the end of the lesson anyway and I've read this chapter of the text book.'

'I find that hard to believe.'

'Believe it. I'll quote you if you don't give me detention.' I shove my way out of the aisle, tripping over chair legs as I go. Smooth.

'An hour detention or fifteen minutes of lesson?' he asks, almost nicely.

I wish. But my hand's already on the door. 'How about a complete recital of chapter five instead of the detention?'

'It doesn't work that way.'

'Obviously.' I slam the door behind me.

The corridor is blissfully peaceful compared to the classroom. I slump against the wall for a second and close my eyes. There's never a moment's rest for my brain. If it's not the endless pushing of background noise, or the crushing presence of other people, I'm smoking off all the anxiety or bingeing on Red Bull. Thankfully, there's just enough time left of last period for me to have a zoot before I go home and pretend I don't smoke at all.

At the other end of the hall, a boy bursts through the double doors. As usual, he's an absolute mess. His trousers are almost below his bum – don't know how he gets away with that – but get this: he has a belt. This means he's bussing them low like that for pure style – which is just sad, and only gets sadder when you add in his weird walk that's like a cross between a lumbering child and a roadman swagger. He does have nice lips – hence his nickname, Lips, by which people refer to him more often than his real name – but I can't even take his lips seriously because they seem to be stuck in this annoying half-smile which he wears all the time.

I glare. 'What?'

The half-smile drops right off his face. He shoots back, 'What are you looking at?'

'Your face.'

'You are as cocky as they say.' Lips circles round me, inspecting, his half-smile now quirking the opposite way. 'Are you a sket, like they say?' His eyes pause at my chest and my cheeks burn – I unbuttoned my shirt at the beginning of last period and I unbuttoned it kind of wide. Not because I'm a sket. There are moments when I just need a little space from seams and buttons. I didn't think much of it at the time.

'Believe what you want.' I shrug. 'I did beat up a girl at my last school, like they say.'

He snorts. 'So you're a *vindictive* sket. Rah. Bet you feel really good about yourself.'

'You're a klutz,' I retort. 'You need to decide whether you want to walk like a roadman or a toddler.'

'Ooh. An *unkind*, vindictive sket. I'm really scared.'

I stomp past, giving him a deliberate barge.

'Bet you didn't really beat on anyone!' he calls after me. 'Not with hair that neat!'

I smile and slide my hand into the zipped pocket of my jacket, where Emerson sits, cold and heavy. I'd get kicked out even if they just found him, let alone if I backed the blade in public. But he makes me feel strong. Invincible.

*

They're leaving without me. I can see them through the crowds which I'm trying to navigate without touching anyone. None of them look behind. Nobody stops to wait for me.

I catch them up somehow just outside the school gate, where the throng of blue blazers is spilling out along the path and crossing the road in waves. Shadavia and the girls are just beyond the bus stop – it's easy to spot them since Kelly's dark red hair sticks out and I know that she'll be directly next to Shadavia. Sure enough, Shadavia's at the front with Kelly, Raquel and Eisha bringing up the rear, and they're clearly not missing me.

It's Raquel who turns first, in time to see some younger girl kicking off because I accidently bumped into her really hard on my way past. I ignore her. My mind's going at a hundred

6

miles per hour – a Red Bull and zoot can do that to you – and I crash into the two of them a bit faster than I meant to. 'You lot tryna leave without me?'

Raquel acts dumb. 'What? Nah!'

'Yes! You think I'm blind?'

Eisha makes a face. 'Shadavia said you texted to say you'd catch us up.'

'Riiight.' I pop a stick of bubblegum in my mouth and offer some to the girls. Eisha happily takes. Raquel does too, but she's watching me like I'm up to something. I'm not.

Up front, Kelly and Shadavia are chatting about Kelly's sweet sixteen party at the weekend. It takes me about twelve taps on Shadavia's shoulder before she turns around. 'What?'

'You want gum?'

Her face softens. 'Yeah, sure.' She takes some and so does Kelly, but Kelly does so almost like it's an obligation. Why would she bother taking any if she's going to look so sullen about it? She gets that look whenever she's within three feet of me, like I smell or something. I noticed that right from the start, and I also clocked that behind that sprinkling of freckles and set of angelic eyes, she can pull a seriously sarcastic lip-curl sort of expression. She might be slightly petite, but her presence certainly isn't.

As soon as we're out of the crowds I start singing. Can't help it. I'm on a high – my energy's soaring like I've regained what I lost during the lesson. Kelly is playing music out loud from her phone and I roll with the vibe. I know all the latest tracks and the lyrics just spill out of me. Knowing lyrics isn't nothing new, especially not to me – there are always those artists that everyone's listening to – but I'm on a different level and it's a wonder anyone sings along with me. Don't know how I do it – somehow, after a little while Eisha is joining in, and then Raquel, until next thing I know Shadavia's like, 'Spit sixteen bars!'

So I do.

Then I take a break to breathe and Kelly stops the music.

Everyone looks at her.

'What are you doing?' I pretend to flick her.

'Way to kill a good vibe,' complains Raquel.

Kelly shrugs. 'My battery's low.'

That's a lie. She was charging it in fourth period.

'Spoilsport alert!' I call out.

Kelly snorts. 'Calm yourself. You're high.'

She's right about that. I'm feeling a vibe that's hardly really there. There's this underlying tension that's got me wondering how many months – maybe even weeks – these girls will be my friends for. And I really don't want to feel it but it's still poking a hole in my bubble, cos I can see the way Kelly's clocking me and that's when I really know for sure – the same way I can tell when I'm really not wanted – that she and I are going to have a whole heap of trouble.

TWO

It wasn't my idea to go to Kelly's party. It was all Shadavia.

'You need to get out and get to know people,' she'd announced, waltzing into my room. She was already dressed up in a cute top and jeans, her green bomber jacket peppered with random badges and old bottle tops, a pink sparkly slide holding her hair out of her face. If it was anyone else, this would be weird. Shadavia somehow gets away with these things.

I didn't take off my headphones at first, or turn the volume down. I was checking out this Lips kid's YouTube channel. He does parodies, reaction videos and other entertainment as a character called Kwame, a complete loser trying to get his come-up with a very critical father.

Shadavia didn't even notice that I was in the middle of a very entertaining video.

'Come on!' she exclaimed. 'There'll be mandem from sixth form and stuff. There's got to be a boy in this borough who'll go out with you.' She threw open my wardrobe doors and started picking through my stuff, admiring the abandoned hoverboard sitting on top of my piles of shoes. Don't ask me why my dad bought me that. Hoverboard, Segway, self-balancing scooter, whatever you want to call it – it's the perfect illustration of exactly how little anyone knows about me. My dad, along with a handful of past foster dads, has often bought me the most expensive things. Even Shadavia was impressed when she first saw my collection of chains and clothes. I'd exchange it all for a real dad any day.

I blew out a breath. 'Everyone already knows me. And if I want the four-one-one, all I have to do is hit Snapchat.'

'We need a DJ.'

'Can't you just put on a Spotify playlist?'

'Kadiiiiieeee.' She dragged my name out extra long. 'Come on, I promise it won't be bad.'

'There gonna be drinks?'

'Bruh, Kelly knows how to throw a party.'

I gave her a long look and almost went back to my magazine. Almost.

It was a pretty good offer. If I wanted to fit in the clique, I needed to be at this thing – but I knew exactly what it was going to be. Everybody full-on raving and me in the corner or outside, trying to drink away all my worries.

I very nearly said no. But Shadavia was sitting on my desk chair giving me cute-puppy-eyes from behind her glasses and just waiting. That was what did it. She wanted me around – she was *begging* me. Who knew how long that would last?

So that's how I ended up walking out the door by her side, swag on point, Shadavia looking like the older sister with her long legs and me in my baseball jersey and gold. I'm lighter-skinned than Shadavia and we don't even low key look like each other. But I can still pretend that we're sisters.

*

There is a lot of twerking and jumping around like dogs. This is what happens when you leave yutes unsupervised with lots of alcohol and a good sound system.

Kelly's house is one of those grand modern ones trying to look like it's Tudor or Victorian or something but totally renovated and modern on the inside: sparkling kitchen counter tops and proper wooden floors, a massive TV rigged up to a speaker system that has the beat thumping all over the house. There's nowhere to escape it. The place is bursting with kids – the living room especially hardly has any room for breathing, around all the drinks held high, the lingering waft of sweaty teenagers and other things.

The kitchen is pretty much empty apart from people ducking in and out to raid the food and drinks collection, and that's exactly why I am holed up in there after three hours of hard-core partying – in my case better known as *pretending* I know how to dance. This is much easier to do when I've lost count of the number of drinks I've had, although I'm not actually sure what it is I've been glugging since I got in the door. Cider? Vodka and Coke? Unfortunately, getting wasted does nothing for the situation with me and large, loud groups of people. Three hours has proved to be my max today. Why?

Ask me when I'm sober. All I know is I'm done hanging out on the dance floor with the armpit smell.

There's only one other person who doesn't seem to be enjoying the revelry and he's slouching at the other end of the kitchen counter, wrapped up in his bomber jacket despite the pressing heat, sipping from a large cup. It might be something to do with Josh's boys – I'm pretty sure I saw Ellis giving him a hard time over his dancing, which is dumb, because his skanking was quite good. Usually he's hovering alongside these boys who make up a music group called Amalgamandem, or AMD, but the last I saw of the other three was in the mosh pit in the living room.

I get up to get my fifth cupcake. 'What's the matter? Ain't got a girl?'

Lips turns his head just enough for me to see his perfect poker face. 'Nah, I just don't like Post Malone.'

'Suuuure. So if I went and made a request just for you, you'd go out there and party?'

'No,' says Lips, 'and neither would you.'

He's right and I'd rather he wasn't. But I'm also intrigued. How did he pick up on what everyone else is oblivious to?

'What makes you say that, Mr-I-Know-Everything-About-You?'

He puts his cup down. 'Nothing.'

Nothing.

I suck my teeth. 'But you're not enjoying yourself.'

'Who says?'

12

I laugh even though nothing is funny. 'Bruv, look at you chilling on your own. Did the mandem drag you along?'

Lips tries not to look disconcerted. 'Nah.'

'Then go out there and party.'

'Ditto.'

'Excuse me?'

'You were over there looking like your rabbit just died,' he says, gesturing to my corner by the microwave. 'So you can't talk.'

'Tch. Shut up and go get a girl.'

A little smile creeps onto Lips' face. He eases himself up and steps closer to me, leaning casually on the counter. 'Yeah? Looks like I got one stood right in front of me.'

And I'm just about to explain to him how I am useless at whining, twerking, and all other forms of gyrating, when somebody swoops in and wraps their sizeable arms around my hips and says in a bad Spanish accent, 'Hola, señorita.'

Josh.

He spins me around and kisses my chest through my shirt. I wrap my arms around his neck and hang off him. My legs are just about holding me up as it is.

Lips looks down at me and the half-smile on his face dies slowly.

Josh scoffs at Lips. 'Find your own ting. I've got Goldilocks.'

Lips' smile disappears completely. He glances at us once more and walks off, muttering, 'She's not a thing.'

Josh walks his fingers down my thigh. I push him off.

Playing hard to get is an exhausting game, even if it's because he needs to know that his hands cannot just wander where they like. People only get that kind of freedom with me when they've proved themselves worthy.

'Why are you out here?' he demands.

'It's bare loud,' I remind him, because no one can deny that it is. 'We could go outside though.'

'Outside? Aren't you gonna be cold?'

'Nah. I'm making a fashion statement.'

He looks me over, smiling cheekily. 'Well, yeah. Short-shorts in September? Come on. It's not summer anymore.'

'I'm not cold.'

'Well, shorts and long sleeves are still a mad combo.'

'S'just how I roll, innit.'

Josh snickers. He doesn't interrogate me like I expected. He nods in time to the music, his mop of curls bouncing, and then grabs my hand suddenly. 'Let's go outside.'

He tows me through the crowds to the back of the house, totally unaware of me trying desperately not to bump into people and tripping over my own feet and elbowing others in the process, until we're out into the cool of the garden where the air is less clogged and dusk is falling. He finds us a bench by the fence, dusts away crispy leaves and old twigs before seating himself. He pats his lap and I sit on his knees. Somewhere to the east someone's having an autumn barbecue and the smell of frying meat is just reaching over Kelly's back fence.

Josh links our fingers and squeezes my hands beautifully tight. 'Is it quiet enough for you now?'

The world continues to sing with the sound of the city, and I can hear it all better now: birds tweeting goodnight songs, the stream of cars scuttling by on the main road, a distant child protesting. It's not drowned out by the heavy bass of Kelly's Spotify playlist, though of course that is still pouring heavily out of the open back door.

'You're weird,' Josh says, like this is news to me.

'I know.'

'And peng.'

'I wish you'd just call me pretty.'

He guffaws. 'You've also got swag.'

'I know that too.'

'And your hair actually kind of is gold.'

I smile. 'That's why they call me Goldilocks.'

He lets his fingers trail from the dip-dye at the ends to the real highlights at the roots – courtesy of my Caucasian half. He has no idea how much close bonding with the gel and the straighteners it took to pull this off, but his genuineness still warms me.

Josh pulls me forward so that our faces are a lot, lot closer together. The sort of close where I can feel his breath on my nose and it tingles, and I can smell the vodka and Coke. The kind of close where his hands are wandering places again. He has a particular thing about my legs. His fingers are light, and I get the feeling this is meant to be all romantic. Actually, it's more like spiders crawling down my legs. Kissing is a very attractive distraction technique, but instead I rest my forehead on Josh's and let him mentally salivate over the idea of it. He tries and I let him briefly before easing a gap between us. Yep, playing hard to get is hard work.

The hands stop wandering but my mind doesn't stop running at a hundred miles per hour. Where is this going? I shouldn't care but I do. Because I need people on my side before everything starts to crumble and so far, Josh looks like a pretty good asset. But there's a reason I didn't start anything. I've learned the hard way that even though having a man might mean having that someone to stick up for you, it's also a fast track to being found out.

Josh pulls away, but his hands are still wandering over my body and it's proper difficult to ignore the way he's rubbing my legs. I ping his curls one by one, but it feels like we're both playing a very confusing game.

'Come on. Let's go get drinks.' Josh slides me off his lap, but I shake my head and plop back down on the bench. No way am I going back in there. I've been pinched and grabbed and pushed enough for one night.

After a moment of indecision, Josh goes off to get us some drinks. I watch him go, fighting that little bubble of fear in the back of my head that's telling me he won't come back. That he doesn't really like me, that it's just a drunk party thing. There's also that little side asking, do I want it to be more than that?

Heart says yes. Heart wants love and friends.

Head says no. Head follows the rules.

I live by the rules to protect myself – and everyone else. It's simple:

1. Don't count on anyone.
2. Act. Always act.
3. Be prepared to lose everything.

Head says follow the rules.

But Josh.

After five minutes pass and my head's a bit clearer, I slowly shuffle back towards the house and shove my way back through the hustle and bustle of the 'dance floor', where there seems to be some sort of dance-off going on. I head to the upstairs bathroom, about to burst with my high drinks count. No sign of Lips.

I take a moment to appreciate the relative quiet of the bathroom before I let myself out. Josh is probably waiting and if I don't want to waste all my work getting him to think I'm worth it, I better hop skip and jump.

But I stay there, standing on the landing, listening to the bass resonate through the house, mingling with conversations and bad singing. I probably hear the footsteps, but I don't really register them – I'm too busy wondering if there's a switch in my head I can flick to make the party atmosphere less suffocating. Next thing I know some boy – Ellis, the one who hangs out with Josh – has his fingers in my bag, which is round at my back, hitched right up under my armpit. I twist and shove him off, but he's already found my Oyster card and is still smirking and waving it well out of my reach. 'What you gonna do, babes?'

Ellis is like a brick with a belly, so I swat him right in the centre of his softness where I know he's a bit sensitive. Keep it playful. Lay the dimple on him. 'Give it, mister.'

'Mister?' Ellis laughs, flattered. I snatch my Oyster card back. One point to Goldilocks.

The music changes from Smoke Boyz into something by Kojo Funds, and suddenly Ellis is bopping and asking me to dance. The word dance makes me feel a bit queasy – my head's all over the place. I just want to go outside again.

Ellis spreads his arm for a hug. 'Come on. One dance?' His fingers dance brushing the back of my leg. I smack his hand away.

He gives me a funny look. 'You're jumpy.'

'Don't touch me like that. Don't touch me at all.'

'Like this?' He tickles my leg.

'Yes!' I swat at him, but he chases me around the landing brushing me in all the most uncomfortable places. I try to dodge him, to go downstairs – stuff like that, to go full stop – but Ellis plays about, messing me around and then suddenly acting apologetic. 'Hey, I'm sorry. Truce. Truce, babes.'

'Just let me go, man.'

'Why you fobbing me off?' He tries to put his arms

18

around me. 'One dance. Come on. We don't even have to go downstairs.'

He reaches for my waist and somehow misses.

I only meant to push him off, but the line was proper crossed and so my fist shoots out too. Bullseye – right on the jaw. Ellis' head jerks back, followed by his shoulders and his windmilling arms.

And then he falls down the stairs.

He thuds to the bottom awkwardly, crunching and banging against the wall, lands on his forearms at the bottom and half slides across the floor into some boys. Then people are shouting and laughing and filming and a few girls crouch by him to see if he's okay – which apparently he is, somehow – and meanwhile I'm just frozen at the top of the stairs, like, how did this even happen?

Josh pops out of the crowd, drink in hand, and stops abruptly when he sees Ellis kissing the floor. His eyes trail up the stairs until they meet mine, silently asking me what everyone wants to know.

I put on a screw-face and stomp down. My feet can just about find the stairs, so it's a relief when Josh reaches a hand out to steady me and lets me fall on him. I cling onto him, glad for something stable to keep me upright. I cling onto him because I don't think I can quite see straight. Not because he kissed me. Not because my heart is naively hoping that he could be different.

'What's going on?' Josh asks, glancing at Ellis.

'He slipped.' My tongue is heavy. I'm ready to go home. Can't deny that.

Kelly pushes her way out of the crowd. 'What's going on?' She clocks me and Josh and sneers, 'Why you sucking up to this troublemaker?'

Josh rolls his eyes and says nothing, so naturally, Kelly turns on me. She gestures angrily at Ellis and demands, 'What d'you think you're doing?'

I don't know what I'm doing, so I'm not entirely sure how she expects me to answer this. I try and push past her but she shoves me back at the stairs. 'Don't come trying to start beef in my place!'

All I want to do is get out of here – I'm on the edge as it is, and having her up in my face isn't helping even remotely. I slap her. Kelly slaps me right back. The air is pressing on me. People are too close and the room is hot with the tension. My face burns where Kelly's hand hit me.

She shoves me again, all, 'Well? Got nothing to say for yourself?'

I stumble back into the wall – extra-clumsily thanks to all that whatever-it-is that I've been drinking. Ellis is up on his knees now, emphatically telling Kelly to get that sket – and she does. Flying fists and cussing and her sharp nails clawing me.

I've always liked the whole pushing and jostling thing. Play-fighting or even the real thing – it's a great attitude burner. I used to get into bare fights just for the sake of it when

I was younger. You fight and people decide they don't want to mess with you. But real fighting is never on my agenda, not when I'm so out of sync. I don't drink and then fight, let's put it that way.

Kelly gets her fingers in my hair and pulls. I don't really feel the pain but a guttural shriek explodes out of me as if it's a reflex – and then I'm going for her face. Only I can't seem to land my hands or feet in the right place. *Don't drink and fight,* my logic reminds me. Too late. But there's no way I'm losing this – phones are out – so I hock up this big lump of throaty phlegm, splat, on Kelly's chest. She stops and gasps as if I've just smashed her mother's best china.

Then Josh steps directly between us, arms spread, drink sloshing onto the floor. 'That's enough!'

Kelly cusses loudly. 'Are you seriously defending this beg?'

Josh swigs from his cup, thrusts it into some girl's hands, and turns to grab my fists. 'I said enough, Goldilocks.' He pulls me close and walks me backwards through the crowd, away from the screw-faced Kelly, who hollers, 'Sometimes you're a real idiot, you know that?'

Josh ignores her and shuffles me towards the porch. He kisses me all over my face, ending with my lips almost shyly. Those kisses make and break me. They are for Goldilocks: the girl on my Instagram, the girl who was raving and pretending she knows how to dance. Not for the girl who wants to go home.

But I can't break Rule #2 as well so I act like I'm

really into it, like I'm proper simmering with rage still. I'm simmering alright, but it's with something worse than rage.

I step back from Josh and clench my fists to contain the burning in my palms. 'I need to go.' But I don't even know if he heard me, my voice is that small. He's too busy staring at the gap between our hands, bewildered and unsure if he's allowed to touch my fingers again. As if I've broken some important bond – which maybe I have. But then I'm just doing what I have to do. Don't count on anyone. Play hard to get. I've dangled the fish; let's see if he comes after it.

Kelly steps through the crowds. 'Get out!' she barks.

Josh glances at her. 'You get out.'

Kelly ignores him and sneers at me. 'Get out. Of. My. House.'

'I haven't done nothing.'

'Just get out, you little sket! We don't need you offloading any of your dirty vibes.' She yanks Josh away, missing how he reaches for my hand once more.

I'm about to break with the effort of holding myself together. There's no way I can let this end on a bad note. Everyone is watching. This has to end the Goldilocks way. Short, sharp and sweet.

'Whatever. I ate all the good cupcakes anyway.' I spit again, right at Kelly's feet. It lands with a satisfying splat on the carpet and that's the last I see of the party before I slam the door between us: jeering and jostling kids trying to get a snap of the scene over Kelly's shoulder.

The euphoria leaves this warmth in my chest. It's just enough to momentarily lift the stress swirling round my head. Just enough to remind me about that gap between who they think I am and who I really am.

THREE

I don't wake with a start. Nah, it's more like a slow and uncomfortable shift from dark dreams to the dark night. The towel I always lie on has this nasty prickly feeling through my shorts at the best of times, but now it's a *damp* prickly towel, and my clothes are clinging to me with that vile wet warmth that a peed-up bed gives you. This is a thing that happens whenever it wants to, the only predictor being a change of placement, but even though it hasn't happened for a while, the familiarity aches.

I repeat the same clumsy routine: fumbling around blindly in my wardrobe for clean sheets, washing off the stickiness with ice-cold water at the bathroom sink, grabbing a onesie and carting the smelly stuff downstairs to the washing machine at arm's length.

I'm setting the washing machine for a hot wash when I hear another pair of feet creaking their way down the stairs. The padding gets a little louder until a tall shadow pops around the corner. I can tell who it is straight away – I see stupidly well in the dark. But obviously the shadow can't tell it's me, because the light flips on. I screw my eyes shut, but the sudden brightness still punches through my eyelids.

'Oh, it's you making all the noise,' says Vince.

'Yeah, it's me.' I cover my face with one arm and look vaguely in his direction. His 'fro, which is fashioned like an upside down capital T, looks even more ridiculous with his Superman pyjamas, even without the large glasses he normally wears. If the light wasn't singeing my retina, I'd probably be laughing at him.

'Quiet as a drunk elephant, you are,' Vince says.

I thought I *was* being quiet. 'Am not.'

'Are too.'

'You should get some ear plugs.'

'You should just learn to be quiet.'

I groan and turn back to the washing machine. It's three in the morning and I barely slept even when I was unconscious. I'm really not in the mood.

Vince steps further into the room. 'What are you washing anyway, at this time?' He peers closer. 'Bed sheets?'

I scoot around him and switch off the light before he can get a proper look.

'Are those bed sheets?' he demands.

I shrug. Act casual. 'I spilled Coke on the bed. Wanted to get it out before it stains.'

'Yeah? And you were soooo desperate, you had to wash it at three am?' Vince snickers. 'I bet you peed the bed.'

'I don't care what you think, so long as you keep your trap shut,' I hiss.

'Where's the excitement in telling people you wet the bed?' he whispers. 'There's already nuff stupid rumours about you.'

'I don't know. Just don't bother.'

He follows me back up the stairs. 'I won't, no worries. No one will know that Goldilocks wets the bed.'

At the top, he catches me by the arm. 'Is it true you pushed some boy down the stairs at Kelly's party?'

It was only three nights ago now, but after the hangover it feels like way longer than that. 'He slipped.' The lie rolls off my tongue too easily. 'He was messing me around and he stepped back, and we were at the top of the stairs, so . . . yeah.'

Vince grins and shakes his head slowly, like an adult that can't quite fathom kids' behaviour. 'One of Josh's boys, right? They're a bunch of idiots anyway. Don't worry about it.'

'I wasn't.'

He grins. 'I saw it on Snapchat but I wasn't quite sure if it was you.'

'Yeah.'

'Respect.'

'Respect?'

'Yeah. Sometimes the goons need to know their place.' He play-punches me. 'As long as you don't push me down the stairs.'

'I wouldn't do that.'

'I'm too nice.'

Too nice.

Ha.

*

Beverly never talks about her music lessons, and judging by the way she's plonking angrily at the piano she doesn't like them very much. If only she could understand the chance she's been given.

Mummy always wanted a piano. Hey, she even wanted a keyboard, but by the time she could afford one, it was irrelevant. She taught me the music notes by singing them instead, and then when I was old enough, she drew out the keyboard so that at least we could pretend. She'd be proud of me if she knew I even managed to get some piano lessons at one of my placements. I don't know how happy she'd be to know that I didn't do that great. Yeah, I tried, but even though I understood the theory from day one, I didn't pick up the rest of it before it was time to move. You don't know what you had until you've lost it.

Someone needs to explain this to Beverly. The way she's plinky-plonking William Tell out of the piano just makes me feel a bit sad. Which is not helpful, given the current state of play.

Charmaine, my foster mum, comes to rally me from my perch on the stairs where I've been inching my way down on my bum. For a mother of four kids, she still manages to look like she means business. Today she's donning a crisp purple shirt rolled up at the sleeves – ironed by the looks of it – and jeans that look casual but not too casual. She's cane-rowed her hair too and it looks sweet, the braids sweeping over her left shoulder.

Charmaine puts her hands on her hips and gives me her usual soft smile. 'Kadie, you need to have some breakfast.'

It almost makes me laugh when foster parents say I *need* to do something. What do they know? They clearly don't know that breakfast is not on the top of my priority list. What is? In reality, the list is too long to go through, but if one thing's for sure, breakfast is way down near the bottom. A zoot hits close to the top because if I get one in before school, I can float my way through the day in a lazy trance. Lately, sleep has been evading me, so by the time morning comes around that hits nearly number one on the priority list. I'm tired – not just physically, but of everything. I could lie in bed for the rest of my life, dreaming about good days gone by, and be happy.

But Charmaine doesn't take no for an answer.

I shuffle down to the kitchen doorway and stand there reluctantly. How five people can make breakfast sound like peak time at Maccy's I'm not sure, but somehow they're managing. A pile of assorted healthy lunch snacks, all homemade, sits on the table for the pickings, with lunchbox bits, utensils and half-made breakfasts scattered around it. Vince's uniform is draped over the back of a chair and he seems to have lost his tie in the pile of washing Charmaine is (or was) loading into the machine. The dishwasher rumbles in the background because I forgot to put it on last night, and it smells like somebody's toast is burning. Amando is dressed up in his work overalls, trying to balance a stack of lunch containers against his chest and looks like he's about to spill the tower everywhere.

'Daddy, let me help.' Shadavia saves his yoghurt from falling and helps him to transfer the pile to his bag. She has her dad's eyes and her mum's smile, something she attested to on Instagram which I admit I was jealous of. *Daddy*. Ugh. *I have to call him Amando.*

My daddy wouldn't let me call him Daddy. After disappearing before I was even old enough to remember him, he then spent three years banging on the door to our flat, spewing out a multitude of stories: he wanted to make it up to us; he could take some of the pressure off; I deserved to meet him; I deserved to know I had a father. Obviously I didn't deserve any more than that, because as soon as I was up in his house, it was, 'You can call me Saul. Or it might be confusing for the girls.'

The girls being his *other* daughters. The half sisters. For him, the "half" was probably justification enough to disown me. For the most difficult four months of my life, I was a shadow in his house. I went to school, I came home, I did as I was told like a zombie, and I cried myself to sleep nearly every night. The only time he hugged me was when I started throwing things around the bedroom and his wife was too wimpy to restrain me. She wasn't even concerned when my anger dissolved into tears.

He left it to the day before it was happening to tell me, his voice as soft as when he tried to comfort me at Mummy's funeral. Except this time it had a sort of emptiness, as if he'd decided to detach himself from something. *It's not working*, he had explained. *This house just isn't big enough. There are other places that are probably better for you.* He sat in front of me and fired excuse after excuse. Years ago, he had desperately painted a fake picture of a daddy who cared sincerely from the other side of Mummy's front door, and then he erased it within hours.

I've never had a dad that I could call Daddy.

With a begrudging sigh, I enter the kitchen and head for the box of fake Shreddies, aka 'Malt Wheaties'. It was definitely a shocker to move here and be told that in this household, *fake* Shreddies are a treat, not an everyday occurrence. Charmaine's been buying me fake Shreddies on the agreement that I'll transfer to something healthier by the end of this month.

I pour half a bowl of fake Shreddies and a cup of milk. The chaos of the kitchen is enough to distract me from my breakfast, but everyone is so engrossed in other things that I could sit here for fifteen minutes behind a book and probably get away with not eating. Amando comes back, ruffling all his children's hair except mine. Instead, he pauses noticeably and pats me hard on the shoulder. I give him a nod.

I pick the fake Shreddies out of the bowl one by one and dip them in the milk (I prefer them crunchy). I'm about halfway through and a glance at the clock tells me there's no way I'm going to finish in time to leave with Shadavia, so I down the milk and tip the rest of the Shreddies back in the packet when no one's looking. The thought of school kind of puts me off anyway.

By the time it's third period, I'm massaging the scars with one thumb – around and around and up and down over the marred skin – and reminding myself what I promised myself when I moved.

Thing is, when Emerson was given to me, I never meant to use him on myself. It was meant to be a self-defence thing. A scare prop. For respect, that's why he was given to me – Emerson was probably the closest thing to a friendship bracelet that I ever got from anyone. Whenever I daydream, I remember that placement clear as crystal. Megan – Megz when she was with me – placing it in my palm like a promise. *Show them you're tough.* It was a joke at the time – I had a lot going for me during those six months and besides, the two of us got too many good grades to do something petty like back out a knife at school. We wanted to do something like start a doodling club. Nobody took this seriously. Nobody seemed to take anything seriously with me until I was moving out.

I rub my forearm. Around and around. Up and down. I'm

out of it, no question. There's a faint headache hovering in my temples. Later, it will probably be a migraine.

Mrs Wells gives me a *pick-up-your-pen-and-work* screwface. That woman hated me from the moment I walked in the door on day one. Told me straight off to get my earphones out, put my tie on properly and don't let her see me looking so bedraggled in her classroom ever again or I'll get a detention. She's probably just passive-aggressive because she knows everyone hates RE. Or maybe she's just seen the front page of the *Kadie Hunte* folder and formed her opinions from there.

I make myself stay still until Mrs Wells shifts her attention. Then I slump in my chair, sliding down until my legs are sticking out far in front of the desk.

'Kadie, can you stay on your side of the table?' The girl next to me, Tia, elbows me hard from the right and tries to shuffle away.

'I am on my side of the table.'

'Well, keep your legs there too.'

Surprisingly, there's an apology sitting on my tongue, but I let the attitude get there first. 'Alright, Stroppy Socks.'

'Just keep to your side of the desk. And stop humming.'

'I wasn't.'

'You were.'

Okay, maybe I was. If anybody ever asked, I would tell them that humming, along with any other musical things that come out of my mouth, is a reflex. Sort of. My brain works on music. I eat, sleep, and breathe music because that's what keeps my head straight, and when I'm thinking, sometimes it just slips out. In a hypothetical situation where, maybe, I am a different Kadie, I'd be humming because I'm doing the worksheet about euthanasia. But this isn't a hypothetical situation: this is real life, and the Kadie I am is working on her caricature skills.

Yesterday I drew a masterpiece of Mr Tucker. He had a big hairy eyeball and big square shoulders, but super-long spindly legs. Today I sketch a satisfactory exaggeration of Mrs Wells' glasses and her nose, which is not as pig-like as it is in the picture but it makes me smother a giggle. Tia's peeking at it out of the corner of her eye and I think she knows who it is, because she's smirking.

Tia's actually okay, when I think about it. She's probably the only brown girl in our half of the year who pulls off a neat look without wearing extensions or makeup. You can tell when her plaits are a few days old, but the fact that she just does her edges and doesn't worry about the rest says a lot. If I ever fell out with Shadavia and needed a backup friend, Tia would be my go-to person. The only problem is that we don't talk much, apart from her asking me to stop shaking the table every lesson.

Five minutes before the bell rings, I fish my air pods out of my blazer pocket and arrange my hair so that it conveniently covers my ears. Then I accidentally on purpose spill my pencil case all over the floor so that I have an excuse to get up – not something I can afford to do every lesson, but some days warrant it more than others. Unfortunately, this is too much for Mrs Wells to handle and so instead of being first out the door, I get to stay and endure a special How-We-Behave-at-King's-Manor-College lecture. The usual.

You should know how to wear your uniform properly.

Your attitude is abysmal.

You should set an example to the younger students.

The kind of stuff that goes right over my head while I'm trying to resist the urge to roll my eyes.

I'm out of that classroom like fire in the hole, half glad that the crowds are gone. Even with Shadavia by my side I sometimes have to stop and physically summon up the courage to step into a mass of jostling elbows. The paranoia follows me like a shadow, but it's something most people will never understand.

It doesn't surprise me at all that Shadavia didn't bother waiting for me. I find the girls wandering down the corridor at the speed of a legless horse, heading in the general direction of the canteen. Naturally, I hear them long before I see them.

'That girl lives for detention, doesn't she?' Eisha sounds almost awed. I'm not sure what it is with her – hands down she's been the nicest to me since the day I stepped in, but sometimes I wonder if she's secretly taking notes. She listens a little too much for my liking. Don't they always say it's the quiet ones you have to watch?

'She's a badass. It goes hand in hand, Shadavia.'

'Yeah, a bit too badass for us.' That's got to be Kelly. No one can drip sarcasm like her.

'Are you jealous?' Shadavia asks, and I can imagine her nudge-nudging whoever's at her side. They all laugh except Kelly, who kisses her teeth.

'No way. And she's not badass. She's just a sket. I'm sorry, but that's all I've seen of her so far. Scatty, mouthy, and full of it.' Kelly pauses. 'Why do we let her hang around with us again?'

'Because she's a joker?' Eisha replies lightly. 'I don't know. She kind of just *arrived*.'

I walk slowly as they amble around the corner.

'Well, you can't exactly tell her *not* to hang out with us,' Raquel points out.

(I wouldn't put it past Kelly, who sent a few Year Nine girls scarpering from our regular bench with just a few words and a hard look.)

'Can't I?' Kelly says predictably, with a mock *what, really?* tone.

'She's too badass,' Eisha deadpans. 'Come on, even you follow her on Snap.'

'Only cos everyone else does. And let's face it, Goldilocks and Kadie are like two entirely different people.'

Shadavia sucks her teeth. 'Everyone's lives look better on Snapchat and Insta.'

'She looks great on Insta *and* in person,' Raquel grumbles. Funny, because she wasn't that disgruntled when I was giving

35

her photography tips. But then she shocks me by adding, 'Her skin is so perfect. And her hair.' She huffs.

'Badass,' says Shadavia, using that tone she employs when she's trying to hold in a smirk. Though sometimes it's difficult to tell whether Shadavia is being sarcastic or not, since she uses sarcasm like it's going out of style.

'Filters, people. Filters.' Kelly again. Of course. 'No one has perfect skin.'

'Badass,' Shadavia and Eisha intone together. They giggle. Kelly sighs.

'Don't get it twisted, I think she's okay some of the time,' Raquel muses. 'But then other times I'm just like *what is this girl doing?* Like when she's hyper one minute and practically introverted the next. She was like that at the party – I don't get it. It's as if she's half in her own world.'

'Yeah, she does have a bit of a split-personality thing going on,' Shadavia agrees.

'Split personality? What, are we in psychology?' Eisha asks.

'She kind of does though.' Shadavia sounds convinced. 'Admit it. Even *I've* admitted it.'

'Has she actually got problems?' Raquel asks, a little inquisitively.

'Problems or not, she chooses to act like a freak,' Kelly says.

Thanks.

'What does it matter?' Shadavia's tone is sharp again.

'She's hanging with us until she latches onto someone else, so you better keep your traps shut when she's around.'

''You seriously think she's going to latch onto someone else?' Kelly is incredulous. 'Think again, fam.'

'She could,' Raquel says a little too hopefully. 'Fingers crossed. It'll be less awkward not having a clueless tag-along poking her nose in everything private, you know? Even if she only ever seems to be half listening. Which is actually pretty annoying.'

For the record, just about everything is private with Raquel.

'You know who she reminds me of?' Kelly says, as they move towards the last set of doors. 'Lips.'

There's a collective groan.

'Oh, please, let's not call him that,' Raquel groans. 'Man's never kissed no one.'

'Lips. Dayan. Whatever you want to call him. He never looks at you when he talks. She's always off in la-la-land when you're speaking with her. Plus, there's the whole Goldilocks versus Kadie thing. I'm with Raquel – yeah, she's slyly peng on Insta, but in real life?' Kelly pauses, probably to pull a face. 'She just hovers around leeching off of us because, face it, no one would've batted an eyelash at her on day one if she hadn't come in with us.'

'Are you slagging off Lips or Kadie?' Eisha demands.

'Both.'

'Lips comes across like he's hard of hearing sometimes,'

Shadavia says. 'I don't think Kadie is. I think she chooses to listen to other things rather than us.'

'So she's a little bit obnoxious,' Kelly concludes.

'Obnoxious?' Raquel asks.

'She's a beg.'

'Being obnoxious and being a beg are two entirely different things,' I say loudly, unable to hold back. 'You gyal need to get your definitions right before you go dissing someone.'

Five heads turn. Nobody looks even slightly fazed.

Kelly flicks her hair. 'Speak of the devil.'

I pop a packet of bubble gum out of my pocket, shake one out for myself, and hold it out as I push the door open with my back. 'Gum?'

No one meets my eye except Kelly, who smiles smugly and lets me shake one out into her hand. I jerk the box a bit too hard and three sticks slide out. She glances at me and raises one eyebrow. But when I don't take them back, she rolls her eyes but instead of giving them to the others or pocketing them or something, she chucks them straight on the floor.

'Are you stupid?' I blurt out.

Kelly pushes the gum into her mouth. 'No, why?'

Her gaze is steady, eyes innocent and piercing at the same time. She holds my attention for half a second, daring me to say something.

I lift my chin defiantly. 'What, man?'

Kelly turns for the door, and promptly starts up a new conversation about the latest kicks she wants. The others trail behind, towards the smell of potato from the canteen. It'll smell even better inside the canteen, but I feel anything but hungry even though I didn't even really have breakfast. If Charmaine knew I hadn't eaten all morning, she'd flip.

Then again, if Charmaine knew this was my school life, she probably wouldn't want breakfast either.

FOUR

Music and I were meant to be. But sometimes I question if taking Music for GCSE was actually the right choice. I feel like a traitor, sitting here with my pen hovering over the worksheet, rolling my eyes cos these questions are so easy it's almost insulting. But then how can I be like that when rapping and singing has been just about the only thing to keep me grounded?

A pen prods me on the arm. Mr Driver leans over me. 'Am I being delusional,' he says, 'or are you doing that "not working" thing again?'

'I know all this stuff. I've done it before.'

He whisks my doodled-on (but otherwise untouched) worksheets away. 'If you can do it, why haven't you filled it in?'

I shrug.

Mr Driver bobs his head. 'If you fill those in so I can at least mark them, then I'll find you something harder.'

I sigh heavily.

'Deal?' he prompts.

'Gah. If I have to.'

'I just want proof,' he says, smiling apologetically. 'I know you're smart. But other people want proof of that.'

Proof schmoof.

A hint of guilt surfaces. *He called me smart. He offered to get me something harder. What more do I want?*

Maybe I should actually try. That's what Mummy would want, wouldn't she?

I grip my pen and set about putting all my thoughts onto paper – something that usually doesn't work well. Outside, the autumn leaves dance through the air, swirling around the PE students running onto the basketball courts. I force my attention back down to the worksheet and reluctantly engage my brain, blotting out the mishmash of keyboard-plonking coming from the Year Seven class next door. Between that and answering the questions, my concentration is pretty stretched, so I only hear the heavy footsteps a second before Lips yanks out the chair next to me and drops into it with a deep-voiced, 'What you saying?'

I don't know why Kelly seemed so incredulous about him. His nickname is obviously because of his lips, and he is kind of cute, if you think clumsy big boys are cute. If I saw a picture of him on Instagram I'd rate it just for the looks, even if he has a slightly weird walk.

I pull one air pod out and cut my eye at him. 'What do you want?'

'Why so sour?'

'I just asked what you want.'

He throws his hands in the air. 'Okay, feisty. I want to do a duet with you.'

'A duet? Some bad boy like you coming talking about duets like you play violin or something? Allow it.'

'Junior plays viola,' Lips says, rocking on his chair. Junior – full name Joseph Morley Jr, but nobody calls him that – is one of our year's top boys. Handsome, yes. (And modest about it.) Definitely not clumsy. 'Anyway, you don't have a duet piece at all. Or an ensemble piece.'

Lips is not asking. This is a fact. (A fact which I've been dismissing.)

'And . . . I want to get a good grade.'

'Good for you.' I scrawl some more answers on my worksheet. Why is he doing this to me?

'So what do you say?'

'Good luck.'

'Why?'

I ignore him. 'Why can't you get an ensemble out of your music group? Amalgamandem? You ain't good enough to produce an A grade with a bunch of singers and a viola?'

Lips plays with his tie. 'I did. I want to do another one for comparison.'

'So you're coming to me?' I snicker. 'Yo, you obviously don't know nothing about me.'

The aforementioned Junior turns to face us from the desk behind us. 'Coming from the notorious Goldilocks? Bruv, everyone knows everything about you.'

'Shut up.'

Junior eyeballs me. 'Why are you playing dumb? My man can sing. He got an A in his performance, you know. And since you brought it up, we have drums, piano and guitar between us, as well as singers. Have some respect for AMD.'

'You'll have to earn your respect with me, man. I ain't sucking up to some J Hus wannabe just cos you sing.'

Lips narrows his eyes. 'I'm not asking you to respect anyone. I'm just asking you to work with me. Partly because you need to if you want a grade.'

Mr Driver ambles over, arms crossed thoughtfully. 'They've both got a point, Kadie. You need to get your coursework done ASAP, and you're both in a good position. You both sing; Dayan plays guitar. You both have brilliant potential, if you can bear to stop glowering at each other.'

Lips stops cutting his eye at me.

'When are we supposed to do this?' I ask.

'Well, perhaps some preparation could be done during lesson, a little at a time, but a recording might have to be done after school.'

The whole idea drops to the bottom of my priority list. More time at school? No way. I mean, the grade would be good . . . but extra hours at school?

Apparently I actually pull a face while having these thoughts, because Mr Driver leans back casually and goes, 'Mull it over for a bit. You need an ensemble and a duet piece.'

'You know he's right,' Lips says, getting up.

And he is. They both are.

But the pure disgust at the idea of staying after school somehow sticks on my face, despite the fact that I try to wipe the thought from my brain, and it's obviously noticeable because when I meet Shadavia at break, she asks me straightaway how Music was.

For half a second, I wonder why she's walking at the back with me and if she really cares or if she's just asking to *look* like she cares. Then I shrug, adjust my face again, and kiss my teeth because I have no words. 'Mr Driver wants me to do an ensemble piece with Lips.'

Shadavia snorts. 'With Lips?'

'Yeah. He sings, apparently.'

'Oh, yeah, he sings.' She deepens her voice and sings, '*I just want a girl to come hold me, yeah I'm a bit low-key, if you got a big heart come show me* . . . Yeah. He made like one song and everyone liked it and things went from there. You've probably seen him chilling with AMD, yeah?'

'I have.'

The others slow down so we mingle, listening in on the conversation.

'Why did I not know this?' I ask.

Shadavia smirks. 'Denial, girl. AMD are lit still, but it's hard to get your foot in the door, if you know what I mean.'

Eisha pipes up from where she's been walking on my right. 'I think you and him would work together, if you got the right style of music. You could do a really good cover.'

'I can't imagine him singing a cover,' Shadavia mutters.

'He can sing,' Raquel muses, 'but he can't quite hold notes enough to do a complex pop song.'

'*Hold Me* was kind of middle-grade still,' Kelly puts in. 'But the six notes he sang in that don't magically make him a good singer. I mean, just imagine him doing Drake. The microphone would probably break.'

They all laugh and start doing terrible falsetto impressions – except for Eisha, who rolls her eyes and looks at me. I shrug. She winks.

*

It catches my eye when I'm not working in science, burned out from the first three lessons. Real talk, the motivation factor is zero, and when I'm running on four hours' decent sleep it's less. I swivel my exercise book slightly to get a better angle on my winking emoji doodle and there it is, scratched boldly into the worn wood of the desk.

CAREY'S MUM IS A SKET

I don't know who Carey is. And I don't know who wrote this. But seeing those words instantly stirs up things that were dormant. My left hand starts tapping with the pen again even though it annoys the kid next to me. I can't help it at the best of times, but when my mind clicks into that mode . . . cheeks aflame first, followed by the back of my neck, hairs on end . . .

The memory's too fresh. Yeah, this time round the desk is cleaner, the letters smaller and faded as if somebody tried to erase it. Last time it was done deliberately next to my space, carved into the wood and overlaid in fat bold marker pen so the bad grammar couldn't be amended.

KADIES MUM IS A SKET

Because they knew *so much* about my mum. That was placement sixteen – that lot had never even seen a picture, let alone heard a story. Mummy was a lot of things – hot-tempered, check. Impatient, check. Disorganised, spontaneous, downright imperfect? Definitely. But she wasn't no sket.

I knew who had done it straightaway, planned to confront the girl after school. As it turned out, we had an altercation a bit sooner than that. She got what she asked for, but I didn't get away. Had to add a fifth school to my list of permanent exclusions. The only good thing that came out of it was that it was so close to the end of the year that they just tossed me in the next school along for the last two months. I spent that time skiving, messing around, and enjoying sucking up to the teachers in seclusion. I came up with some good poetry during those months.

'Kadie.' Miss Pigeon taps my desk with her pen. 'Come on! Work! This is your last warning. Don't make me tell you again.'

'I am working.'

Miss Pigeon gestures to my doodle-filled but otherwise pretty-much-empty page. 'That doesn't look like working to me.'

'I'm working on my doodling, Miss.'

She sighs. 'Do the task, Kadie, and you need to write down your answers. I've told you multiple times.'

'The answers are in my head.' Then, because I'm in that kind of mood, 'I told you multiple times.'

She ignores the last bit. 'Yes, well, unfortunately school requires you to write them down. If you don't want to, you can stay at break time to redo the work.'

I tut and scrawl the date.

'And don't you dare tut at me!' She taps the desk again and swans off to the next table.

The classroom chatter rises and falls as a group on the other side of the room bursts into laughter. It melts into the heated debate going on at the table behind me. Teachers think they've hit the nail on the head, sticking me at the front. It's like a whirlwind down here, all the conversations twisting together until they're just noise upon noise. If I were more like Superman, maybe I could filter out what I want to listen to. Unfortunately, I'm just Kadie Hunte.

I slump against my hand. Why would I want to listen to the lesson anyway, when I can just listen to the hullabaloo pressing down around me? Teachers always wanna come asking why I'm always so distracted. Yeah, windows are usually a magnet for my attention – maybe because the world is out there and I'm in here. But usually no one's interested when I tell them that maybe I'm distracted because I straight up *don't care*. The more you care, the more you have to lose – it's as simple as that. It took me a while to realise that the older I get, the less compatible I become with classrooms. Shame nobody seems to understand this. Shame I can't just wear a hat that says DONE WITH EVERYTHING/EVERYONE. Or, better yet, I PLAY BY THE RULES.

Something hits me in the back of the neck. I start so hard that I knock my knee on the table. Shaking my blazer viciously, I discover a note from Shadavia down the back of my shirt.

Uno the answers together for questions 5 and 7??

I scribble the answers and fling it back. A few minutes later she throws me another: *what about question 9?*

'Kadie!' Miss Pigeon swoops in and seizes the note I was about to toss over my shoulder. She unfolds it, reads the message, and crushes it. 'Cheating, I see?' She checks my book, eyeing my (slightly lazy) writing. 'What is all this?'

She picks up my exercise book and deftly tears out the current page. All the heads at the nearest table swivel in our direction.

'Wha—You can't do that!' I protest.

'I can if I think you're being lazy,' she says, placing the separate page down beside my book anyway. 'Here. Last chance: write the whole thing again, neater and without the doodles.'

Neater and without the doodles.

That's got my heart proper thudding. I thought I was past

the days of people doing that. Of course not. Where else would Rule #3 have come from? No: now it's the teacher's turn. Rip up Kadie's work. Mock Kadie's work. Why doesn't she just shred the whole book? I see the way she clocks me. It's all light tones and smiles towards all the other students and then for me the gleam is replaced with a kind of hardness, an impatience that shuts off the warmth in her eyes. I've not even been in this class two months and she seems to hate my guts.

I sit there staring at the fresh page. That scribbly style *is* my writing. Why do teachers have to jump on the idea that smart girls should have perfect handwriting?

Okay, true say I could probably do it if I put my mind to it. There's a lot I can do if I put my mind to it. It's just the 'putting my mind to it' part that I don't get on with. First, *effort*. Second, it doesn't change who you are. Or who *they* think you are. When it's likely that I'll be in a different school, a different borough even, by next year, it's kind of just like . . . what's the point? I'll have to start from scratch. Third . . .

Miss Pigeon is circling back around, hovering at Shadavia's table, commending all of them for their perfect answers. Never mind whether or not *I* had the answers. No rest for the wicked.

'Can I have my page of doodles back?' I ask loudly.

Miss Pigeon cuts her eye at me. 'Sit down,' she says, with that impatience that teachers get when your name has two strikes on the board. I sit down with a humungous groan. I could've answered these questions standing on my head about ten times by now. Instead I'm being forced to write it again for no reason other than Miss Pigeon having a personal grudge because of my track record. I told her writing is *so much effort* and she just laughed. Said that was *nonsense* and moved on, because face it, why would anyone believe the words out of the mouth of the naughty girl?

The middle pages of my exercise book crumple when I grab them in my fist. The paper comes out in two pops, *tack-tack*, as it loses hold on the staples. I toss the double-page on the desk and grip the next one. *Tack-tack*. And the next. *Tack-tack*. As the classroom chit-chat pushes against my ear drums, Miss Pigeon's voice drowns against the sound of class work and far in the background, a siren, and the main road. *Tack-tack*. Yeah, I can do it too.

'Kadie! Right, I've had it with you. Get up.'

'Why?'

'You've had your chances.'

Chances? What chances? I might as well have put my name on the board the moment I walked in this class from day one, the way she's treated me. I didn't ask to sit at the front, in the middle of everything. Didn't ask to have her looking over at me with one beady eye all the time.

'I don't care. I really don't.'

'Fine. You still need to get up.'

Does she think I didn't hear the first time?

Well, I did. I might be badass, and I might be distractible, but I'm not deaf.

'I don't. Care!' I sweep everything off the desk. The ripped-out pages flutter to the floor and the felt-tips I was using spiral across the floor, rolling everywhere. 'See? THAT'S HOW MUCH I CARE.'

'Get out!' Miss Pigeon shouts. 'Stand outside!'

I roll my eyes and kick my stool back so hard that it topples over with a loud bang. I go to reach for my bag – no point staying in this dead lesson – but the way Miss Pigeon has positioned herself, my bag is on the other side of her feet.

'Leave the bag and go and stand in the corridor,' she orders. 'If I have to tell you one more time, that's an hour after school.'

I reach for my backpack anyway, but Miss Pigeon is stood firmly between me and it and she's determined not to move. Everyone's watching while I try and edge around her as she blocks my way, as my palms get hot and my fists form. All this because she wanted me to write out some dumb questions. She could've just asked me the answers and been done with it, but no. No. It's never that simple.

'Tch. Let me get my bag.' I need a break. Somewhere quiet, away from all these faces eager for some beef. Somewhere to wind down the information spinning in my head.

Miss Pigeon barks at me. 'Do as I asked and go outside!'

'Let me get my bag or I swear down . . .' The prickling heat on the back of my neck, in my cheeks. Something's about to split inside of me. The murmur of mocking voices echoes around my head, ringing like my seven o'clock alarm. Piercing and relentless. It's gonna go off, just like before. I can tell because the background noise sharpens and suddenly my blazer feels a lot less comfy.

Miss Pigeon is talking but her words don't take hold in my head. I don't even try to let them. Somebody brushes past, heading to the door. *Pastoral. Get House Leader.* Because Miss Pigeon's not mean enough to make me do what she wants. Because I'm a nutcase rudegyal and only the hard core teachers can make me budge. Because only their voices can get past the nutcase exterior. So they think.

I'm yelling now. 'Give me my bag! Give me my bag and stop picking on me!' A pot of pens flies off the desk and scatters in front of Miss Pigeon but she doesn't move an inch. The murmur-murmuring in the background is filling my ears still, so much that I want to plug them. Words mashing into each other like Raquel grinding her chewing gum.

WEIRDWHYSO

WHATWRONG

ISSHESERIOUSLY KADIE

OUTSIDEGO WOW

If there wasn't a teeny little corner of my brain that cared, I'd just punch her and be done with it. Get kicked out, permanently excluded from this stupid school and moved to another stupid school and another stupid placement and another stupid life in a long straight of them.

But I don't.

Instead I march out of the classroom, hollering over Miss Pigeon as she tells me I'll get detention. I walk out anyway, thumping the walls as I go. Thump and swear, thump and swear at the top of my lungs – that sort of drowns out the sound of everything else spiralling inside my head.

Thump and swear all the way down the corridor to Learning Support, where I duck into a shady corner behind the table football set and shut my eyes. It's quiet in here, but inside my head is a riot.

FIVE

It is almost guaranteed that there will be a reaction. That much I can think about coherently as I slip out of Learning Support between lessons, where I'm sure I was spotted by a member of staff, but not soon enough for them to confront me. Miss Pigeon's got my bag still, and it's just about reaching time for lesson two. Time for me to get my bag back.

I'm a bit too slow though and soon the corridors are crammed with blue blazers all trying to jostle their way to second lesson. There's supposed to be a one-way system but it fails miserably when there are no teachers managing it.

I take the stairs to the second floor and sprint down the corridor in the wrong direction, stopping at points to avoid the hustle and bustle. But by the time I hightail it down to Miss Pigeon's classroom, her next class is already well under way.

I hammer on the door. Miss Pigeon opens it half an inch. 'Yes?' Her hostile glare is set to melt my face off.

I put on my best screw-face. 'Do you have my bag?'

'No. Somebody took it away.'

Her bluntness makes the heat well up again. Fudge! I just got rid of all that and she wants to go rake it up again?

Miss Pigeon goes to slam the door shut but I stick my foot in the way. 'Who took it?'

She sighs. 'A member of staff removed it, Kadie. They wouldn't have had to if you had stayed put outside the door as you were asked.'

I shove the door open further. 'Where did they take it?'

'If you don't mind, I'm trying to teach,' she says. 'Go to Pastoral. That's where they would have taken it.'

Of course.

Now I'm going to have to go there and compete with my Year Leader and all those other intervention-y people who think they can make my life better. I've pretty much just shot myself in the foot.

Maybe I should have just stayed put like I was asked.

Maybe she should have just let me get my bag.

I kick the door so hard that it rattles, twice. 'You shoulda just given it back to me then!'

And there's more winding up inside where it's already burning badly in my fists and feet. Sure, I should have stayed put. It would have been simpler that way. But she should have just let me get my bag. And she should stop staring me down with that look that says *beat it you bratty foster child*, as if fifteen minutes ago her eyes weren't alight with excitement as she discussed genetic disorders with my class.

– but somebody else jumps between us a mere moment before it spews out. 'Aha! Just the girl I've been looking for.'

Andi. My counsellor. One of those cheesy people who says you can call her by her first name, like that instantly makes a wonderful rapport between the two of you. Hardy ha ha.

Andi beckons to me. 'Mr Norris took your belongings,' she says softly. 'Come over to Learning Support and we can have a chat and find your bag.'

'Why?' I demand. I don't want to calm down. I want my bag with my phone and my precious Snap and Insta where the other version of me lives. I want my bag so I can go home and disappear into the world of Goldilocks and forget everything that just happened. I'd rather be anywhere, *anywhere* on earth, than school. 'Where's my stuff? I need my stuff! I can't go nowhere without it.'

Andi repeats herself about my bag. Miss Pigeon quietly shuts her classroom door. I glare through the window for a few moments and then reluctantly follow Andi.

In Learning Support, Andi sits me down in her office in one of her admit-all-the-crazy-thoughts-in-your-head comfy chairs and gives me some space. She failed to mention that someone had dropped my bag off in her office, but I spot it as soon as she points me to the chair. I snatch it up from the floor as soon as she turns around, sling it on my back. Things feel so much better with that weight on my back. Most of my important things are in that bag – just in case. You never know. If something kicks off and I don't get to go home, at least I've got a photo of my mum, my iPod, a notebook full of all drafted song lyrics, some weed and a little cash. Yeah, it must be a comfort thing.

I jiggle one knee nervously, sliding out my phone as Andi sits down in the chair opposite. Here it comes.

I check Snapchat. People are already messaging me.

Kelly: *what in the world was that?*

Shadavia: *are you okay, sorry for getting u in trouble*

Josh: *mad are you alright?*

Raquel: *ummmm so are you really a psycho murderer??*

And worse still, someone has filmed it and put it on our group story like it was some sort of spectacular phenom. (Don't ask me how, since phones are banned in school.) That means it's visible for over two days – longer if it gets shared – and anyone in any of our contacts can see it. That would be hundreds – I repeat, *hundreds* – of people.

My stomach turns over. Why is something as simple as me losing my temper so entertaining?

Andi leans back in her chair. 'So can you tell me what happened back there?'

I slip my phone into my blazer pocket and shrug. 'She was just winding me up. As usual.'

'I mean before that. When someone radioed me to ask me to come and give Miss Pigeon a hand.'

Silence hangs between us, broken only by the sound of the clock ticking.

'I did hear reports of swearing and shouting,' she hints, so gently that I have to roll my eyes.

'I wasn't the only one shouting,' I say truthfully.

'No . . . though you were the only *student* shouting.'

'She ripped up my exercise book.'

Andi nods slowly, tapping her finger to her lips. She fixes me with her dark eyes and smiles a little. 'Do you remember when we talked about telling the full story?'

I remember zoning out during that talk, listening to the audio filtering through the wall from next door.

'What I'm saying,' Andi says, 'is did Miss Pigeon *actually* rip up your exercise book? Into shreds? Because that's what you're making it sound like.'

I groan. 'She ripped a page out.'

Andi raises her eyebrows, trying to prompt more out of me. 'And that was where it started?'

'That was it.' And I'm half hoping we'll leave it there, have some biscuits and talk about music. But naturally, Andi's not letting up. As counsellors do. 'I heard that there was a lot more to it than that.'

'Sounds like you already know.' I stand up. 'Since that's the case, I ain't gotta talk, so I'll just be going.'

'I'm not sure that you're ready—'

'I'm gone. Bye.'

I cross the room in two steps, swing the door open and slam it hard. That's a copyrighted Kadie manoeuvre.

Andi pops out of the room after me, calling my name. I

break into a sprint until I've gone around several corners, and then I take the quickest route to my locker. I probably have a couple of minutes max before she comes here, so I shrug my blazer and tie off quick-as and swap them for my jacket. Three minutes later I'm slipping out of a fire door at the side of the school, worming my way through the car park, wearing an NHS lanyard I borrowed from someone a while back as a skiving decoy.

Freedom.

It's about a twenty-minute walk back to the Lucas' house and I stretch it. Ambling along with my air pods in, I detour, following Princes Avenue until I reach the bridge over the train line and zigzagging back the other way, trying to memorise the criss-crossing streets of houses in various shades of brown. I might have escaped school, but there's a feeling simmering inside somewhere, whispering to me, telling me I need to wind down some more. Otherwise I'll come up against another obstacle and BANG! Off I go.

I wander across the green where Vince took me to play basketball the first week I arrived, following the shortcut that's been trampled diagonally across the expanse of grass. This autumn's been dry so far and the ground is still cracked from summer, the cracks peppered with old rubbish and BB bullets. I imagine kids spending their summers frolicking on this green. Reminds me of the green near the flats where I grew up – Croydon, right out in the boondocks, in a block so far away in distance and time that it's a whisper in my mind.

I hold onto that whisper like a lifeline, especially in the middle of the night when I'm staring at the ceiling. That flat was cramped and cracking in more corners than not, but I still loved the view. From my bedroom I could sit and watch the endless stream of life on the main road. From the living room, I watched the world like a TV, since we didn't have one; the green and the park were almost always occupied, even at night. From outside the block, you could always tell which window was ours. Mummy taught me to make paper dolls when I was five, and as soon as I could make them myself, there was a different string of them hanging in the window every few months. When I figured out how to get even more complex, I upgraded my design, cut and coloured one as neatly as possible, and left it there like a silent wish until it faded. Eight girls and one man joined hand by hand.

The thought of the past kills my good mood. I sigh to myself, swing my bag off and fumble around until my fingers find Emerson at the bottom. Ice against the fire of my hot hand. After five counts, I let go.

It's okay, I tell myself. *It's going to be okay.*

But it's not going to be okay.

Because I'm going to get home and Charmaine will be there, and even if she hasn't already got a phone call she'll still be so vexed she'll probably take away my privileges. No Wi-Fi, no computer – no Goldilocks. Then there will be screaming and red hot hands on my part, and she'll be running the risk of pushing me over the line. It doesn't normally happen this soon, but that doesn't mean it can't.

Nobody wants that to happen, so I pull out a little weed and roll a zoot. It doesn't take long to smoke, but then I don't want to go home smelling strongly like weed so I spray myself with perfume and wander around a little more, letting the high settle in. I picked up smoking four placements ago down in the south west. It pays to bun a zoot every now and then, even if you're not a regular smoker. Some places everyone does it as casually as they play football. Other places it makes you look a little bit bad, the kind of bad that people leave because they don't want to cross you. Which is just the kind of bad I like.

By the time I reach my street things have cooled off inside my chest, but the baby evergreens sat in pots around the front doorstep still manage to look happy enough to irritate me. I resist the urge to boot one of them over and quietly go through the gate to the back garden. Vince entrusted me with his back-door key – apparently it hasn't been long enough that Charmaine and Amando trust me with a front door key yet.

As I guessed, the kitchen is occupied. Just my luck. Vince's silhouette is bobbing around in the kitchen by Charmaine. Smells like someone's cooking patties – the window's open enough that I can almost taste the spice in the air, and it makes me smile. I'll take a proper Jamaican patty any day. I edge closer until I can hear the washing machine competing with Kiss FM, which is blasting from the living room. Yeah,

Charmaine has this obsession with the throwback songs that they play on Kisstory at eleven. The kind of stuff my mum used to listen to.

I close my eyes and press my forehead against the wall. Charmaine is the last person I want to see right now. I'm not sure if it's her eyes, or her voice that's so soft but firm, or maybe just that she smiles warmly all the time – something about her makes me ache for my mum.

I've done enough aching for today. If I don't have to see her, I don't have to disappoint her. Simple as. The moment I get inside, I'm going upstairs.

Guess what? Getting inside unseen is easier said than done.

I wait patiently, flattened against the back wall of the house, until I see Charmaine disappear into the dining room for a minute. Cue! I slip in through the back door, not wasting the time to shut it properly, and sprint through the kitchen. Unfortunately, Vince is just around the corner and I smack straight into him.

'Wehey!' he protests, nearly dropping his armful of books. 'Wait, where did you—'

'Sshshhsorry!' I dodge around him and practically dive for the stairs. Charmaine's coming this way, fast. I make it to the top of the stairs and launch myself at my bedroom door with all the stealth of a rhino.

'Yes, I know you're here,' she calls, so casually that I'm actually slightly annoyed.

I crawl the last two feet into my bedroom. Charmaine is at the bottom of the stairs. 'I know you're here, Kadie, so there's no point hiding. What's going on?'

'I'm slowly closing my bedroom door.'

'No you're not. I'm talking to you.'

'I'm going to my room. Forever and ever.'

'It's one-thirty.' She makes her way up to the landing. 'Please explain what you're doing home so early.'

This is the part where she wants me to fess up and get all weak and guilty because I broke the rules. Usually problems arise here because I've broken *their* rules, but I won't break mine. There's a tactic: give the cold shoulder, but not so much that they want you out. Yes, let a bond form – but just enough to keep things going. Not enough to push the stakes too high. You want them to want you around, but you don't want them to feel like they've lost something if things kick off and someone gets hurt.

It's taken far too long to learn my lesson with this rule.

I push my back up against the closed bedroom door. 'I got sent home.'

'You did not,' Charmaine replies sharply from the other side. Wow, this woman is not giving up.

I sigh at the feeling of déjà vu. 'If you know, why are you asking?'

'Because I want it from you.'

'I had a fight with a teacher. I left. I came in through the back door. End of story.'

Charmaine sighs. 'And what about the hour detention you were supposed to be doing today?'

She's probably already had a conversation with Andi and a bunch of other know-it-alls about what will happen regarding this, but I say, 'It's gonna have to wait, innit?' Then I get up and barricade the door with a very deliberately-placed wedge of wood.

'Kadie!' Charmaine hammers on the door. 'We're not done!'

'I am!'

'Come out here now!'

I get up and collapse on the bed. 'No.'

After a long moment, she sucks her teeth. 'We will finish this discussion later, young lady – don't think you've gotten out of it. And until then you can say bye-bye to your laptop for another twenty-four hours.'

She confiscated it yesterday night after I gave her a little bit too much lip.

I listen to the floor creak as she retreats and pads back down the stairs. Then, without an ounce of guilt, I shuck the school uniform, burrow under the bedcovers and prepare for hibernation. There's a migraine waking up inside me.

SIX

'Kadie Francesca Hunte! If I have to tell you to be quiet one more time, I am going to lose it with you!'

I plop back into my chair at the table and stick My Little Pony – Rainbow Dash – on the radiator by her magnetic foot. 'I am being quiet.'

'No. You're humming and talking. And as much as I love it, it's not quiet. Siddown and finish your homework.'

'I did my homework already.'

'Whatever. I need some quiet from you. Total silence, in fact.'

I get back to playing while the smell of pizza wafts out of the kitchen. Mummy keeps promising that one day she'll make me real pizza with cheesy crusts just like the Domino's leaflets we get in the post, but then she just keeps on buying the ready-made ones. She says it's because she's always too tired to cook properly. She never seems too tired to have a book full of numbers and weird symbols open in front of her. I'm meant to be doing my Literacy homework but it's boring and I don't like writing, so I made a paper aeroplane out of it when Mummy took a break from glaring at me.

Plaiting Rainbow Dash's hair is confusing so I twist it up as best I can, tie it with a ribbon, and practise my poems in a whisper. 'I count red buses like it's life or death, me and Mummy are alone cos my daddy left. I missed first play for IQ theft, smarty pants, Mummy says I'm blessed.' I slip off my chair and pad over to the window overlooking the busy main road. Gazing out of the window helps me come up with creative poetry. And at home I can gaze out of the window as much as I like without getting told off.

Suddenly Mummy is grabbing my arm. 'You can't sit still for a minute, can you?'

I try to pull away, but her hand is well and truly clamped around my wrist. She drags me to the centre of the living room and points to the jelly stain on the floor from last year. 'Stand there. If you can't sit and do your homework quietly, at least do me a favour and learn some self control. Stay there until dinner or until I say so.'

It's hard trying to be as still as a statue. Another plane rumbles through the sky, probably going in the direction of Heathrow. All the songs I know float around my head, like they always do in silence. Silence that isn't silence with the oven humming as it cooks our fake pizza and the ice cream van singing down the road even though it's only April. I sway to the tune. One cornetto, give it to me, delicious ice cream, from Italy . . .

Mummy's lips move soundlessly and her pencil dances across the page, scribbling weird shapes and lines. I roll up my shirt around my hands and flick my feet in the air so that my inside-out, loosely worn socks flip-flap. Like I'm doing keepy-uppies – with an imaginary ball, because I can't play football or any kind of ball to save my life.

Mummy cuts her eye at me so I stop doing imaginary keepy-uppies and concentrate on the songs in my head. Mostly Donell Jones and Beyoncé because that's what Mummy plays when she's not staring at a text book. This is the first month of my life when she hasn't played him. Her record and CD collection hasn't even been dusted recently.

I try to keep it all inside, but eventually Donell Jones wins over and a song starts to seep out of my lips. My arms swing to the rhythm and I whisper it as quietly as possible, but that's not quiet enough for Mummy.

She's up off the sofa in a flash, hurling her text book on the coffee table. 'Ten. Minutes!' she yells. 'That's all I ask of you, girl! You can't keep hush for ten minutes?'

'I—'

'Wasn't a question. Go to the bedroom. Now.'

I ball my fists. 'Why? I wasn't doing anything.'

'You were distracting me! G'wan, get out of my sight.' Her eyes are ablaze, their twinkle turned red hot. She points down the hall. I snatch up Rainbow Dash and run to the bedroom, slamming the door.

I don't understand. I was just singing.

Normally she loves it when I sing.

If there's any moment when I'm ever – even for a split second – glad that Mummy can't see me, it's always ones like this. The morning. Getting out of bed. Or rather, not getting out of bed.

I have an alarm clock, but I've been switching it off a lot recently. The sleeping situation last night was as peak as ever, so when I'm rudely awoken by Charmaine at seven-forty, my first thought is not that she's opening the curtains all the way (which I never do) – but that I'm actually asleep in the first place. Especially since I had to change my sheets at two in the morning.

I drag my pillow over my head and turn over, wishing someone could invent decent earplugs. Recharging when your mind is as volatile as mine is hard work and requires a decent amount of sleep. Not, say, five hours.

'Kadie, it's time to get ready for school.' Charmaine tries to take my pillow away, but I've had that battle a billion times before. I hold onto it proper tight with both arms until she gives up and pulls my blanket off instead.

I respond with an unintelligible grunt. 'So tired.'

Charmaine doesn't get this. Or maybe she just doesn't want to get it. She says something that is muffled because I am under my pillow with my ears plugged, trying to pick up my dream from where I left off.

'I'msickandtiredleavemealone.' I grab the blanket again.

'You seem well enough to be rude,' she says, and I can hear her shaking my container of meds. The thought of downing them makes me feel worse. I cuss loudly so she knows this.

Our conversation goes on like that for another few minutes, with me waking up enough to get very dirty-mouthed and her making threats to ground me or confiscate my tablet/phone/

internet. By the time we're done, both of us are vexed. I hear Charmaine rummaging on my desk, but by the time I sit up to yell at her to leave my stuff alone, she's already confiscated my laptop, tablet and headphones.

I huddle up in my blankets and lie there, ignoring my phone pinging and the sound of everyone else getting ready for school. Thanks to Charmaine, I don't get back to sleep. But neither do I get out of bed. The energy just isn't there.

By the time I *do* make it to school, morning break is about ending. Not that that matters – chilling with the Shadavia clique is stressful and I had breakfast at home. Charmaine coincidentally made this stack of waffles the exact same hour that I woke up. She makes me laugh, that woman. She rang the school to say I'd be late and everything, and then dropped me off. What! The second I got up I'd been trying to come up with ways to get around the inevitable punishment – so it was a real shocker to amble downstairs and get that soft smile from Charmaine as I came into the kitchen. She did also calmly inform me that we would be having a discussion later, to negotiate some better behaviour, but at that point I really couldn't care less.

I amble my way to Maths, avoiding the crowds like usual, sipping on the Coke I nabbed from the cupboard when Charmaine wasn't watching.

Shadavia and Raquel are lingering outside our classroom when I enter the Maths corridor, their backs to me. The halls have quietened down and I'm not wearing anything on my ears lest I break the precious school rules, so I can hear their every word.

'. . . Spoilt little brat. She does whatever she wants.' Shadavia.

Raquel toys with a purple curl. 'Are you jealous cos she's skiving?'

Shadavia sighs angrily. 'No, I'm just . . . I don't get why we even took her in. It's like they *like* having dodgy kids in our house. But then everyone acts like she's an angel. Or some princess. Tch.'

'Yeah, I've noticed that.'

'Exactly! I honestly don't get what's so special about her.'

Raquel rolls her eyes. 'You know what mandem can be like, though. Ellis never shuts up about his light skin ting.'

Shadavia examines her own light-brown hue uncertainly. 'It's not even just the boys, though. It's everyone.' She curls her lip. 'I hate her. She's just one of those people I want to punch.'

'Maybe you should punch her.'

They both laugh.

'Time to get in here, girls!' calls Mr Johnson.

Raquel cracks her gum. 'Maybe she'll just keep on skiving all the time and get kicked out and then we'll be done with her.'

'I'll still have to live with her.'

'There must be a way to get rid of her.'

Shadavia is about to follow Raquel into the classroom,

but she turns her head just enough to glimpse me, about six steps away. She pretends like she hasn't seen me but I know she has.

As soon as we're both sat down, I slip out my phone and message her on Snapchat.

I heard you btw

She messages right back. *Yeah and what*

Did you mean what you said

Yeah

Really?

Why would I say it if I didn't?

Then: *besides I'm just speaking the truth you are a spoilt brat and you've got my mum kissing the ground at your feet*

I rub the back of my neck viciously. *Shut up you don't know anything*

Yes, I do I live with you

Your a mess, can't even dress yourself properly

That gets me. The way the words appear on the screen make me feel like a joke.

I shoot back, *Watch yourself*

She replies. *All bark no bite*

So not true.

My fingers fly across the screen. *Charmaine does not worship me*

There's a gap as she pays attention to the register, pretending to look engaged. Then: *No but she doesn't discipline you either cos you're a BRAT*

She adds: *you might have been badman at your last school but everyone knows you're a beg*

I reply, *you don't know anything*

She fires right back. *I know you're lucky my family wanted you*

Then, just for good measure: *kmt you think your too nice*

The rest of the class is obediently doing the starter activity. Across the room, Shadavia twirls her pen in one hand, casually jotting some answers in her book and looking entirely innocent even though she's pushing the line and she knows it. I stick my phone between my thighs and hold my breath. Crack my knuckles. Squeeze my eyes tight shut. Count to ten.

I open my eyes. Shadavia is watching me out of the corner of her vision. I throw her a screw-face. She gestures rudely.

I wait for the ideal moment. *I know you. Your too soft to say things to people's faces come on you would never punch me*

She replies, *smh*

Just for the lols, she shakes her head in real life.

No seriously

I reply, *If you can say it to Raquel you can say it to my face, come say it to me and we'll see what happens. I'm waiting.*

I wait for her reply all lesson, watching her across the room. But my phone stays silent. She's pretending the conversation never happened and if we both close the app without saving, it will be that way. The evidence will be erased, even if the emotion stays. Snapchat's great like that.

*

At lunch, the group automatically heads for the canteen. I lag at the back, half hoping maybe that's not where they're going, but I might as well be delusional.

I stop as we get near to the door. 'Yo, anyone want to chill outside with me?'

Josh, Ellis and Aidan don't even hear; they're busy arguing about something. The girls just innocently ignore me.

Kelly glances over her shoulder and curls her lip. 'We're going inside,' she says bluntly. 'It's too cold out.'

I squint up at the hazy sky, then look to Shadavia for help. She suddenly develops the need to find something buried deep in her blazer pocket.

'It's not that cold,' I protest.

Raquel inspects her impeccable nail job. 'You're the only one who thinks so, hun.'

'You sure about that?'

'No,' says Kelly, 'but we're going inside anyway.'

'Sorry, Kadie, you're on your ones,' says Aidan. He meets my eye when I glance at him. The look in his wide eyes is actually halfway apologetic, but Kelly's already turning to the door with an airy, 'See ya. Wouldn't wanna be ya.' Aidan follows her.

I switch my attention to the girls.

'Well?' demands Kelly. 'Are you lot coming? The queue's getting long and I'm not missing the pizza.'

'Pizza!' yells Ellis. 'Let's go!' He shoves Aidan through the door, squashing some Year Seven girls, and bulldozes towards the counter. Shadavia follows their lead and Raquel goes with her.

Josh glances at Eisha, then at me. 'I'll come back out and sit with you as soon as I've got my food, yeah?'

I raise one eyebrow sceptically. 'As soon as?'

'As soon as.'

'Pinky promise?'

Josh looks at my outstretched hand. 'Pinky promise?'

'I'll be waiting right here.' I do my super-cute dimples-flaring smile and flex my pinky.

Josh links his pinky finger with mine, rolling his eyes. 'You wait here,' he says.

He disappears into the canteen crowds. I sit down on the nearest bench and carefully open a packet of breadsticks. Let's count the seconds.

Ten minutes later, I'm still waiting.

My phone buzzes. Snapchat. I sigh, glance about furtively, and slip it out.

One message from mr_J05H!E. Josh.

Likelihood of betrayal? About ninety per cent.

The snap is of half a discombobulated sandwich sat on the table. *sorry babe your half cute but still butters*

Then a screen-shot picture from my Instagram from mscutiegreeneyes: *bum too big for dem skinny legs and arms he never wanted you*

Then mr_J05H!E again: *sorryyy I'm staying here*

They all blink off the screen after three seconds.

Josh has just dumped me via Snapchat. And we weren't even going out.

I drop my phone in my pocket and take myself off to the lockers to abandon my blazer. Fine, then. Be that way.

Back when I was younger I used to get upset for days over people declaring that they didn't want me around. One day you're in the group, the next you're invisible. It used to make me angry. Now it doesn't make me anything. Expect nothing from anyone, and you never get disappointed. Follow the rules, no one gets hurt – not me or them. Yeah, there's always that little part of me that longs to be in a group, but groups never understand.

The plus side is, now I don't have to tell anyone or make up excuses if I want to walk off site at break to get high. I just go. And no one cares.

SEVEN

'Eight o'clock, Kadie?' Amando's eyes are blazing. 'Eight o'clock, on a school night? It's not good enough.'

I'm never good enough. The fact that I decided to come back to school at the end of break today is not good enough. The fact that I sat through History and English and even did PE is *not good enough*. And let's just forget the fact that I just spent several hours doing something productive.

Occasionally, I allow a teeny part of myself to wonder if Amando could be any different to the ones before – like when he comments on my swag.

And then there are moments like this that completely kill all my fantasies.

'Where have you been?' he demands.

I curl my lip sullenly. 'At studio. I texted Charmaine to say I'd be late back.'

Amando shakes his head. 'That's not how it works and you know it.'

'I had a song to finish.'

'A song,' he repeats. 'What kind of song?'

'It's called *I got you*. J Hus, Not3s sort of afro swing vibe.' I beat box the rhythm for him.

Amando purses his lips. 'That's . . . great.'

I blunder on, half hyper and half aware that I can distract him. 'Great? This is sick! This is the last song on my EP. I'm so gassed. Why d'you think I've been practically living at studio? I have a 79k fan base that I'm working on as well.'

Amando raises his eyebrows a bit. 'And what's this EP called?'

'A.D.H.D. *All Detentions have Dreamers*.'

'Interesting title.' Ironically, the interest has disappeared from his face. 'Fair enough. I'm happy that your extracurricular activities are challenging, but that doesn't justify deliberately flouting the house rules.'

Then he starts going on about something or other but I'm starving and I really need to wee so even though my ears are hearing him, I'm dancing about everywhere and not even slightly listening.

Above us, the landing creaks minutely. Amando probably doesn't notice it but I do and I can tell by the way it creaks that it's Shadavia, and she's trying to eavesdrop without being obvious.

'Kadie!' Amando barks. 'Stand still and look at me when I'm talking to you!'

I look at him and manage to keep my eyes there somehow. While I'm focusing on that, I crack my knuckles and tap tap tap on my leg while Amando talks at my face. The dishwasher is rumbling like an empty stomach and someone's got the TV switched to the politicians squabbling in Parliament. I don't think Amando realises how strongly the smell of coffee lingers on him. He thinks he knows everything. He thinks I'm missing out on revision time and sleep. What he doesn't know is that these two things are both non-existent. Also, he seriously thinks this-and-that punishment is going to stop me from staying out late. He can do what he likes. I'll just stay later at studio.

The moment he's done I bolt upstairs, blurting out a half-hearted, 'Yes Amando!'

Once I'm all wrapped in my onesie (emblazoned with the all-important words SLEEP IS ALL I NEED), I head downstairs to grab something to eat. Family dinner's already come and gone, which only makes me sad for half a second.

Charmaine floats in from the living room, clutching an empty mug. 'I put your dinner in the left-hand oven,' she tells me, but she's already stooping to take it out. Cheesy lasagne, green beans, garlic bread. She hands the plate to me with a little smile. 'Careful, it's hot.'

Not a word about my late arrival. Ookay.

I settle down at the table and wait for Charmaine to begin the lecture. Instead, she reaches a tray stacked high with cookies out of the other oven and offers one to me. 'I thought I'd try my hand at Subway-style raspberry cheesecake cookies. Let me know what you think.'

I take one suspiciously. She beams at me, stacks the cookies into a container, and disappears out the door.

I've been alone in the mostly-silence for about fifteen minutes when Beverly comes barging in, clutching a fluffy pink pencil case and a piece of crumpled paper, moaning, 'Mummmyyyyy—'

She stops when she sees it's just me. With a dramatic sigh, she tosses her piece of paper onto the table and watches as it floats all the way across to the other side and falls on the floor at my feet. She stares at it and sighs again, brushing her mad 'fro off her forehead.

'Homework?' I ask.

Beverly gives me a sullen look that only a nine-year-old kid can muster. 'Stinky, stupid homework.'

'Are the homework police onto you?'

'Yes, but Mummy said she'd help me with it.'

'I can help you if it's Maths.'

Beverly pouts. 'It's adding and minusing big numbers and I don't get it and it's boring and it's mean to make us do it. Why can't we eat ice cream instead?'

I spike a piece of lasagne and carefully put it in my mouth without getting any of the sauce on my chin. 'We can't eat ice cream instead cos the point of school is not to have fun and rot your teeth.'

'Well, school should be fun.'

'Do you find it fun?'

Beverly snorts, blowing her curls far off her forehead. 'Pssh, no. School is so dead.'

I throw my hands up. 'High ten! I'm not the only one!'

We high ten.

I push out the chair next to me. 'Come to Kadie's School of Maths.'

'Only if we rock, paper, scissors it. Otherwise I'm not doing it. I can't be bothered.'

'Fine.' I grin. 'Ready? Rock, paper, scissors.' Beverly scrambles to get in time and comes out with paper while I get scissors.

'Too slow. I win! Let's go.'

'No! That wasn't fair!' she protests. 'One more time!'

So we do. Rock, paper, scissors. I'm a rock, she's scissors.

'Smash! Let's go.'

Beverly's pout doesn't get any smaller. She collapses into the chair and flops onto the table, hugging the pink pencil case. 'How are you going to help me if you're rubbish at maths?'

I scrape up the last of my lasagne. 'Who said I'm rubbish at maths?'

'Mummy and Daddy did. They said your grades are terrible.'

'A grade is just a number.'

'Or a letter.' Beverly lifts her head to look at me. Her eyes are big and brown and cute, but they also seem to want to know stuff. 'So you're good at maths?'

'I'm sick at maths, thank you very much.'

She pulls a calculator out of her pencil case and starts putting in a sum. 'What's a hundred and ninety-six times two hundred and seventy-three?'

'Fifty-three thousand, five hundred and eight.'

'Five point three times seven point nine?'

'Forty-one point eight-seven.'

'One hundred and forty-eight divided by five?'

'Twenty-nine point six.'

Her eyebrows arch. 'Ha! Four hundred and ninety-seven divided by six. Bet you can't do that!'

I frown for about five seconds. 'Eighty-two point eight three recurring . . .?'

'You *are* good at maths!' Beverly sits up properly. 'How are you good at maths if you're never at school?'

I sway from left to right on my stool. 'Let me guess. Mummy and Daddy said that, too?'

'Ummmm . . . yeah.'

'I bet they have a whole folder on Kadie Hunte, don't they? With all the itty bitty details.'

Beverly completely misses my sarcastic tone. 'No! They just talk about you. A lot.'

'Of course.'

'Daddy complains about you. He says you're a bad influence.'

'Wasteman.'

'And sometimes I accidentally hear them.'

'Not your fault.'

'And accidentally remember what I hear.'

'No comment.'

'So you *do* go to school?'

'Yes! Rah!' The notion that I never go to school irritates me.

'Shadavia says you skive most of the time.'

'She's telling porkies.'

Beverly leans forward so that her hair nearly tickles my nose. '*Do* you skive lessons?'

She holds my eye. I hold her eye. I want to lie. I can't.

'Not every class.'

'So you *are* a naughty girl?'

'I have my reasons.'

'What reasons?'

I open my mouth and close it. Twice. Beverly watches me and waits.

I look away. 'School is stressful, okay? And I ain't got no one to hang around with.'

'What about Shadavia?'

'What about her?' I don't try to hide my scathing tone.

'I thought you were in her squad.'

'Was. Past tense.'

'But you still walk to school with her!'

'Not often. And when I do, I take a detour as soon as she meets Raquel at the park.'

Beverly frowns deeply in surprise. Her eyebrows do a

disgusted sort of Mexican wave and she looks like she wants to go all Sherlock Holmes on the situation, so I tap-tap her homework sheet with my finger and say, 'You're digressing, bruv.' Which she is.

Beverly looks at my finger and slouches. 'Maths makes me floppy.'

'*School* makes me floppy. How about if we make up a rap about maths first?'

Her pout disappears. 'A maths rap?'

'Yeah. We can take it in turns to make up a line.' I make a vocal scratch like a DJ scratching a record and, dropping a beat, I jump straight into it. 'Maths is a subject we all need to know . . .' I point to her.

Beverly sits up, wearing a thoughtful face. It takes her a while. 'Without it you're dumb and you'll live on death row.' A smile flickers across her lips.

'Yeah. You got it. Check out my answers to see if they're right . . .'

'If they're not then you'll have to put up a fight!'

'One more line,' I say between the bass drum and the hi-hat. 'Schools make it seem like maths can't be fun . . .'

'But if maths isn't fun it'll never get done!' Beverly's pout has turned into a big grin. 'Can we make it longer?'

'Maybe later. When that homework's done.'

Beverly gets her head down and starts 'trying' to do her homework. She gives up after two seconds. 'I'm stuck.'

'You're stuck, or you're bored and can't be bothered?'

'I'm stuck. In boredom.'

'Right.'

I seize a pen from her pencil case and walk her through the first two sums. Beverly watches me struggling to make the pen write neatly and says nothing except, 'You keep writing your threes backwards.'

She doodles on the side of the page while I talk, answers my questions without looking at me, and scrawls the answers with a Dead Bored expression.

I smile, borrow some scrap paper off the fridge, and start writing lyrics. After my hours in the studio I'm still buzzing and the words just pour out of me. I can barely read my handwriting, but my brain is like a safe when it comes to words. Most of the time.

Of course, it's just when everything's all going well that Charmaine has to walk in. Beverly is halfway through her sums and I am in the middle of the kitchen, spinning on the desk chair from the living room and composing more bars.

'Girls, it's gone bedtime,' Charmaine says dryly.

Beverly carries on with her sums. 'I'm nearly done.'

'I thought I told you to do that yesterday.'

Beverly lolls her head and turns her innocent eyes on her mum. 'It *fell*.'

I bite the inside of my cheek. If Charmaine is at all amused she covers it pretty well with a curt, 'Don't give me that. Just get it finished and get to bed. It's past nine.'

Then she turns on me while I'm still trying not to snort

with laughter. 'As for you, Missy, you are seriously pushing it. You're not off the hook for coming home late.'

I clench my jaw. 'I'm helping Beverly.'

'It looks to me like you're spinning around on the desk chair, which you know full well should only be at the living room desk.'

'Kadie's helping me, Mummy,' Beverly says. 'She's really good at maths. Kadie, what's eight hundred and sixty-four times fifty-six?'

My brain cogs go. 'Forty-eight thousand three hundred and eighty-four.'

Beverly smiles sweetly at Charmaine. 'See?'

Charmaine slow-mo blinks and folds her arms. 'That's great, but I need you in bed before nine-thirty.' She raises one eyebrow at me. 'Both of you.'

'Okay,' we chorus.

She leaves.

Beverly squints at me. 'You did a bad thing, didn't you?'

'I stayed at studio till past seven o'clock and skipped detention so I could get there for half four.'

She whistles and goes back to her sums. 'You are a naughty girl! I knew it!'

'I want to be a music star. I paid good money for that studio time.'

'But you don't have to break the rules.'

'I do, fam. I really do.'

'No you don't.'

'I do.'

'Why?'

I kiss my teeth.

Beverly raises one eyebrow. 'Why?'

'Cos if I don't break the rules, the rules break me.'

She frowns. 'I don't get it.'

'You won't. No one does.'

She finishes, writes her name on the sheet and piles everything up to leave. 'That's stupid. How am I supposed to get it if you don't explain it to me?'

I go to retort but there's no smart reply waiting on my tongue.

She has a point. But I'm not explaining everything to a kid. How would I?

'Don't answer that,' Beverly says, seeing the look on my face. Then she lunges forward unexpectedly and throws her arms around me. We teeter on the back end of the stool for a long moment while I try to adjust myself to hold up her weight. 'Don't just throw yourself on me! I don't want to accidentally punch you.'

Beverly adjusts herself on my lap and squeezes me from all sides. Her hair is in my face, and although it smells good – some sort of fruity flower something-or-other – it doesn't taste that good. I press my face into it and squeeze her back. 'That's good. Great.'

We hold each other so close that I can feel her warmth ebbing into me. Her heart beats in sync with mine.

Beverly lets me go. 'Thanks, Kadie. Good night.'

She kisses me on the cheek. I freeze, caught off guard. The suddenness of it reminds me of the party, of the fleeting thing with Josh. People are unbelievably unpredictable. You have to watch them twenty-four/seven, and even then they'll still catch you off guard – buttering you up with hugs and kisses and then suddenly changing their minds about something.

I can control me, but I can't control the people around me. But that's not Beverly's fault. Anything good can turn sour in an instant. The memories still flash into my head at random moments. Luca, turning the flat upside down looking for his money that we hadn't seen, grabbing Mummy even though her tears should have answered his question. Hadley Oxford, swinging a book hard into my temple while his daughter stood and watched. Sequan, throwing his arm too hard around my shoulder, grinning.

It's hard to tell until some time has passed, but you can't just jump into something when you don't know anything. How do you know who's going to turn gifts into weapons or when hands are going to grip and swing you? How are you meant to tell which smiles are fake and which smiles are looking only at the surface, blinded by twisted thoughts?

You don't. Not in my case, anyway. After enough smacks you figure it out.

EIGHT

I amble into the house after an evening in the studio, casually sucking a mint to kill my weed breath. The smell of rice lingers; the others have already eaten.

Shadavia hollers a greeting as I come up the stairs. 'She's back! What up, my girl?'

I pause, trying to gauge whether she's being nice or not. 'Oh, dis and dat, you know.'

She bum-shuffles into the doorway of her room. 'Good session?'

'Sick.' I sing a couple of bars of the song I've been recording. '*How we gonna lose, when we getting dough? People wanna chat but I'm out here doing shows* . . . You're gonna see me drop a preview on my Snapchat soon, bruv.'

'Can't wait.' She grins. A proper, authentic grin, not that fake one she gives me at school. Then she says, 'How come you weren't in Maths today?'

I snort. 'I didn't want to be.'

'And what about English?'

'English is a dead ting.'

'But don't you care?' She studies me. 'Don't you have loads of catch-up to do because you moved?'

I cross my arms. 'Don't get it twisted. Of course I care.'

She smirks. 'Just not enough to be in class.'

'Yeah. Not enough to be in class.'

'Well then, isn't it a good thing *someone* got your homework for you.' She thrusts a handful of stapled pieces of paper at my feet – 'That's English.' – followed by my Maths homework book and a worksheet. 'That's Maths.'

My jaw drops. 'You got my homework for me?'

Shadavia looks unconcerned. 'Uh, yeah?'

'Why?'

'Why not?'

It's moments like this that make me feel bad at school, when I take my frustration out with pen and paper. If Shadavia saw some of the caricatures I've been drawing of her squad, she might not be so nice to me. If she saw some of my exaggerations of her nose (which isn't really that fat), I can guarantee she would never get my homework for me again.

I glance at the Maths homework. 'Tch. I can do this standing on my head.'

Shadavia cocks one eyebrow. 'You want to slip me some answers?'

'No, you lazy blob.'

'I help you, you help me?'

'I can explain it to you.'

She sighs. 'Ugh. I guess.'

'You can pay me in chewing gum. One stick per question.'

'Deal.'

Surprised at the outcome of our exchange, I thank her again, toss the homework on my bed and head downstairs in stealth mode to find something to eat. Unfortunately, I only make it to the living room. I'm creeping past, all Batman, avoiding Charmaine and Amando lest they lecture me about curfews and revision, when Beverly pops out from behind the door and jumps on me. 'BOO!'

I scream.

Amando pops his head out of the office just down the hall. 'Play nicely!' he orders. Then he sees me. 'Ah, Kadie! Can I talk to you for a sec?'

My heart plummets.

Defensive shields: check.

Attitude: check.

Screw-face: check.

The office is cluttered. Two shelves, stuffed with books, loom over the desk where Amando is sat with his ridiculous reading glasses. Behind the coat stand there are two world maps tacked on the wall, plus a mirror behind the door, and a huge blind hanging beside the three aloe vera on the windowsill. I immediately feel claustrophobic and confused.

I try to ignore the mess on the desk and end up focusing on a framed picture of Amando and Shadavia on holiday. Looks like a selfie.

I want one of those. One that I can frame. One that I won't have the burning desire to delete in roughly three months.

Amando sits back in his desk chair and looks at me. 'I didn't know you were an artist,' he says.

He's got my attention now. 'What?'

Amando shuffles the pieces of paper on his desk until he finds one with the distinctive squares of a typical maths book. I recognise the page – it's filled with various clumsy caricatured heads. Someone's ripped it out of the middle of my maths book.

'Where did you get that?' I demand.

'It came in the post,' he says. 'Your teacher sent it to me.'

'My teacher?' I snort. 'Rah, what for?'

Amando picks up a postcard from the multitude of papers. It has some cheesy design on it – the alphabet made with rubber bands or something – so there's no way it's something exciting. But he looks ridiculously thrilled as he reads, 'I would like to award Kadie this postcard for not only paying attention for four weeks straight, but for getting one hundred percent in every paper and piece of homework I have issued since the start of term. Though these pieces of homework are usually late, the success rate is clearly an indicator of her unique mathematical ability. I hope she dosen't waste this talent." He glances at the drawings, then at me. 'And these caricatures are pretty amusing, even if your teacher would rather you not do them in his class.'

There are no words in my mouth. Amando is smiling. *Smiling*.

I study him closely and eventually manage to say, 'Are you okay?'

'I'm very good,' he replies. 'I'm proud. Impressed.'

I curl my lip at my drawings. They're not that brilliant. He must be saying that to flatter me – I mean, pictures come easier than letters sometimes. I am no Picasso.

Amando offers me the postcard. 'You can tack it up on the fridge if you want.'

'What for?'

'Because you've done well.'

'I thought you had no hope in me.'

'No hope?' Amando tries to hide a smirk. 'No. I just had to adjust my expectations a little.'

'Great. Thanks.'

'That's not a bad thing. Everyone's different.'

But paying attention in class isn't anything special, is it? That's following the rules. That's being *normal*.

'It's a stupid postcard.'

'It's still an achievement,' he insists.

Now I really feel like he's pushing this just to make me feel good. The caricatures are not that sick. And let's face it, a couple weeks of paying attention in one class? Shadavia would kiss her teeth if she knew I was getting a hallowed postcard for something like that. Amando's just trying to make it look like he cares.

Maybe he does care.

'You could always just stick it in your room somewhere,' he tries. 'I mean, a hundred percent, all the time? That *is* something you should be proud of. I took Maths at school, all those yonks ago, so I can attest to the fact that Maths is not an easy subject.'

If Mummy were here, she would probably be like, 'And imagine what you could do if you actually went to class and *listened* all the time.'

It's a struggle not to cut my eye at the piece of card in his hand. I want to believe that he actually genuinely means everything he's just said. I really do.

I am also not going to break the rules.

Amando bites his lip. 'No?'

I snatch the postcard, rip it in half, and toss it in the waste basket at his feet. Then I'm gone, leaving him sitting there, agape. There's a little spot of guilt in my heart from the half-disappointed look in his eyes. But it's not my fault. I don't want a stupid postcard reminding me about my problems. I want a selfie with a dad who cares.

NINE

Don't ask me why Mr Driver is so chill. I rock up to his class like six minutes after the bell, which my green card is no justification for. Everyone's all seated in a circle doing a class activity when I skip up the corridor, higher than the stratosphere, singing some rap song. '*Blud you're a liar, liar, liar, blud you're a liar*—'

I slam straight into the door and bounce off. On the other side, Lips, Junior, and a handful of other people smother their laughter. I grin, turn the handle, swan into the room, and run to my seat. 'You didn't see nothing.'

'Sit down quietly and get your planner out,' Mr Driver says coolly, but he pauses whatever he's saying while I dump my stuff down and straddle my chair backwards. He doesn't challenge me a bit, although he does bother asking me questions on whatever it is he's droning about – stuff I already know. As the high wears off, I rest my head on my arms on the back of the chair and answer with my face in my blazer sleeve. Everything Mr Driver is saying just floats around in my brain like water in space.

After lots of blabbing, we're sent off to do more boring

revision. I rock my chair backwards and forwards for a while, squinting at what's scrawled on the whiteboard. It's too far away and I can't read it, so I hop my chair around one-eighty degrees so I'm facing the desk and get a pen out.

Mr Driver hands out a bunch of unchallenging worksheets. I start colouring in the corners straight away, and that's exactly what I'm doing when he comes straight back to me, pulls out a chair and sits down.

I rock my chair and give him a huge smile. 'Sorry I was late, sir. There was traffic.' People traffic.

Mr Driver purses his lips. 'Did you think about the duet idea?'

Of course I have. I've looked for the best kind of songs for us to do. I've practised old stuff and been touching up on my singing lately. I've also envisioned every single way it could possibly make my life better, and every single way it could go wrong.

I shrug. 'A bit.'

'That's great! I think you and Dayan should get talking ASAP about what you want to do, because we need to get this project going.'

Then he sits the two of us straight in one of the practice rooms and leaves us to it.

I'm straddling my chair backwards and chewing bubblegum when Lips comes in. He slams the door, and turns his chair backwards like mine before sitting on it.

'You got the ideas for this, yeah?' I blow a bubble, pop it with my pen, and carry on chewing.

'Are you for real?' Lips demands.

'Yeah.' I'm not sure why he's so angry.

'Then let's do this and don't mess me around.'

We stare each other down for about ten seconds before he reaches for his notes.

I try not to mess him around. I really try. But it's more fun to play clown than actually get on with it like a boring good student.

With his class Apple Mac balanced on his lap, Lips opens YouTube and begins making suggestions that I counter with other suggestions. We play each other songs off the Mac and it takes us nearly all lesson to find a performable song that both of us like: 'Give me Love'. Ed Sheeran and Demi Lovato.

Lips finds the guitar score and plays it, sight reading, on his guitar. His forehead furrows a little as he concentrates, but he loses the angry pout. I know that feeling. I saw it all the time on Mummy's face.

Halfway through, he fumbles the notes and stops suddenly. I pretend I haven't been staring at him for the past minute, but judging by the smirk on his face, he knows.

'So you'll be fine to learn the part, then?' he says.

'Yeah.'

'You better.'

I grin mischievously. 'You don't trust me.'

He gives me that poker face from the night at the party. 'I just want a good grade. I've seen your stuff on YouTube. You're perfectly capable.'

My phone does its Snapchat noise, ever so quietly, and I slip it out of my blazer. Maybe this time it'll be one of my friends from the last placement, one or two of whom promised they'd stay in touch.

It's not. It's the group story. The one that nobody uses anymore.

Somebody's reposted one of the pictures from my personal story that I posted at the weekend: more swag, nothing special. It makes me feel pretty good after a week of being stuck in school uniform and getting slagged off left right and centre.

Lips strums aimlessly and stretches his legs into my personal space. 'So . . . you wanna do me a freestyle or something?'

'A what?' My mind is on the Snapchat repost. On the caption over the picture.

Skinny legs fat belly nose too long for your face well that sums you up #butters

'A singing freestyle. So I can hear you.'

'You just said you've heard me on YouTube.'

'What's wrong with right here and now?'

I look at the picture. In it, I'm bussing a Converse T-shirt and jacket, couple gold chains on my neck, hair slicked into a nice bun, my special edition pink Nike Airs. The authentic Goldilocks mixed-brands tomboy style. I might have put a little weight on since I got here, but I'm not fat. I'm really not.

'Kadie?' he prompts.

I close Snapchat and dunk my phone in my pocket. 'I can't.'

'But—'

'I just can't. Not in the mood.'

'You were a minute ago.'

'Well, I'm not now, okay?'

Lips recoils. 'Alright, Miss Moody Pants.'

He leaves the room, slamming the door. Again. Why does he always slam the door?

TEN

I'm on my own. Head ducked, hanging around outside Mr Driver's room doing Mission Impossible with a can of Monster that could get me another detention.

Peeking through the door, I spot AMD chilling: Junior, Lips, and the two other boys – Michael and Reuben. Reuben's a sixth former so I don't see him around much, but I've encountered Michael and Junior enough that it doesn't surprise me to find them here.

I can practically feel their vibes through the classroom door. They're not being loud or anything, but I can just feel them. It's just the way they're talking and laughing and no one is sitting there on the fringes looking left out.

Junior glances over then and notices me watching them. I make a point of busting the door open backwards and entering loudly. 'What's good, everyone?'

Mr Driver is way more delighted than I expected him to be. 'Kadie! You made it!' He rubs his hands together and comes over. 'I have some good news for you.'

'Good news? Like what? Are they granting me my predicted grade without taking the exam?'

'No!' He looks far too pleased with himself. 'I spoke to your year leader about your six hours' worth of detention that was about to land you in almost a week of isolation. We have agreed that they can be wiped off your slate if you spend that exact amount of time here, in Music.'

'Here?' I exclaim. That's almost just as bad as having to serve the detentions.

'Yes. The time can be used for practising your performance pieces and revising.'

I bite my tongue to stop myself from groaning and cussing. 'Sick. Thanks.'

Mr Driver is genuinely concerned. 'You know if those detentions continued on as they were, you'd be on a behaviour report.'

'Pretty good achievement for the first two months of the year.' I smile cheekily.

Mr Driver leaves me alone. The bell rings and I sit down, one earphone in, watching as AMD splits up to go to their desks, and Reuben leaves the room.

Lips moves his stuff to his desk and prods me on the way past. 'Don't think I didn't see you checking us out.'

'Checking who out?' I ask innocently.

Lips waves a finger at me. 'Yeah, I saw you.'

'So what?'

'Why so glum?'

'I'm in *school*.'

'But Mr Driver sorted out, like, your biggest beef with the system.'

I titter sarcastically. 'My biggest beef? Ha!'

Lips hitches his trousers up to normal height. They sag right back down to his bum. For a second, he looks about to carry on this useless exchange, but then he closes his mouth and drops into his chair. He doesn't say another word to me until Mr Driver sticks us in one of the practice rooms to get some work done.

For the first half a minute, we sit there in silence. The awkwardness makes me want to laugh. It's not as if either of us is socially incapable, and it's not as if we haven't been compiling plans over WhatsApp or anything.

Finally, Lips says, 'Shall we get started?'

I shrug. 'Whatever.'

He blinks. 'Seriously? That's still your attitude?'

'Dun know.'

He sucks his teeth. 'Look, I'm not stupid. I can tell you want to do this.'

'Really?'

'Yeah. I can.'

'Can you tell what I'm thinking as well?'

'You're a joke.'

'Ha ha.'

Lips leans back in his chair. 'I'll make you a deal.'

I rock my own chair onto its rear legs. 'What is this, *Deal Or No Deal?*'

He ignores me. 'You do this thing to the best of your ability, get us A grades, I'll get you studio time. Good studio time, free of charge.' He clears his throat. 'And maybe you can come chill with us.'

I snort. Partly in disgust, partly in disbelief. 'I don't need studio time.'

'Yeah? I can guarantee you I've got better links.'

Probably true. I glare and scowl anyway. 'Tch. You ain't got nuff girls already? You can't be so desperate that you're offering a *friendship* for a grade.'

'I didn't say friendship.'

'You implied it.'

Lips sighs and folds his arms. His creased-up school shirt, only half tucked into his trousers, bulges awkwardly. 'What's with you? You love music.'

'You don't know anything.'

'But what have you got to lose?'

I close my eyes. My mum said the same thing once. 'Music is a wonderful thing,' she told me. 'It's beautiful, and it's powerful. If you're going to put your whole heart and mind into making good music, you have nothing to lose.'

That was probably just her opinion. I put my whole heart and mind into making music and I still had a lot to lose. She was just the start. How many times can you lose everything?

My music is the only thing that keeps my head straight. I'm not having that taken away from me by any more buff little rudeboys who only want one kind of love.

I open my eyes and glare at Lips.

'What did I do now?' he demands. 'I just asked a small question!'

I rock on the back legs of my chair and give him a cool look. If he thinks he can get me on board by pulling me into his clique . . . I'd like to just oblige. But it's never that simple. I ain't no sket. I'm not about to support that rumour, and I'm certainly not about to break the rules.

Lips stands abruptly, knocking his chair over. 'Tch. You're a joke! I can't believe you.'

He leaves and slams the door.

I let my chair drop back onto all fours. What a stroppy socks. He must've meant what he said sincerely, then.

I swallow back a touch of remorse. Maybe I shouldn't have been so quick to wind him up. Even if it's cute when he pooches out his lips with frustration.

He doesn't come back after a minute, so I wiggle the mouse to wake up my Apple Mac and check him out on YouTube. Sure enough, the first song that comes up is that one Shadavia was singing: *Hold Me*. The instrumental is an afro swing sort of vibe, mellow but with a tempo that carries you along. The kind of thing kids would bop to in summer. He sings and raps on it, and he does it well. He's proper good at the singing and the rapping and even the music video is on point. He might run like a klutz but he sure knows what he's doing with his music.

Comforted, I find my favourite recording of Ed Sheeran and Demi Lovato singing 'Give me Love'. Little does he know, but I've been listening to as many versions as possible, absorbing all the different ways to sing one song.

It was my mum that taught me to sing. She was definitely right about music being powerful. Singing put down the foundations of my confidence. I stopped worrying about the fat lisp I had back then. I'd wanted to rap from day one, but never did outside of the flat because people – adults and kids alike – took the mick. Seven years on, I don't have the lisp anymore, but I've definitely still got the power.

'Do you know why I put you on the naughty spot?'

I sniffle. 'Because I was naughty at school.'

'Correct.' She shifts me on her lap and touches her warm lips to my shoulder, next to a frill on her dress. 'Screaming and hitting when somebody says something you don't like is a very bad thing to do, babe. And so is talking back to an adult.'

'Laurence said I sound stupid. He said singers can't have a lisp so Simon Cowell will give me a big red X. I don't like it when people say things like that.'

'I know. But you can't just lose it when you get vexed.' She smooths down a stray curl from one of my plaits. 'And you need to control that fast mouth of yours. It's only going to get you in trouble.'

I pout. 'What about your fast mouth? You shouted at Mrs Zhang Lee.'

Mummy closes her eyes. 'All you need to remember is that you should never behave like that.'

'Like you when you yelled at Mrs Zhang Lee?'

'Yes. Like that. You're better than that.' She leans back against the sofa cushions, sliding down until she's nearly lying flat, and tries to make herself comfy. Shifting so that I'm lying next to her, I lean over and run my hand over her messy curls. She always puts them in a neat bun, but they've come out and are sticking up all over the place. I hold her hand in mine and rub my forefingers on her newly done nail varnish. She looks different in the pictures we have on the wall. Her face glows. But now she always has dark bits under her eyes which might be from all the crying she does when she thinks I'm sleeping.

'Can I sing?' I ask.

She opens one eye. 'Don't just sing, Goldilocks. Sing to me. Sing me to sleep.'

'Can we do "Amazing Grace"?'

She smiles. 'How sweet the sound? Go on, then.' Then she adds, 'It doesn't matter what anyone says, babe. Your voice is the most beautiful thing I could hear before I go to sleep.' She touches my nose with one finger. 'Don't ever forget that.'

So I do. Just the way she taught me. And she echoes, her voice soft as silk and in perfect harmony, stroking the top of my head as we sing. By the third verse, her voice is fading to a whisper, her hand almost still on the back of my head. I put my head on *her chest and sing the last verses of 'Hallelujah' to her heartbeat. Then I breathe in her work-and-cooking smell until my own eyes close.*

I press play. I've got a love-hate relationship with this song. It was more Lips' choice than mine, but the lyrics are so relatable to me that it almost hurts. Okay, so maybe it's a love song, but romantic love isn't inherently that different to family love, is it?

I turn the volume all the way up on my Mac, but I still drown it out through the first verse, into the pre-chorus, then the chorus.

I'm moving onto the second verse when I glance up and see the two faces pressed at the door. The door opens and Mr Driver steps in. I momentarily forget the lyrics and cuss.

Mr Driver raises his eyebrows. 'Kadie, that was impressive.'

I duck my head.

Mr Driver looks at Lips. 'Are you sure you're going to have a problem?'

Lips scowls.

'If she sings like that for the final piece, you'll both be sorted,' Mr Driver says reassuringly.

Lips pouts some more. 'She thinks she's the baddest.'

'Well, if you play your cards right, maybe you can make her good.'

I screw up my face. 'Don't count on it.'

Lips rolls his eyes. Thing is, though, Mr Driver's correct. I might not be acting like it, but I am seeing some serious pros of this duet thing. Excluding the 'deal', Lips still runs with Amalgamandem. He might not be the most popular of the group, but he's still got status. He wants to work with me so badly that he's offering *free studio time*.

I'm not turning down that offer.

Maybe this is my chance to change the state of play. And if I do it well enough, I might even end up at the top of the league.

ELEVEN

He turns up with no notice. I am passed out on the bed, the door barricaded, with a very polite door hanger illustrating this. When the hammering on the door rouses me, I am a lot less polite.

'WHAT??'

The knocking comes again. 'Wake up. There's someone—'

I only hear half of what's being said. 'GO AWAY.'

Shadavia pokes her head in. 'Lips is at the door.'

'WHAT?'

'Lips is here.'

She slams the bedroom door.

'What?' I sit up.

Why is Lips knocking for me at four-thirty in the afternoon?

I drag myself out of bed, rubbing my eyes fiercely. He's chosen the worst possible time to show up. Most of my room is organised in a very obsessive-compulsive manner, which should be a good thing – it helps me find stuff, anyway – but looking around, I suddenly get this flush of humiliation.

There are the freakishly precisely organised areas – like my desk, on which everything is white, or my colour-coordinated wardrobe, or my recording equipment painstakingly arranged at perfect angles. And then there are the pockets of chaos: my school bag spilling open onto the floor, my uniform in a twisted heap on top of it, those little areas that haven't been tidied since I last had a moment and threw and kicked stuff. And then of course there's me, stumbling around like a headless chicken.

I dive into my wardrobe for fresh clothes. It takes me twice as long as it should to find something. By the time I get downstairs, trying to adjust myself inside short-shorts, I'm still groggy, half-blind and beyond incensed. No way is Lips at the front door. They must be hallucinating. He'd have texted me if he was so desperate to practise that he just *had* to come over.

Charmaine is at the bottom of the stairs watching me as I lumber down. 'Are you expecting someone?' she asks sceptically.

I glance past her at Shadavia, who's glowering by the porch door. 'Yeah.'

Or I would be, anyway, if I'd checked my phone at quarter to four and seen his texts.

Vince is lingering at the front door, about to unlock it. He gives me an amused glance as he eases the door handle down. 'So you invited Lips round for a tea party?'

I shrug. 'He invited himself.'

'He invited himself?' Vince laughs dryly. 'Okay, that's a first. Man thinks he's a big shot, huh?'

I try to sound optimistic. 'We needed to rehearse.'

Vince opens the door and peers out and his expression changes as we both see the person on the other side, who is casually spinning in circles on a hoverboard, hands in pockets.

'Oi, big man.' Vince doesn't have to raise his voice to get anyone's attention. Lips stops spinning. 'What are you here for?'

Lips grins at me. 'Goldilocks didn't tell you?'

'I want to hear it from you.'

'We're rehearsing our duet piece.'

Vince watches him like a hawk as Lips steps into the house and puts his Nikes carefully to the side. 'Well, you're certainly making an effort, aren't you?' he says, leaning back for a good look.

I swallow back some rudeness. His outfit isn't bad. None of this Adidas from head to toe like most boys – just the jumper, a snapback wedged on top of his tufty hair and jeans that are not too roadman but a teeny bit too skinny for his backside. The only thing that doesn't match is the bulky guitar case on his back, the tip of which is nearly scraping the ceiling.

I cut my eye at Vince and take Lips straight upstairs to my room. Thankfully there was a space under the bed to shove my school stuff. Granted, it's not perfect, but that's not my fault.

Lips blinks hard in the low light and instantly looks lost. 'Why are your curtains shut in the middle of the day?'

'I was sleeping.'

He tuts. 'Cool. Can we open them a bit, so I can actually see where I'm stepping?'

I look at him.

'Like, for real?' His eyebrows come together. 'My vision is rubbish at the best of times. I don't want to break anything.'

I reluctantly open the curtains, squinting so that the light doesn't burn my eyes. Lips doesn't show any sign of having to adjust. Instead, he takes in my organised chaos – a makeshift recording studio – and a completely out-of-place smile lights up his face. 'This is so—'

'Let's get one thing straight,' I say loudly. 'Don't ever turn up at my house like this again and expect me to be sociable. Ev-er.'

'Turn up at your house like what?' he asks with that annoying innocence. 'I texted you a reminder. We talked about it in school.'

'We did not.'

'We did. You said it was cool.'

'And THEN I said it WASN'T cool.'

'Right before you left to skive last period?'

'Yes!'

'And you obviously didn't hear me saying I'd be coming anyway.'

I fight back a snarl. 'I'm tired.'

'From what?' he smirks. 'You basically did nothing in class at all today.'

'Nunya.'

'Well, it's my grade too, you know.' His voice is firm and big and very indignant. I don't know why, but this irritates me. A lot.

'I don't care. You can't just turn up to my house like this! You're lucky I was awake enough to answer the door.'

Lips just looks at me. 'So why did you make the effort to answer the door?'

I grit my teeth. He wants me to answer that. I can see it on his face.

'You're a joke,' I grumble.

'So are you.'

'Wasteman.'

'Wastegyal.'

'Shut up. You're in my room.'

'Do you wanna get a grade for this or not?' he demands.

My bedroom door swings open and Vince steps in. 'Everything alright?'

I sigh.

'I can drop kick him out the front door if need be,' Vince says without an ounce of guilt. He casts Lips a grey look. 'Hear that, mister? Any trouble and you're out the front door jazz-style.'

Lips turns slowly, head lolling like he's hard done by, and half-glares at Vince. 'I wasn't doing anything.'

Vince eyeballs him suspiciously.

'It's fine,' I say wearily. 'We'll manage.'

'Sure?'

'Sure.'

Vince retreats and pulls the door to.

Lips looks at me. 'Does "we'll manage" mean "we'll rehearse"?'

I roll my eyes.

'Is that a yes?'

I stomp across the room and straighten my bed sheets. Lips watches me, smirking, and sits down on the floor with his guitar.

Then he asks suddenly, 'Are you wearing anything under that shirt? Because I don't think your foster mum would be totally okay with me being in here when you're half naked.'

I turn to him and force myself not to roll my eyes again. Lips looks right back at me, innocently waiting. He raises his eyebrows. I hold his gaze, waiting for some cheeky comment or even that half-smile. He spreads his hands. I roll my eyes super slow and lift the baseball jersey I'm wearing so he can see the shorts underneath.

'Oh. What a relief.' Either he's actually being serious, or he has an extremely good poker face, but it's not so much that bothering me than the fact that he even thought such a thing. Why on earth would he think I'd let him in my room if I wasn't dressed?

Unless he really thinks I'm a sket.

I wouldn't put it past myself, *if* all that nonsense was true. But it's not. So I'm slightly vexed.

'You want something to eat?' I ask tightly.

'If it's going.'

I stomp downstairs and grab us a drink and a packet of crisps each. When I get back Lips is running through his part, and I'm sure I catch his eyebrows doing expressive Mexican waves before he sees me and stops abruptly. Kelly was wrong about him singing a cover. If you heard him sing without seeing his face, you'd never think he's so awkward.

I sit on my desk chair and swing from left to right. After some thought, I ask if he wants to record straight off so that we can play it back. My room's not the greatest studio, what with the bed and the wardrobe and the carpet, but it's better than nothing at all. Lips retunes his guitar and agrees with a tense shrug, positioning himself a little too close to me at the mic. He doesn't seem to notice how I stiffen.

He finds his first chord. 'Ready?'

I'm not ready, but I nod anyway.

He starts the intro to the song. He starts out flawless and goes on with a few fumbles. I twist my shirt in my fingers.

We are almost perfect. Almost. His voice is dreamy in a kind of deep-voiced, proper inner London sort of way. He doesn't sound like Ed Sheeran and I don't sound like Demi Lovato, unless Ed Sheeran articulated himself like Stormzy and Demi Lovato had the remnants of a lisp.

If Lips thinks anything bad of my singing, he keeps it to

114

himself and just nods when we reach the end. But after two run-throughs, he still wants to go through it again.

I spin on my chair. 'Are you mad, bruv?'

'No, I just think that bit in the bridge where you do the solo could be a bit . . . stronger.'

All the time we've spent on this – the discussions of how to divide the lyrics, when to harmonise and all that – and he decides to tell me this right now.

'Your plucking could be a bit more consistent.' It's a harsh fact, but the truth is, he hasn't quite mastered the song to an Ed Sheeran level just yet.

His nostrils flare. 'I've been practising every day,' he retorts. 'Do you practise every day?'

'Why does it even matter?'

'Because this is a Music GCSE, Kadie. It's a grade.'

'No, this is us trying to do a cover and failing miserably.'

'We're not failing.'

'We are.' I laugh bitterly. 'You can't play Ed Sheeran, okay? It's too complex for your fat fingers.'

His fingers aren't fat.

But I'm tired. And vexed. And strung-out.

Lips turns away and snatches up his guitar case. 'There's nothing wrong with it. It just needs more practice.'

'I don't know how you're so positive about that,' I mutter, grabbing a Red Bull from my hidden stash.

He kisses his teeth. 'Someone needs to be positive, since you obviously don't know how to.'

'I know when and where to be positive.'

'No, you just don't believe in yourself.'

'I believe in myself just fine.'

'Then why are you so reluctant to practise?' he demands. 'Why are you wasting my time with this stupid argument when we could be doing something towards an A? Sometimes I wonder if people are right about you being a wastegyal.'

I shoot to my feet. 'This was your idea, not mine! Why do you flipping CARE so much?'

Lips is shocked speechless at the volume of my voice. His mouth opens, closes, opens, closes.

'Why?' I slam my Red Bull down on a coaster. 'You don't even know me. We slagged each other off in the corridor! I didn't aks for your help. Nobody aksed you to give it to me. Nobody said you should rely on me to get a better duet grade than you already have! Why do you care if I get an A or an E?'

Lips shifts from foot to foot and twists a tuft of hair at the base of his neck. Have I scared him off?

When he lifts his head to face me again, he's doing that irritating lopsided smirk. 'I don't . . . I don't think I've ever seen you smile.'

'What?' I feel demeaned.

'You wear that screw-face all the time. D'you even look in the mirror?'

I'm on the brink of yelling for Vince. 'Yeah? So?'

'And you have a filthy attitude problem . . .' Lips shoulders his guitar case and heads for the door. 'Look . . . if you could just get some tropical vibes on instead of that ice queen demeanour, maybe we could do a collab. It would be sick, like if you had a Not3s and Lady Leshurr mashup. You know. If.'

He leaves me standing there, stunned.

A collab?

Lips and Goldilocks on a track together?

I can see it, and I'm stopping my heart doing pirouettes at the idea. Because Rule #3. Take things one step at a time.

I'm supposed to be seeing him out but he's already halfway down the stairs before I follow him. By the time I make it down to the porch, he's putting his shoes on. I watch him loop the laces through the Velcro without tying them and I don't say a word. He's knocked all the cockiness out of me.

Lips shoulders his guitar case and off he goes. 'Catch you later.' He says it more to the door frame than to my face.

I stamp up the stairs, officially in a bad mood. But now I've drunk Red Bull and there's no way I'm going back to sleep. I flip my door hanger to HELLO WORLD, I'M AWAKE and lean on the door frame, exhausted. Forget dinner. Forget homework. I just need sleep. Without wet sheets.

I bang my head on the door frame a few times. A little energy diffuses. I do it again and again and again. Wow. Why did I stop doing this?

'Kadie?'

Oh, I remember why.

'Are you alright?' asks Beverly. 'Daddy says you lose brain

cells every time you hit your head. You don't want to get dumb.'

I sigh. 'What's up, bruh?'

'I really liked your performance.'

'You what now?'

She gives me a hug from behind. 'I really liked yours and Dayan's singing.'

A weird feeling of warmth settles in my chest. 'Bae! Thank you. At least somebody liked it.'

'Shadavia doesn't like Dayan,' Beverly says into my back, 'but he's really nice, and his singing is so good. I don't understand big sisters.'

My ears prick up. 'Why doesn't she like him?'

'I don't really know. My BFF told me that her cousin's older brother's girlfriend said that he asked for her number and she curbed him in front of her whole squad and called him names or something. And then a few months later she got a bit drunk at a party and tried to kiss him but he wasn't having it, and she somehow managed to fall over and make it look like he pushed her off.'

'Classy.'

Beverly peeks under my armpit. 'I think she's sad because she started everyone calling him all sorts of names even though he's not any of them.'

'He is a bit awkward,' I admit. The words are a betrayal, like the pot calling the kettle black.

'She's also angry because he embarrassed her,' Beverly

adds, thoughtfully. 'I saw the video and it was like a Tom and Jerry moment. A vase fell on her head.'

'That's her own fault.'

'Lips isn't a wasteman, though.'

'Nope.'

'Even though they all call him that.'

'They?' I ask.

'Mostly Kelly. She slags him off when she comes round and they spend forever looking at his YouTube channel.' Beverly grins. 'And that's why Mummy says you shouldn't get drunk.'

'Because awkward guys might push you over when you try and kiss them?'

'Yeah.'

We both snicker.

'I don't get people,' Beverly declares.

I snort. 'Huh. That makes two of us.'

TWELVE

Counselling makes me feel pretty brain dead. Which is why I roll a zoot the moment I'm out of the door, lighting up in the toilets as the bell goes for lunch. If I'm discreet I won't get caught. I even tuck my hair into a beanie and pull my jacket over the top so that my blazer won't get the brunt of the smoke.

My phone goes off like mad as it receives tons of texts. I sigh to myself, rolling my eyes, but it's not Josh or anyone else I don't care to hear from. It's Lips.

where are you Kadie mandem wanna talk to you
why did you have to miss music it was amazing
they loved the duet

I emerge from my hiding spot, binning the zoot at the first opportunity. The crowds have spilled out of the corridors now and people are everywhere, faces and identical blazers and a mishmash of backpacks and handbags. So much moving colour. I linger at the side, keeping a wide gap between myself and the chaos. This would be the perfect place to get jumped. My brain's already conjuring up imaginary shoves from behind, dredging up old echoes of collective laughter from everywhere from bedrooms to kitchens to changing rooms and playgrounds. I pull my jacket further around myself and do my best to be invisible.

'Kadie!' A hand smacks down hard on my shoulder.

I whirl around. 'What?'

Junior spreads his arms. 'Why'd you skive Music?'

'I didn't skive. I had counselling. And one of those stupid progress meetings.'

'Told you, bro,' Lips says from behind.

I peek around Junior's shoulder. Michael and Reuben are trailing out of the doors of the Languages block, surrounded by a flock of girls. I'm pretty sure neither of them has ever willingly spoken to me before but their faces actually light up when they see me.

'Ayyy, it's the golden girl!' Michael hollers.

Junior adjusts his hat and grins. 'You never told us you and Lips had recorded your duet already!'

I smile. That's what happens when there's a fluke good day. I had one, so Mr Driver recorded us 'performing' after school that very afternoon. After all the time I'd spent daydreaming about all the things that could go wrong, it all fell into place kind of magically.

'Mr Driver was so pleased,' Lips says, smiling at me – a proper smile, not the half-smile. 'He played it to the class and everything.'

Junior nudges me. 'You two are a great combo. Your voices really work.'

The face-to-face compliments are making my face get hot. I struggle to keep my smile from getting too big. 'Thanks.'

'You know what I think?' Reuben says, looking directly at me probably for the first time. 'The lot of us could put together a pretty good ensemble cover. Drums, guitar, piano, violin, voice—' He points to each of the boys and I – 'We could pull it off.'

'Bruv, we ain't no boy band,' Michael snickers. But nobody disputes the idea. Actually, the lingering girls start grovelling, until the boys turn towards the Arts block. Everyone knows that's where they hang out, but the gaggle of girls gets the cue and goes in the opposite direction as the boys amble off.

Guess I'll just go eat lunch in a discreet corner.

Lips turns to me and jerks his head at the group. 'Come with.'

My heart seems to do a double beat in my chest. 'Really?'

He shrugs. 'I'm not leaving you on your ones. Come on.'

The others wait until Lips and I fall in step with them and off we go. I feel like I'm going in slow-mo all of a sudden. The way the boys position themselves, everyone makes way for them as they cut through the crowds heading in the opposite direction. It's probably because Junior walks so upright, with lanky Michael swaggering at his side.

On the way to the Arts block we pass the Shadavia clique. As usual, they're dragging their heels and talking dumb talk, the boys kicking a Coke can along and yelling at each other. It's been a long time since I walked so tall, so proud. I make a point of pretending not to notice their faces of disbelief. It puts a defiant smile on my face. I'm floating on a kind of real happiness I haven't felt for months. Rah, I'm *smiling*. That's a first.

Inside Mr Driver's room, AMD make themselves comfy in the corner where they always sit. I pull out a chair, sit on it backwards, and pop some gum in my mouth.

Compared to hanging out with the Kelly clique, hanging out with AMD is heaven.

Mr Driver greets us and pretends not to notice when Junior sets some bashment playing from his phone. Year Eleven privileges, I guess.

Junior stretches out in his chair and launches into a quiet chat about media with Reuben. Lips and Michael set about discussing things like who's better at FIFA (Junior) and who's got neater hair (Michael – that boy never parts with his pick). Michael and Lips exchange food and the four of them get into a debate about whether Ghanaian or Nigerian jollof rice is better. No one seems to give an ABC about the fact that I can't stay sat down.

I can feel Junior watching me at points, but that's just what he does. He stretches on a regular basis and eats his crisps quietly, taking everything in and looking like he's just rolled out of bed. Reuben, who's an amateur producer under the name Rubix, always seems to have a fancy camera around his neck and doesn't seem to mind being the only sixth former. He clocks me every now and then with this cautious tilt of the head, but like the rest of them, he acts like I'm as normal as anyone. Funny, that. I fit in with a bunch of boys miles better than the Kelly clique. Compared to those frosty looks Kelly used to shoot me, the boys' lazy banter is like love.

But it's Lips who is the icing on the cake.

In his comfort zone, suddenly another side of him comes out. His bottom doesn't touch his chair for more than a minute – instead he's lingering over Reuben and Junior's game of poker, commenting from under his hood in the same roadman voice he always uses. Then Mr Driver makes him remove his hoodie and asks him to sit down. Lips reluctantly perches himself on a chair next to me and proceeds to comb his mini 'fro with a large purple pick which, he admits, he has stolen from Michael. Against all rules, I really want to touch his tight curls with the tips of my fingers – and I'm sure he's got an inkling of this because he keeps glancing at me, that half-smile easing its way onto his face. Embarrassed, I hide my smile behind my sleeve.

Michael notices his stolen pick and a tussle breaks out as he retrieves it, ending with Lips spilling someone's water bottle all over the table. Lips exclaims loudly in a Ghanaian accent, his roadman voice all but gone, and pulls multiple faces as he frantically dries the spillage with his hoodie. Mr Driver still gives us a stern warning. Lips exclaims some more.

Michael spends the rest of break trolling him for his clumsiness but to my surprise, he doesn't switch back to brooding. He even catches my eye and gives me a full-on smile and a playful wink.

When lunch ends, I'm quite disappointed.

*

The fire alarm comes without warning, as they do. Thanks to my lack of effort in the past three years, I've been dropped about two classes lower than I should be, so there I am sitting at the front of third set English – miles away from Lips and the boys – daydreaming and only marginally listening to Mrs Soares droning on about Dr Jekyll and Mr Hyde. I pretend to take notes and doodle instead, listening to the echo of other classes floating up the hall through the open door.

Mrs Soares made a mistake putting me at the desk right by the door – not that it would really make a difference anyway because as far as I'm concerned, any effort I make just goes to waste. I'm just going to end up at a different sixth form in six months' time and never mind uni – I'm probably headed for Tesco at this rate. Even if I tried, the system's not exactly designed for foster kids to do well. Especially if they get pinballed around like me.

So there I am shading in the lines in the margin instead of doing the warm-up question when this piercing, screaming, wailing noise blasts into the classroom from the corridor. Ducked heads bob up, followed by excited whispers. Mrs Soares is on edge straightaway.

Squeezing my eyes shut, I count the seconds. *One*

Mississippi, two Mississippi, three Mississippi – Please don't let it be a fire drill – six Mississippi, seven Mississippi –

It cuts off. Mrs Soares is trying to maintain order, but already the anticipation has spread. Everyone is on the edge of their seats as we wait for the second bell to go that will signal us to evacuate. My stomach tumble-turns inside as fear clamps around my heart. I hate the swirling chaos of people crammed in around me. It draws out a panic I can't explain, turns me into an uncontrollable mess that nobody can ever know about. *Please no fire drill please no fire drill please no—*

It goes again. Screaming, piercing, rattling its way through my body with a power no sound should have. I plug my ears, but it's too late: the alarm has already churned up the fear I'd stuffed far down below and it drags it back up by the ear as Mrs Soares directs the class into the corridor, shouting about how to behave. I rise obediently to the screech of chairs scraping on the floor. The sound of everyone evacuating crams itself into the corridor – the stamp of restless feet, the excited chatter, the fire alarm screaming screaming screaming the way my brain is screaming at me to get out of here.

The corridor was such a different place earlier, with the boys there and all of us bantering just enough for me to ignore the squeezing surroundings. Now the whole world is alive with glee because lesson's come to an abrupt stop. Theories are being thrown left to right – who burned their toast, who blew something up in science?

No one bothers theorising with me.

Students pile into the corridor, pressing so close front and behind that it feels like the oxygen seems to have disappeared, crushed into heat and suffocating chatter. Classes mingle one into the next as the whole school forms a stream of blue blazers heading to the basketball courts. Somewhere far up ahead I catch a glimpse of Lips' head of tufts; Junior is recognisable just from his laid-back walk, even at this distance. A sudden desperation to be with someone settles on my shoulder like a heavy hand, but the boys are too far away for me to even shout to them. At least there would be someone to help me not to think about the crowd squeezing the air out of my lungs.

'Kadie, you alright?' a girl asks, tapping me from behind. I jerk away and nod fiercely, but apparently ferocity isn't enough: another girl chips in with, 'Why you looking so vex?' Like it's a joke. A few kids laugh because they can. Somehow I tune into the roar of the whole school heading for the courts, and the noise of feet stamping and voices rising and falling drowns them out. Normally this wouldn't be too much of a problem. Today the pushing of the crowd has my head spinning and my heart slamming around in my chest with the nerves, the fear of so many things I can't figure out how to say. How do you explain that sometimes everything can be too much?

Out on the basketball courts, we line up by class in the autumn sun – Year Sevens at one end, right up to Year Thirteen at the other – while the teachers order us into straight lines as if it's life or death. Then it's the wait. In my great experience, these agonizing waits can be anything from fifteen minutes to forty. Fingers crossed it's the former.

Alone in the midst of everybody else's bemused chatting, I suddenly feel very aware of the fact that I'm on my own. This usually wouldn't bother me, but right now my solitude has left me alone with a barrage of thoughts and other things tumbling around my head.

There is nothing worse than being on your own.

After glancing around, I quietly slip my phone out of my blazer pocket. I've always carried a picture of my mum with me. Sometimes just a glimpse of her face is enough to cull the suffocating loneliness.

I pop the case off slightly and slide out the laminated photo. It's always comforting to know it's there if I need to look at it: a snapshot of one of our good days, a rare moment when she was smiling. Probably on one of her random days off work between jobs, when she'd turn round and announce that I wouldn't be going to school that day. She was unpredictable like that. Not that you would ever know by looking at the photo, the way her arms are thrown around my shoulders, her head tilted slightly as if to say, *come on then* – and me, with my eyes closed mid-laugh.

My fingers are trembling slightly as I rub my thumb over Mummy's face, fighting to keep my breathing steady as the thunderous presence of thousands of students melts me slowly. Mummy never quite believed in my quirks. I told her about what went on in my head sometimes. *The sound of everything is* real, I insisted. *It never leaves me alone. There's never silence.* She rolled her eyes. She was probably tired, but still . . . maybe she just didn't want to believe that I'm not perfect. Or maybe just a bit mad.

Still, if she were here, she would hug me. Tell me to breathe. Remind me that I can get through this. Think of a song.

'Woah!' Somebody jogs me suddenly. My phone flips in the air, hits the tarmac and skitters towards the 11F line.

'Oops!' Aidan's grinning widely. He's quite handsome actually. In a different world, he would totally make good friend material if he decided to show his non-wasteman side. I ball my fists. He's *so* lucky that my phone landed face-up.

We both lunge for the phone, but Aidan gets there first, scooping it up and peering at the photo that's still sticking out of the top of the case.

'That's cute,' he says after a long moment, and slides it gently out of sight. 'You checking what the time is?'

'Yes. Give it, please.' My heart is going wild again. *No. No, no, no—*

'Come get it.' Aidan holds it out of reach. I inch closer, not wanting to play his game, but his arms are fractionally longer than mine. I grab for his hand. He dodges. I try to get a hold of his blazer sleeve. He dances further away, in and out of the line, out of the crowd and back again. I lunge again and he twirls out of my reach.

'Oi! Is that a phone I see?'

Aidan spins around to find himself face to face with Mr Kulendran, tech teacher-cross-grizzly-bear. Mr Kulendran has a handy couple of extra inches to glare down from, which he does. Aidan steps back. His grin's been wiped so far off his face it's pretty much over in the gutter.

I throw Aidan a pointed look. 'Can I have my phone, please?'

Mr Kulendran frowns disapprovingly and holds out his hand as if to accept the phone. Aidan's hand twitches as he glances between us. His half-second of hesitation is enough. Even as I swipe for it, my phone is already in the bear paws. Aidan doesn't even have the decency to try and put up a fight.

Why can't people just help me out for once?

I shove my way into Mr Kulendran's face. 'He took it from me! I need it, sir—'

'It should be in your locker,' he says.

Okay, yeah, it should be – but how do I explain that I need it? I need things to help me stay calm. *Stay calm.* If I could, I would have Emerson with me, but I can't risk him getting found and it isn't like there aren't other ways to help diffuse the thud of emotion in my temples. Remembering Mummy just so happens to be one of them. But I daren't leave a picture of her in my blazer because it would end up getting washed in the washing machine at some point.

'I need it, sir.' My voice shakes.

'If you need it so badly you can get it from me at three thirty, after a detention.'

'No, you really don't get it.' I'm holding on, I really am, but by my fingertips. 'I need it *now*.'

'I'm not discussing this anymore.' Mr Kulendran turns away, putting the phone in his pocket. My throat feels dry and my palms . . . *No.* They're getting hot. *No, please—*

'Please, sir. Please! I need it! You can't just—'

Mr Kulendran's not even listening. He's walking towards the gate, where the classes are slowly beginning to filter back into the building. There goes my phone.

I shudder and curse under my breath.

'Sorry, Kadie.' Aidan rests a hand on my shoulder. 'It was just a joke. I didn't mean that to happen.'

I whip around, knocking his hand off. 'You "didn't mean that to happen"? Bruh, you practically gave him the phone!' My voice is big and I'm right in his face, breathing the heat of my face and fists out onto Aidan's chest. Just for good measure, I shove him. He barely moves.

Somebody behind me laughs and I make the mistake of glancing in that direction. More sniggering. Maybe it's not coming from the other Year Elevens – there is so much noise swirling, all trying to get into my head, that things are getting jumbled. Which is frustrating. Which doesn't help at all.

'What's going on?' demands Mrs Soares.

'Kadie's phone got nicked by Mr Kulendran,' someone says helpfully.

'It shouldn't have been out,' Mrs Soares tells me. 'Sorry, but that's the rules.'

'It wasn't even me!' I yell. 'Aidan had it!'

Mrs Soares beckons gently. 'Come over here.'

'No. I just need my phone.'

She's saying more, but I can't hear anymore – only partly because I'm choosing not to – and that same phrase keeps going round and round in my head. *I just need my phone. I just need my phone.*

Someone's calling my name but it gets lost in my head as I turn and head back towards the school. I need to get away. I need space.

'Hey. Are you okay?' Aidan again. He's following me. 'Seriously?'

I don't stop walking. 'Bruh. Do I look okay?'

He purses his lips, a little lost. 'No, actually, you look like you're about to burst a blood vessel.'

'Leave me alone.'

'We're not allowed to go back inside yet,' he says, right as a teacher says the same thing.

I push through the gate anyway. Play the stubborn student and people sometimes leave you alone to simmer down by yourself. Whether or not you actually need the space is sometimes irrelevant.

'Kadie. Wait up.' Aidan's *still* behind me.

'Get lost.'

'No. Look, I'm sorry. I wasn't trying to be an idiot.'

'You can say that again.'

'You're cold, you know that?' he says.

I stop dead in front of a teacher who's about to tell me I can't go back in the building yet. 'If I'm so cold, why don't you go away before you get frostbite?'

He shrugs violently. 'Why don't you learn to take a joke?'

I turn fast, possessed by a combo of anger, lingering distress, and straight-up choice. Aidan takes my fist square in the left eye, so hard that he reels back. Suddenly I'm yelling again, yelling words I can't even make out over all the bits of everything twisting in my head like brambles, tearing me up from the inside. He needs to know that nobody talks to me like that. He needs to know he crossed a line and that's why I'm vexed – but now that I've let a little loose I don't know if I can rein it back again. Aidan's shouting at me now, holding his eye with one hand.

Teachers flock our way like it's the gold rush and already they're saying those toxic words—

Come on

Breathe

Calm down

My head feels like it's going to explode. What with all the shouting, I feel like I've opened the valve on the pressure. Throwing that punch and screaming at Aidan – that was me in control.

But now too many people are trying to guide me, to make me sit down, to divert my attention, to stop me going towards the other students. Suddenly I'm letting off too much steam at once, allowing the heat in my chest to speak volumes. Why? I can't tell you why.

The teachers have their arms spread, as if they're trying to herd me into a corner. I get gobby. 'Oh, so I'm a danger now? No, I'm not gonna sit down. I'll sit down when you leave me alone. Don't touch me! Why don't you just give me my phone back, then? WHY DON'T YOU JUST GIVE ME MY PHONE BACK?'

But they won't. Obviously. They just keep saying those toxic words.

I shove my way through the teacher barricade, wrestle my way past a few arms and burst out of the crowd. Where? I don't know, but I'm running, making a beeline for the car park.

Round the front, in a corner, I crouch behind a car until I'm sure nobody is coming, biting my lip hard. What a sight to behold. The notorious Kadie Hunte, kicking off again. Bet somebody caught it on camera. I've set myself up for more misery.

On the way out, I take out my frustration on the wall, because the wall can't get injured. The pain kicks in with the second and third hit, but it takes some more before the agony matches the grazed knuckles and the rage has been diffused a bit.

A bit, but not enough.

Still not enough by the time I get home to an empty drive.

When I remember that my key is next to Emerson at the bottom of my bag, in my English classroom.

Exhausted, I collapse on the doormat. The rules are sitting at the back of my mind, pushing into my conscience like a pin – *don't break us, don't break us* – but I've got no fight left; my angry fire is burned out. There are no words left to describe how utterly useless I am.

I put my head on my knees and sob.

THIRTEEN

'Kadie, I need you to trust me.' Charmaine has no idea what she's asking. She has no idea of anything. Bloody, bruised knuckles and a grazed knee from where I tripped up don't tell the whole story, even if she found me slumped against the front door, red-eyed and shaking and not looking at all like myself.

I would've been busted if I'd used my secret key to let myself into an empty house, but even that would have been better than seeing her look of horror as she pulled up in their big VW van, parking it askew in her hurry to get out and ask what was going on. At least then I wouldn't have had her on my back, telling me to come back down ASAP as I went upstairs, planning to shut myself in my room – only to discover that the tidying fairy had been by. Not only had the tidying fairy been by; she had cleared up my organised mess *and* found the wet towel and clothes I hid under my bed. After a pretty good dry streak, I'd had a really bad night. In the end I rinsed the stuff out in the sink and was waiting for an ideal opportunity to wash them in secret, but the sheet was a matter I hadn't even considered.

Apparently I don't need to. The tidying fairy has swept away all traces of last night *and* changed my sheets, right down to the duvet cover.

That means somebody knows. And if somebody knows, somebody could ask. That sends my heart spiralling into a wild, fearful beat.

I don't want to talk about the bed-wetting.

I don't want to talk about school.

I am in hell. I just about got out of my uniform, and now I don't want to do anything.

'Kadie.' Charmaine raps on the bathroom door gently. 'I can't help you if you won't respond to me.'

I stretch my fingers out slowly. The skin around my knuckles is starting to turn a sickly purple where it's not bleeding. There's no way I'll be writing with my right hand tomorrow.

'I'm not going away, you know,' Charmaine adds. 'I'm not putting my feet up until I know everything is okay. Which it clearly isn't.'

Reluctantly, I reach up and slide the lock back, before moving so that my back is against the bath tub instead of the door. Minutes later, Charmaine is sitting cross-legged beside me, holding a first-aid kit and a piece of aloe vera fresh from one of her biggest plants. And by fresh I mean dripping with sticky greenish liquid that has a potent natural smell which I'm not sure if I like.

'I'll start on that knee, shall I?'

She works quickly, saying nothing to my red eyes and messy hair as she swabs my knee and covers it with a plaster that doesn't match my skin tone.

With my knuckles, she wipes the sticky juice that oozes from the cut end of the aloe vera stalk. 'Keep them like that until it dries,' she instructs. Then, as if this is all normal, she adds, 'Do you want something to eat?'

I shrug. My appetite's gone for a road trip. Though come to think of it, my throat is really dry and actually – bar a Red Bull and, like, a slice of toast – I haven't eaten since yesterday. I'm absolutely starving. Also dog tired. And my head hurts.

I plod downstairs after Charmaine and rest my head on the kitchen table – awkwardly, since I'm trying not to get aloe vera on anything.

Charmaine puts the kettle on, plops a glass of warm milk in front of me, and settles herself down at the other end of the table behind a Lorraine Pascale cookbook.

I lift my head slightly. 'Why are you being so nice?'

Charmaine looks up from her cookbook. 'That's what I'm here for, and I'm well aware that we're in a bit of a pickle.'

'A bit?' I croak. Some wry laughter finds its way out. 'A BIT?'

My stuff is still at school. Any rep I might have had is down the drain. I'm on a one-way road to exclusion just from skipping detentions. It's not a bit of a pickle, it's enough to be several jars' worth of old, mouldy pickles. In fact, for some people *I* am the pickle.

'You invaded my room,' I say into my forearms.

A page turns. 'Yes ... I was picking up your piles of organised mess to go in the wash – which is something *you* should be doing, by the way.'

I sigh. 'It was a one-off. Nightmares again. You know how it is.'

She turns another page. The embarrassment swells in my chest again, and everything else too. Scenarios play out in my head. I can already hear the sickening ping of my phone. The urge to check my DMs is always there – part of that yearn for acceptance I guess. Don't know why I always want to know what people are saying. I *know* what people will be saying. Imagine what will happen when Amando gets home, when Charmaine tells him. I can practically hear the echo of a slap already.

'You can tell me whatever you want,' Charmaine says coolly. 'I'm not going to judge. We've had some crazy times in this house.'

She speaks for everyone, does she?

The swelling rises up my throat and chokes me. My head pounds. I let loose a mouthful of cussing into my sleeve. There are no tears left in my eyes but they still sting like mad.

When I don't say anything for a long time, Charmaine adds, 'It's alright to have weaknesses, you know. Nobody's perfect.'

Yeah, and some of us are more imperfect than others.

I listen to the rhythm of my leg jiggling restlessly.

Charmaine hasn't moved. She's waiting for a response that's never going to come because I can't, I really can't put myself out there. Even though there's *still* that little dot of hope. The what if. What if I talk and someone listens?

The kettle finishes boiling. Charmaine fixes herself a pink herbal tea of some kind and puts together a tray of snacks, which she rests on the table between us before going back to her book, munching chilli crisps.

I slump there and watch her for a long time until she fixes me with those dark-dark eyes and asks, 'Red velvet or coffee cake?'

I prop myself up on my elbows. 'What?'

'Red velvet or coffee cake? For dessert?'

I sniff. 'Red velvet. Why?'

She shrugs. 'I feel like making something.' Then she stops. 'Hmm. I don't have any food colouring, though. I might have to attempt to use beetroot.'

'Beetroot red velvet?' I try not to curl my lip. We had beetroot last week and it didn't go down very well with anyone except Charmaine. 'Go for the coffee cake.'

She laughs and offers me a cracker, homemade. I take one, spread cream cheese on it delicately. Wow. It's almost exactly like a shop cracker except slightly less salty, with a stronger, wheaty flavour. Charmaine can really cook.

She rings the school while we sit there and tells them bluntly that I'm at home and won't be back for the rest of the day, as my 'emotional state' is 'quite worrying'. They want to know why – what's wrong with me, in detail – because apparently everybody knows I caused a scene during the fire drill.

I sip my milk to distract myself from the angry words forming on my tongue. It wasn't just a show. It wasn't.

Charmaine cuts the office lady off by asking about my stuff, curtly telling them she'll pick it up from reception at three-fifteen, and hanging up.

'Why'd you do that?' I demand.

'What? Tell them you won't be back?' She raises one eyebrow. 'Would I be a good mum if I sent you right back to school?'

'By school standards, yes.'

'I'm not running by school standards.'

'But aren't you vexed?'

'Vexed isn't quite the word I would use.'

'But I peed up your bed.' I catch my breath, surprised with myself, and look away.

Charmaine shrugs. 'I'm not angry,' she clarifies. 'I'm concerned.'

'I'm sorry I'm a problem.'

She shakes her head fervidly. 'You are not a problem.'

'That's what they said at my last school. I overheard my head of year calling me a major problem that needed to be solved, or something like that. They chucked me out the following week.'

Charmaine arches her eyebrows. 'There was quite an

incident at that last school though, mm?' She says this with firm casualness, without looking up from her book. Why is she so good at that?

I play with my mad mop of hair, pulling at strands and checking to see how much of the curl is coming back. In all my time here, none of them have said a word about what happened at my last school. Of course, Shadavia and Vince have picked up bits and bobs from rumours, but nobody really knows the full story. Nobody knows the reason I flipped in that class but me, and who's going to listen to the notorious Kadie Hunte after she attacked another student?

I glance up and realise Charmaine is looking at me, maybe slightly expectantly.

I shrug. 'This girl kept winding me up.'

'"Kept winding you up"? As in, multiple times in one day, or consistently over time?'

I twist a strand that is holding onto its straightness. The end is split and gold when I hold it up to the light. 'Both. She found out about me being in care and couldn't get over it.' My voice trembles unexpectedly.

'So she started teasing you.'

'Yeah.' That I could take – it was nothing new after all – but of course she had to take it up a notch. 'Then she got bored with that, started getting chatty about my mum.' My heart shivers just thinking about it. 'She kept on saying stuff that was way out of line until I just lost it. Like, Incredible Hulk kind of lost it. Except I didn't turn green.' Instead I

142

grabbed a chair and launched it. Then a textbook. Then a fistful of her hair. I was probably lucky I didn't get arrested for minor GBH.

Charmaine has put her cookery book down on the table and is fully listening to me. She tries to smile at the terrible Hulk joke, but her eyes are sad. 'Is that what happened today?' she asks gently.

No. Yes. Maybe.

I shrug. It's hard to pinpoint what was going on in my head earlier. Sorting out thoughts isn't generally a problem from day to day, but it always is when I'm frustrated or upset – when the world is pounding me from all sides and I'm trapped and looking for the place where I belong.

I drain the rest of my milk and get up to dump the cup in the sink. 'I don't know what happened today.'

There's a moment of silence. I mentally cross my fingers. *Please don't ask me any more. Please don't.*

When she definitely isn't going to press the matter, I ask tentatively, 'Are you going to try and help me?'

Charmaine empties the last of the chilli crisps into her palm. 'I *am* going to help you,' she corrects me. 'There is no *try*. Especially not with that kind of emphasis. I'm going to do something to help you if it kills me.'

I nod. 'Okay, well, you have to promise me something.'

'That depends on what it is, but ask away.'

'If you can't help me, don't move me to another family. Not even respite.'

143

Charmaine blinks, her forehead half-furrowed. 'Um . . . why would we . . .?'

I extend one hand, baby finger protruding. 'Pinky promise.'

'Kadie—'

'Pinky promise.'

'We'll get through this,' she says firmly. 'We'll find a way to make things work one way or another. There's always a solution – it's just that we have to find one.'

I love how she says *we*, not *you*. But I still repeat myself so aggressively that my voice cracks. 'Pinky promise.'

Charmaine links her pinky with mine. 'I promise.'

'You won't throw me away if you can't help me?'

I stop for a moment, like, rah, I'm really saying it. *Don't throw me away*. And I'm looking straight at her.

'You won't throw me away if you can't help me?' I repeat the words slowly, calmly. That little voice in the back of my head is silent.

Charmaine smiles. 'I promise.'

FOURTEEN

Amando and Charmaine are talking about me and they think nobody can hear. Every door between the kitchen and the stairs is closed, so nobody normal can hear them, but my ears are freakishly fine-tuned today.

'. . . but even so, it's not going at all how I thought it would. I just don't understand anymore. I didn't understand before.'

Charmaine is silent and Amando goes on. '. . . I'm not sure if I even understood from the beginning. There are so many things I thought I got.' He sighs. 'Does she even want a father?'

'I think so.'

I want to think that Charmaine is right, I really do. But Amando? So far this man hasn't shown me anything but antisocial skills and where's the uniqueness in that? He might be a step ahead of all the other 'dads' I've had in the past – at least he's above the slapping at least – but at the same time, he's not much better than any of the others. Love does not show itself in gold chains and Adidas. Especially when you have a daughter whose Converse collection is growing faster than her Adidas collection.

'Does she *want* me for a father figure?' Amando sounds weirdly nervous.

'Of course,' Charmaine tries to reassure him. 'She just doesn't know what to do with you.'

I know exactly what to do with him.

Rule #3. Be prepared to lose everything. It's already happened before. It took some years and lots of placements for me to see the trend, get the picture. The dads are the hardest to win, the easiest to lose, and the least understanding. If they don't try, you don't waste your effort. Follow the rules. Stay safe.

'RAH!' Vince grabs me by the shoulders, his fingernails digging in, and gives me a good shake the way he likes to do. Taken by surprise, I lose my balance, regain and turn fast, smacking Vince in the eye as I skitter to the other side of the hall.

'Ow! You idiot!' Vince protests.

'Why've you gotta do that?' I demand.

'It was just a joke!' he snaps, still holding his eye. 'Why can't you take a joke?'

I stamp into the living room to get away from him – my mind's still trying to decipher what I've just heard – but Vince follows me. 'Little sket,' he goes on, like this is supposed to help. He shoves me. 'You think you can do anything, don't you? Being fostered doesn't mean you can do anything, just because your real family's messed up.'

That strikes a nerve. 'Tch. Coming from you!' I reach for the nearest thing – a *National Geographic* from the coffee table – and lob it at him. The pages twirl as it flies past Vince's head and thuds on the wall.

There's a rush of footsteps. Amando's at the door, flanked by Charmaine. He fills most of the doorway.

'What's going on?' he demands.

'Kadie punched me in the eye,' Vince says before I can get a word in.

'Don't forget that you—'

Amando gives me a disappointed look. 'You owe him an apology.'

'Man came up and grabbed me first. Like, come on, respect my personal space.'

'That doesn't make it okay to punch him.'

'It was an accident!'

'You still need to apologise.'

I exhale through my teeth. It's always me. Especially where the 'father figures' are concerned.

'We're waiting,' says Amando.

I wait.

'Kadie, I'm warning you.' Amando sits on the arm of the sofa, just the way Charmaine tells us not to. 'You can apologise now, and keep things easy, or you can choose not to apologise, and take things down a route which is much more difficult for everyone.'

I let my brain listen to the TV and the fridge humming, and the sound of the girls upstairs. In my back pocket, my phone does its Snapchat noise. I step back and take a peek.

People have been messaging me non-stop after they started posting captions everywhere about my semi-accidental meltdown during the fire drill. As usual, somebody somewhere had a conveniently placed camera and now that shaky video keeps getting shared and shared so it's never going to disappear, and random people keep sending me DMs and posting on my Insta saying stuff like

you really are a freak just get lost

wow anger management problems much

Ngl did not expect her to get restrained

surely goldilocks is a different person to this mess

who is this kadie hunte girl

'Kadie.' Amando's voice has officially reached stern levels. 'We're waiting.'

'I'm not apologising until he apologises for starting it.'

'She's a waste of space, Amando, just allow it,' Vince grumbles. He tries to go, but Amando holds him back.

I open one of my messages. It flashes up for two seconds: a white bottle of some chemical. And the caption:

Your voice makes everyone want to be deaf just go drink bleach

Amando grabs my phone as the message disappears. 'We're waiting for an apology.'

'You're not getting one 'til Vince apologises.'

Vince throws his hands up. 'I don't get what I'm apologising for, but whatever. I'm sorry I grabbed you.'

He storms out. Charmaine darts after him.

I shout after him, 'I'm sorry for hitting you. It really was an accident! Okay?'

'No,' Amando says, putting his arm out to stop me leaving. 'Not okay.'

I snatch my phone back. 'Nothing I do is every okay with you, though, is it? You're never going to be okay with me until I'm out of your house forever – let's face it – so why don't I just get my orange juice and get out of your hair?'

His mouth opens in shock and hangs there. 'You, young lady, have crossed the line a long time ago and you are going to feel my wrath.'

'I already *am* feeling your wrath!' I snarl. 'You don't care about me one bit! You'd probably be happy if I was dead! Then you'd have one less problem under your roof.'

'Oi! Cut the cheek!' His voice swells. 'Put your phone on the coffee table and sit down. Clearly there are a few things you need to understand about how this house works.'

'I know how this house works. The cookie jar is always empty, we leave the house keys on the hooks in the porch at night, pocket money is based on the effort you put into your chores and doesn't exclude foster kids—'

'You're pushing it, Kadie. Pushing it.'

The lyrics to a Not3s song pop into my head. I sing, '*I said I'm pushing I'm pushing I'm pushing up—*'

'I'm not going to ask you again,' Amando warns.

'Fine. Your loss.'

He moves to block my way out. 'Look. First off, I expect you to have some respect when you're talking to other members of this family. I don't care if it's one of the kids or me or Charmaine, but you need to start having some respect.'

'Yeah? Then maybe you can start having some respect for me too.'

A muscle twitches under his eye. 'Pardon?'

'I said maybe you lot can start respecting me too. Just because you think I'm a beg doesn't mean I'm always out to do something wrong. I just want my orange juice.'

'It takes two to tango,' he says. 'You've got to use respect if you want to be respected, and you're certainly not using it now.'

'Neither are you.'

'Okay. Sit down.'

I scramble past him, over the arm of the sofa, to the door. 'Why? I just want my orange juice.'

Amando starts to call me back, but I slam the kitchen door between us. By some miracle, he doesn't come after me.

My phone starts singing and dancing with a call from Lips. I answer it, balancing a carton of orange juice and a handful of biscuits against my chest. 'What you saying?'

'What you saying? I've been meaning to call you, Little Miss Naughty,' he says. 'Can I drop round?'

'Why?'

'Why not?'

'You ain't coming up to my room, bruv. They got me on lockdown.'

'So I can come?'

'Sure you can.'

I sit outside the front door to wait for him, slurping my orange juice. There's a chilly breeze, but I don't feel it much apart from when it shifts my crazy curls back and forth. My hair needs straightening. I'd like to braid it some time, maybe even cane row it, but I can't seem to pull off a neat set of braids. Back in the day, my mum used to do them. Usually she did them so tightly that I almost wished I'd never asked. Once or twice, I had a foster sister or a friend who'd do it. But good things don't last forever.

The sound of the front door opening catches my attention. I duck my head and prepare to get yelled at or smooth-talked by Charmaine.

'Ah. Thought I'd find you here.' Amando pulls the door shut behind him and sits down next to me, hugging his jacket around him.

After an awkward moment of silence, he says, 'You have a pretty impressive taste for bling.'

My empty juice carton crumples in my fist. 'No one says "bling" anymore.'

He rubs his beard. 'Ice. Gold. Whatever you yutes call it these days.'

'What do you want?' I demand.

'To apologise.'

Great. Here comes the adult sob story.

'You're not going to ask what for?' Amando enquires, leaning forward to get a look at my face.

'I don't care what for.'

'I just wanted to say that next time there's an altercation I'll try and do things differently.'

'Differently how?'

Amando stares at the ground for a long time. 'I don't know yet. But something will change.'

A classic promise. I bite back a sneer.

He looks at me. 'You don't believe me?'

I screw up my face. 'Why should I believe you? Why should I believe anyone?'

Instead of answering, Amando changes the subject. 'I don't want you out of my house, and I would most definitely care if you were dead.'

'Prove it.'

Amando's mouth hangs open. He moistens his lips and stares at the floor, silenced. I wait, but there is no revolutionary apology, no promise for a different future, not even a hint of interest in why I am out here. He gets up, murmuring, 'Don't stay out here too long. You'll catch a chill.' And then he's gone again.

Lips rolls up – literally – on a hoverboard, wrapped up in a puffer jacket and carrying a Co-op bag bursting with food. He steps off the hoverboard like it's a royal chariot, restless arms swinging, and lumbers my way. 'What you saying? Long time no see.'

I blow smoke out of my nose by way of an answer. It feels like it's been forever but it's only the second day after the fire drill. I got two days' suspension – plus another three days of seclusion when I return – for fighting, along with a lengthy list of previous sanctions – non-attendance to about three different detentions, incorrect uniform, misconduct in lessons, non-compliance . . . the list goes on. Seclusion is pretty good if you ask me. I get to sit in a quiet room in Pastoral and read books while pretending to do school work. That sort of makes up for the stress of losing my head in front of everyone, and also bulks up my *don't mess with Goldilocks* rep.

'Alright?' Lips sits down next to me on the front doorstep, knocking my leg as his knees spread themselves wide. His hands find something in his pocket to play with almost instantly.

I pose and take a snap of us without his permission. 'I'm fine.'

'Then why are you sporting such a screw face? You've had two days off school. What's not to enjoy?'

I lower my phone. 'That's two days of being cramped up in the house with Charmaine practically holding me on a leash. Cookery lessons, laundry – come on, who wants to hang up

Shadavia's bras and Vince's smelly boxers? You'd be wearing a dark face too if you were in my shoes.'

Lips laughs. 'Is that a hint of sarcasm I detect?'

'No. I was being serious. And like that wasn't enough, I also got extra Maths work because I'm supposed to be a genius.'

He snorts. 'Poor you! I bet you got that extra work done in like ten minutes.'

'Fifteen.'

'Same difference. You got to do it in the comfort of your home. Meanwhile, I was sat doing the same work in a lesson so boring I could have died.'

'I'll be sure to bring a defibrillator when I come back,' I say dryly.

Lips' smile widens as he gets the joke. 'Thank you. Miss Pigeon's lesson are pretty dead right now as well. She's so unobservant. I managed to make three rubber band people while I was sat on the front row, right under her nose.'

His restless hands dip into his coat pockets and a moment later a little red person is dangling from his fingertips, fashioned totally from rubber bands.

I take the little person in my hand and play with the little looped legs and arms. The faceless round head is kind of cute. I make the person dance on my knee and Lips produces another rubber thing – a dog. With a collar made out of wire.

'Captain Rubber Butt,' he explains, making growling noises.

They dance some more. I can't stop the giggles that start slipping out – and I don't think it's just the greenery. They dance together until Captain Rubber Butt does an imaginary number two on my kneecap and runs away down my thigh.

Sighing away my laughter, I blow the last of my smoke into the air and realise I've been swaying from side to side for a couple of minutes without thinking about it. It happens sometimes, particularly when I'm smoking, and it's not even like I do it consciously. It just happens.

Crushing my zoot underfoot, I make a conscious effort to stop moving. *Act.*

'I bet everyone's talking, aren't they?' I ask solemnly, staring out at the road.

'Sharing is more like it,' Lips mumbles.

Great.

'Snapchat?' I try and sound nonchalant like I was before I saw the video.

'Snap. Insta.' He somehow manages to look as distraught as I feel and for some reason, that makes me a bit angry.

'Not me, though.' Lips holds his hands up. 'Not me.'

I skip demanding proof of his loyalty. 'What about the mandem?'

He looks flustered. 'Erm . . . I don't know. I'd like to say yes.'

'You don't seem to know them very well.'

He says nothing and taps the foot pad of his hoverboard. One hand bounces Captain Rubber Butt on his thigh and the other zips and unzips his coat repeatedly, so I can see the bigger, heavier (and possibly much faker) gold chain hanging over his shirt. He really likes the ice, this boy. That's weird. He's just like me. I half hoped Charmaine and Amando didn't notice because I don't feel like they promote that kind of thing, but I've been wearing gold caps on my teeth for a couple of days now, and today I'm wearing two heavy (real) bracelets on each wrist and my mum's old chain (also real) around my neck.

'Why did you come in the first place?' I ask, to drown out the sound of Lips' incessant zipping. 'Cos I'm pretty sure it wasn't just to show off the hoverboard.'

He grins mischievously and bumps me hard with one shoulder. 'Nope. I came to get you to ride it.'

I look at the hoverboard and feel my face fall. The thought of my own hoverboard – a birthday present untouched – hurts. I'm not sure how and where but it hurts. Mostly because he obviously didn't know that I'm actually incapable of riding one. Much like the roller blades that I got for my eighth birthday. It felt like more of a statement gift that anything. *Hey, kiddo, I'm not here but at least I can buy you cool presents! Have a Nintendo!*

'Whoa, screw-face supreme!' Lips shuffles away. He hops up and onto the hoverboard and does a few little manoeuvres, singing softly.

I get to my feet. Watching him enjoying himself on his swag machine, I almost say yes. Almost. Then I imagine getting on the hoverboard, leaning forward too far and falling flat on my face. Like on the jungle gym. If I didn't break my wrists, there would probably be a video, or I would go into a 'hoverboard fails' compilation for the world to laugh at, and there would be a load of hashtag this and hashtag that.

My face contorts back into its usual scowl. No.

'Hey, chill,' Lips says, waving his hands in front of my face. 'You could kill me with that look.'

I glare at the hoverboard.

Lips grabs my hoodie. 'Look, I came here to see if you were okay.'

'You came for me?' I sound very sceptical.

His perpetual zipping/unzipping starts up again. 'For you. We care.'

I snort sarcastically. 'You speaking for all of AMD?'

His shake of the head is subdued, but I'm so vexed I miss that. 'Bruv, no one cares if I'm okay.'

'I care.'

'Why?'

He falters.

'Why?'

He throws his arms in the air. 'You're kind of quirky. And you remind me of me . . . somehow.'

'Somehow.'

'Yeah.'

'And that's why you care.'

'I guess.'

'Pretty vain reason.'

'If you like.'

'Well, good for you.'

'It's good for you, too.'

'Yeah, right.' I stretch the rubber band man's arms as far as they go.

'You were literally on your own. Like, every day.' He says it so bluntly that it sends this pang of anger through my body like an electric shock. He watches me out of the corner of his eye as if just checking my reaction. 'But now you've got us, yeah?'

'You think I don't know?' I suck my teeth. 'Let's see how long it lasts.'

'Don't be like that.'

'Like what?'

'Like ... like that.' He waves one hand emphatically, hunting for the right word. 'Like you don't trust anyone.'

'I don't.'

Lips stands up and swivels his hoverboard in a smooth half-circle. 'Maybe you should.' He smiles. 'Maybe you should start with me.'

He rolls down the drive like riding a hoverboard is nothing. I overflow with jealousy.

'Hey!' I bounce after him. 'You forgot your rubber guy!'

Lips does a half turn to face me. He wobbles, steps off the hoverboard, and steps back on again. 'Keep it,' he says. 'I have loads of them.'

'Are you sure?'

'I'm sure.' He turns to go. 'And his name is Homo Sapiens Rubber Butt. Take care of him.'

He starts to roll away, stops, and turns back. 'Oh, and you don't have to call me Lips all the time.'

'But that's your name, innit?'

'No. My name is Dayan, but everyone calls me Lips because everyone likes Lips. Singer, rapper, YouTuber and all-round funny boy . . .' He smiles and shrugs. 'But I save Dayan for special people.'

FIFTEEN

I used to be one of them – one of the loudmouths, Snapping when we aren't supposed to be on our phones, complaining about lessons, throwing random questions at the teacher.

I still sit at the desk next to Shadavia as if I'm part of the group. Which is awkward, to say the least – for me. Not for them. As far as they're concerned I might as well not be there.

Of course, this doesn't stop me from doing origami. Mr Bud doesn't usually approve, but apparently making ninja stars is better than lining up rubber shavings as if I'm going to snort it.

I can feel Kelly giving me the evil eye every time I make a fold. My guess would be that she was hoping that her silence would make me move seats or make Shadavia put her bag on my seat or something. Actually, the two of us are just sitting side by side ignoring each other. This sometimes makes me want to laugh when I look around the room and see everyone else in their chosen groups of twos and up, chatting away or reading or whatever. What makes me so special as to deserve the silent treatment?

Mr Bud rises from his desk, plods over and places a pink sheet of paper on my desk with one fat hand. 'See this?' he says. 'This is your post-exclusion report.'

'I can read.'

'Good.' He straightens. 'Then make sure you read the targets, fulfil them all, and get it back to me at the end of the day.'

I sit there, squeezing my fingers under my armpits, and look at the pink piece of paper.

Targets:

- Complete all required lesson work
- Stay in seat unless told otherwise
- Keep hands and feet to herself
- Wear correct uniform

'You were doing fairly well,' Mr Bud says, sitting his huge self on the edge of the desk. 'What happened?'

I cut my eye at him and slide down in my seat, leaning far back so that if he tips the table it won't hit me. When I say nothing, he goes on. 'You need to get your act up. You're walking a fine line between staying and going and we're only a few months into the academic year.'

'I'll be just fine.' And I'd be better if he didn't do this spiel in front of Shadavia and Kelly.

'I hope you're right.' His sarcastic expression irritates me. 'You have a lot of potential, and a lot of it is going to waste.'

'Well, yeah, it does when no one lets me go to lesson.'

'You know why that is. And I have heard that whenever given the opportunity, you skive all the core lessons, which is as good as preparing to fail.'

'So you think I'm wasting my potential?'

'I think you need to get your priorities right.' He taps the report. 'Don't let me down.'

I shove the report in my bag.

'Nice shade of pink,' Shadavia mumbles. She reaches over and takes a ninja star.

Kelly is smirking at me with an air of fake sympathy. What with her mixed complexion and the dark red hair, it's actually quite difficult for her to pull this off in my opinion; she's pretty, but she just has a face that doesn't do sympathy very well. Even with the smattering of freckles.

I give her an innocent look and ask her if she wants the origami eagle. Or maybe the bear?

The expression on Kelly's face is unreadable, but I'm willing to bet she's calculating whether to reject the offer or act like a little princess and take it. She shrugs indifferently and opts to take a ninja star. *Five quid says she bins it before the end of the morning.*

Mr Bud dismisses us early for first lesson. Shadavia doesn't say a word to me as we shoulder our bags and head for the door. Part of me wants to say goodbye just to spite Kelly, but then my phone pings in my blazer pocket and by the time I've pulled it out, Kelly and Shadavia have gone.

I drag myself in the direction of PE, gearing up for an argument with Miss Harper about my missing kit. As soon as I hit a quiet patch on the scenic route, I slide the phone out and check my messages.

It's Lips.

come have lunch with us again. we all want you around

My heart swells. I reply. *I'll be there*

I'm there when break rolls around, but my throat is all tight – last time I was chilling with this lot, it all went to pot half an hour later.

There's a moment of silence when I come into the room, apart from Lips, who jeers and does a little dance.

'You look tense,' Michael points out.

I sit down backwards on my chair like I always do. 'I am tense.'

He reclines in his chair so much that it's a wonder the plastic frame doesn't snap. 'Relax. No one's gonna hurt you.'

'You sure about that?'

Michael laughs. He has perfect teeth. 'Yep. We're not bad boys.'

His smile makes me feel a little warmer inside. I unwrap the pitta bread Charmaine made me this morning. She even cut it in half for me.

The boys talk and I try to listen, but I'm half in my own world waiting for something bad to happen. Waiting for someone to say something.

'Hey, Kadie?' Michael says from across the table, where he's combing his hair with a pick.

'Mm?' My mouth is full of pitta and lettuce.

'We're chilling at Lips' place this afternoon. You wanna come?'

Lips throws a ball of foil at his forehead.

Michael leans towards me with a sly grin. 'Oh, sorry. Bad-a-man over there wanted to ask you.'

I snort. A piece of corn jumps out of the side of my mouth. 'I'm open.'

Lips rocks his chair far back. 'We're just chilling. Maybe doing some recording.'

'At your house?' I ask.

Michael does an eyebrow wave. 'He's got a proper studio and everything. You need to see it. It's not as good as the one we pay for, you know, but it's good enough for practising. *And* his mum does banging Ghanaian cuisine. More time I just go just for the food.'

I look at Lips for confirmation. He smiles smugly and spreads his hands. 'Well? You down?'

I give him a big smile. 'I'm down.'

He shoves me and I shove him back. Break goes on. My throat's not so tight anymore.

SIXTEEN

The mandem are already at Lips' – Dayan's – when I rock up, just finishing a zoot to calm my jittery nerves. Dayan actually full-on smiles when he lets me in, and then gives me a playful barge. I shove him back. I can see that becoming our thing.

The boys are already up in the 'studio', a small room tucked away at the back of the house that is maybe a small extension. I can hear the music through the door, which is marked with rainbow-coloured letters shouting SENSORY ROOM!

I give Dayan a questioning look. He clears his throat. 'That's old stuff. Ignore it.'

'What exactly is a sensory room?' I whisper.

'A room for your senses?' He eyes his toes.

'But it's a studio.'

'It's a room where your senses get stimulated. Treble, bass and all that.'

I suppose he's right. He's clammed up as well though, so I turn my attention back to the studio.

Michael's voice is soft, switching smoothly between English and Yoruba. The Afro beat's got a chill, dancehall kind of feeling and the two together give me this irresistible urge to bop.

I bop/swagger to the living room, where Junior's got his feet up next to a pile of snacks ranging from KFC wings through to Tesco value crisps and jollof rice (Ghanaian, presumably).

'Make yourself at home.' Dayan wrangles a chicken wing from the box and settles himself at one end of the sofa, his legs hooked over the armrest. He retrieves a MacBook from the floor beside him and gives me a full-on cheeky grin.

I look at the food. I've already eaten loads today. The last thing I need is to tuck in and then have to look at the #butters comments. The stupid thing is, I am normal-sized – not fat, not skinny. Charmaine makes me eat healthy enough. So why does it matter what they say?

I make myself comfy on the other end of the sofa with a bowl full of rice. It's only after I've started eating that I realise the sofa is a lovely beige and I am a messy eater. Bad combo.

I set about enjoying the rice and start on some Maths homework with my free hand – until Dayan starts playing instrumentals out loud and I have to put both down, because I can't listen to music properly and eat tidily and do homework at the same time. I pop a Coke open instead even though the caffeine's going to get me far more gassed than I ever need to be.

Reuben produces the beats himself and they're actually calm. He's obviously spent a lot of time practising the art.

They have a good rhythm and the melodies fit really well together. They've even got the kind of professional quality that you'd hear from other artists on my favourites list – J Hus, Belly Squad, NSG. They're the sort of thing everyone gets bopping to in summer time when it's muggy and there's nothing to do.

Michael and Reuben come in and make themselves at home. Reuben looks sort of surprised to see me, as if he didn't expect me to show, and sits as far away as he possibly could in a corner littered with revision flash cards. It might just be me being paranoid, but I'm pretty sure he keeps cutting his eye at me. Michael, on the other hand, stretches out in the armchair next to me, polishes his spectacles and gives me this proper cute smile before tucking into his chicken.

It's the first in a long time that I've been comfortable. I'm not on guard, not trying to hold in the bounces and the random thoughts. Bopping to tunes has always been a weird sort of outlet.

Junior starts dropping lyrics, just messing around, and everyone chips in. We play with words and notes like puzzle pieces, pretend-dissing each other while other songs play in the background. Gradually, I forget about the world outside. The homework we came here to do sits scattered across the room, untouched.

As we freestyle it becomes clear that the boys are working on something. The bits and pieces that they put together just have that well-practised sound and it gets me bopping, excitement making me restless. Then Michael sits up suddenly and says, 'Hey, we could get Goldilocks on this track too.' He glances at the others, then at me. 'How would you like that?'

The others are nodding thoughtfully. Suddenly all eyes are on me. I chew my lip uncertainly.

'You blew her away with the suggestion,' Reuben says with a chuckle.

'I'm serious though,' Michael insists. 'You just put down some really good bars in the last ten minutes. That kind of stuff needs to be on a track.'

'I agree,' Dayan says, giving me a flicker of a comforting smile. 'Don't sit on all that.'

Every one of their faces is about as sincere as they could possibly be, but I still don't know what to say. No one has ever given me such an abrupt opportunity to jump on a tune.

Shrugging, I shift for the billionth time and spring to my feet, accidentally kicking my empty Coke can across the room. 'Whoops!' I scoop up the can on my way across the room and stop, catching Michael smirking. 'What?'

'Are you sober?' he asks.

'Course she's sober,' Dayan says. 'I'm not serving alcohol.'

'But she's like a flipping jack in the box!' Michael sounds incredulous, but he can't keep the smile off his chops. 'Come on, the longest period you sat still for was, like, a minute.'

I shift from foot to foot. 'You counted?'

'I counted.' He glances at Dayan. 'You watched me count, right?'

'True dat.'

Reuben laughs. 'Coming from you, Crazy Legs.'

Dayan stops bouncing his legs.

'Crazy legs?' I ask, confused. I hadn't even noticed that he was moving.

Junior grins properly for the first time that afternoon. 'Cos my man can't sit still.'

'It's not just that!' Dayan protests. 'There are a bunch of back stories!'

'But that's, like, the main one, right?' Junior says unrepentantly.

Dayan shakes his head and goes back to what he's doing, pretending not to notice the others sharing smirks as the moment turns slightly sour. It doesn't even seem like a nickname that completely fits with someone who is restless, but whatever – as long as they're not talking about me. Reuben says something under his breath and the three of them burst into raucous laughter that doesn't include Dayan and I. If we were at school it would be different, but here, in this moment, their laughter feels like a tiny line they've drawn between us. Maybe I'm reading into it too much, but there's something about the fact that Dayan doesn't share in the joke at all. Instead he stops watching his friends laugh without him and turns his face up to mine for a moment, as if asking me a million silent questions.

I take that as my cue to leave.

Dayan had pointed out the toilet earlier so I venture

upstairs, trying too hard not to notice how many family pictures there are peppered along the walls. You'd think after six years of dipping out of other people's houses it would stop poking at me. It doesn't.

At the top of the stairs I lean on the banister and listen to Dayan's house creaking, the quiet of the road out the front, the birds tweeting faintly and the bass kicking from the living room speakers. When I'm convinced to the core that I'm alone, I pull my jumper off over my head.

The cool air on my arms is such a relief after being cooped up in a blazer for the whole day. There aren't many chances between getting changed to safely expose my arms, so I have to make do with acting like my shirts aren't itching and rubbing all the time.

Looking down, I catch sight of my arms in the light and shudder inwardly. Would Dayan really have me round if he knew what I hide under my sleeves? I see the way the boys study me sometimes when they think I'm not looking – you can practically see the words *caramel darling* in their eyes like stars. There's nothing caramel darling about these arms.

I sigh, rubbing the soft inside of my jumper on my cheek. There's one open door between me and the bathroom and I don't mean to stop, not really, but the picture of Donell Jones stuck to the outside of the door snags my attention and before I know it I'm peering through the open doorway, gazing in. A record player sits on the dresser beside a precarious pile

170

of tattered books, next door to a shelf crammed with CDs and records. *Actual* records. If I really crane my neck, I can just about see that the wall above the bed is crammed with photos, none of them framed but one in the centre. Obviously his clothes are strewn across the bed and a chair at the foot of the bed where his blazer hangs.

My eyes flit back to the pictures. I've never met a boy who has pictures of his mum and dad above his bed.

It's suddenly hard to breathe. I blink and find myself shutting the bathroom door and falling towards the sink, gasping, my head reeling. Sometimes it's so easy to convince yourself you don't need or want something. And sometimes the craving for it hits hard when you least expect.

I run the heel of one hand up and down the other arm, feeling the bumps and hating myself for leaving Emerson in my coat pocket. The need to hold him has my stomach tightening and my eyes watering. I try to listen to the music downstairs but whispers of other things get in the way.

You're breaking the rules.

You know how it ends.

You'll never be one of them.

I'm always telling Charmaine that she's just saying stuff I already know that I don't need to hear again. Ironically, now I find myself wishing she were here. I need her endless patience. I need someone.

There's a hard knock on the door. 'Goldilocks, you in there?'

I slip my jumper back on hurriedly and wrench the lock back. 'Can a girl not take a dump in peace?'

Dayan steps back. 'You were long, that's all.'

'What if I was just constipated?'

He pulls a face. 'I don't really want to think about that.'

I smile, but it feels plastered on after my overwhelming moment of emotion. Desperate to get away from the scene of crime, I head for the stairs. As I go, Dayan leans over the banister and says, 'Did you go in my room?'

I stop and shrug. 'Not really.'

'The doorstop's moved,' he says, 'which means you stepped through the doorway at the very least.'

'Blame Donell Jones,' I blurt out.

Dayan glances at the picture on his bedroom door. 'What, did he wave you in?'

'Him and the record player, yeah.'

He eyeballs me. I hold his gaze and then, with a deliberate nonchalance, continue down the stairs.

'Why you walking away from me?' Dayan demands, his voice slipping into the roadman tone that he uses in his YouTube videos.

I smirk slightly without looking back. 'Because I can.'

Dayan sucks his teeth. 'Rah! How you gonna chat to man like that?'

I can't help it. A snigger of amusement slips out.

'And now you're laughing at me. Yo, what's your problem?'

When I turn he's coming down the stairs, a mock angry

172

pout on his lips. The expression on his face is so near and so far from the one he sometimes wears at school that I find myself laughing. He pushes past me with pretend aggro, muttering, 'Nah. I'll spin your jaw, bruv. Watch yourself.' Then he's turning around, asking me if I want water in his normal Dayan voice. It's not the first time I've seen him switch personas so abruptly, but it's definitely the first time I've seen him do it definitively and in public. He's just stood up in front of me and drawn a line between himself and another version of himself – something he usually confines to his YouTube channel – and for some reason, the unexpectedness of it touches me. For a boy so quiet, he certainly knows how to act.

Question is, why does he only do it on camera?

In the kitchen Dayan flings open a cupboard and reaches up high for a jug, revealing the skin of his lower back and an inch of the Cookie Monster's face grinning on his boxers' waistband. I wonder absently if he has a whole collection of Sesame Street pants, and if boys can be judged by the kind of prints they have on their underwear. What, then, would Junior and Josh and Aidan be wearing?

Dayan presents me with a glass of water, interrupting my inappropriate thoughts. I take the glass but I find myself blurting, 'You don't have Coke?'

'Sodas? No!' Dayan puts a hand over his heart, feigning shock. 'You know what my elders say about sodas?'

By 'elders', of course, he means Kwame's dad, which of course is also him. Let's just say, Kwame's dad is very anti carbonated drinks. I genuinely laughed out loud when I watched the video, and it's even better now in person as he whisks off his cap and, reverting to his Ghanaian accent, launches into a spiel about why sodas are bad for your teeth.

When he's finished, I shake my head in disbelief, itching to ask him why he never does this at school – why he seems to save it for these snatches of time when it's just the two of us.

'It's so weird that you seem to know my videos back to front,' he says, downing half a cup of water in a few gulps.

I shrug. 'It's weird that you seem to know my Insta back to front.'

'Touché, touché.' He puts the cup down. 'Hey, random question.' He stops and his eyes fall on me. I swallow, unsure of where to look as he studies my face warmly.

'How would you feel about an Insta-relationship?' He edges closer and suddenly his arms are around me, his body pressed up against my side, his nose inviting itself into my hair. He's soft when he's dressed casual, smelling faintly of coconut oil and sweat.

'Yeah . . . no.' I push him off.

'Really?'

'You heard me.'

'Come on, though. Just for a laugh,' he insists. 'People would actually stop bothering us! We wouldn't even have to hold hands in public or anything. Literally, all you'd have to do is post one snap of the two of us within inches of each other and people would jump on it.' He gives me the biggest pout I've seen all year, like a child who's been denied TV time.

The offer is tantalising, but I already know how that goes. I can practically feel the kisses looming, the pressure on zips and clasps. I hold my own. 'Yeah . . . no.'

'Think about it.' Dayan rearranges the magnets on the fridge. When I don't respond, he lowers his voice and continues. 'I really need something to stop the mandem laughing at me. Even Reuben doesn't take me seriously sometimes.'

'Oh, and that thing is me?' I suck my teeth, annoyance washing over me as our moment of humour fades.

Dayan tries to recover the light tone. 'Well, you're cute . . . I'm cute, so—'

'Don't push it.'

'Man. I feel like I'm in Sass Central.' He focuses on the magnetic letters on the fridge, rearranging them so they begin to spell AMALGAMANDEM. He lets out a long breath as he moves them, pursing his lips. I fold my arms and wait for him to keep pushing it, but then Michael bursts through the door, an impatient look on his face. 'Are you two bringing more food or what?'

'We are. We got distracted.' Dayan opens the fridge and takes out a bottle of juice and a small container of cupcakes.

'He was trying to chat you up, wasn't he?' Michael says, grinning at me.

I roll my eyes and push him playfully out of the room. 'My lips are sealed.'

Michael protests as I barge him down the hall, but he lets me. Dayan brings in the food and quietly cuts his eye at the back of my head. It's not his fault, but now I've got this lingering feeling of guilt for constantly pushing him away. He keeps backing me, and for what gain of his own?

Because he wants a girl. So he can shut the haters up.

Or maybe he genuinely just wanted me in the friend zone.

Maybe I want *him* in the friend zone.

Maybe we're both a little bit alone.

I shouldn't be, I really shouldn't – but the thing is, I've already breached Rule #1. Don't count on *anyone* – especially if they look like a good asset. What am I doing, sitting here discussing the finer points of how to identify who's farted in class, if not breaking the rules?

I'm trying. Trying to have a life.

Yep, justify it.

Justify it now, because later, there will be consequences. Won't there?

SEVENTEEN

I don't know if it's me, but something's changed. I'm still trying to stick to the rules, but it's extra difficult when things are popping off.

At the weekend, mine and Lips' first collab – 'Ay Yo' – got uploaded to YouTube. The visuals are directed by Reuben, the beat a kind of 'undefined' style that Amalgamandem are looking to create. Grimy, but with a rhythm that's more Afro beat. My social media's been buzzing just at the preview, Snapchat and Insta streaming with comments.

My confidence is renewed as the views keep scrolling up, easing into three hundred thousand by the end of the week. By the time we gather two weeks later to shoot a video for my new single – 'Playtime' – I'm still peaking. The group is one of the biggest I've had in a long time, and probably the most authentic. There's a real difference between people tagging along just because they want to be in your video, and people coming because they really care about supporting you.

AMD are at my side, along with a small camera team from LinkUp TV. My budget's not big at all, but Lips pulls some strings and manages to get Ozz, a recording artist and director from my recording label, to show his face – a helpful addition. Reuben and Junior have also managed to gather a few other faces to bulk up the squad – some cousins who could do wheelies and shoot three-pointers, a handful of fan-girls from the school a few miles away. I invited Shadavia along for some reason, and she seems to have forgotten suddenly that I'm supposed to be a freak, but she did (unfortunately) drag along Tia and Raquel as well. Not that that matters. So long as there's no sign of Kelly.

Shooting music videos is one of the few things I'm good at, but with Raquel and Tia there it feels like there are constantly eyes on me. Putting together a smooth, engaging music video is actually more complex than it looks. It's about knowing how to manipulate your surroundings; how many people to have, whether you want a cinematic video or just something to stimulate the eyes while the music plays. I'd sat down and planned how I wanted things to look, and now with everyone hanging around watching me, the pressure is on.

'Playtime' is slightly different to my normal upbeat style. Even after the audio was finished I couldn't put my finger on what kind of vibe it had. Somebody had commented on the Insta preview that it makes you want to saunter into class late with a bad excuse, but I was still mulling it over on the journey. On the deeper side of things, the song is a low-key tribute to all the different people I've met since I started bouncing from home to home. When you're on your own all day at school, you learn to observe the world around you, and you learn that break time is the most interesting time for people-watching. Some kids get forgotten as soon as it's playtime. For others, the playground is free rein for them and their squads. It just depends whether or not you draw the short straw.

Junior's cousins have turned up in their school uniform, ties hanging loose and school shoes swapped out for worn Nikes. They happily showcase their wheelie skills for the intro, which we shoot outside the back of Rowan Brown Primary. The rest of the heads – AMD, the fan-girls, Shadavia and co – fill in at the sides, bopping and easily pulling off the image of the popular kids. Shadavia acted a bit flaky when I asked her if she wanted to come – 'I've got tons of homework as well though . . . Yeah, cool, but if it's dead I can leave, right?' – but she's turned up in her best Shadavia look, bussing the jacket with the badges and those mustard Adidas gazelles she only uses on special occasions.

Watching all the others getting into it makes me flush with hot pride and a deep thankfulness that this time I managed not to draw the short straw. I relish the moments when the camera is on me, focusing on me alone on the swings, against a wall, walking down the path. If you discount the rules I'm not an actress, but there's something about standing up in front of a camera that puffs me up with confidence. It's a different kind of acting. Makes me want to turn up the music. Even Dayan gets into it, looking particularly pleased when I select him to star as the lonely boy in the background, head down and feet dragging. It's not a cinematic video as such, but, as Ozz says, 'You're definitely trying to put out a message, aren't you?'

As we're wrapping up the shoot, Tia somehow ends up by my side.

'Are you going out with one of them?' she asks, out of nowhere.

I give her a sideways look. 'No, why?'

'Just wondered.'

'What made you wonder? Snapchat?'

'Michael talks highly of you.'

'Michael?' I snort. 'Man's just gassed. Everyone gets gassed when I'm around. In case you didn't notice.'

She raises her eyebrows and snorts. Yes! I played the arrogance card right.

'I don't care if you hate me,' I add.

Tia is on her phone. She takes a moment to reply. 'Why would I hate you?'

'I sit next to you in RE.'

'No comment.'

'Seriously, though. If you don't like me, don't show up to my next shoot. I'm not a stepping stone to Insta likes.'

Tia opens and closes her mouth several times. 'I don't dislike you. You're just . . . Why are you so weird half the time?'

'Define half the time.'

'At school.'

I jiggle one foot. 'We all know school does things to our brains.'

She rolls her eyes. 'Come off it, Kadie. Everyone knows—'

'I know what everyone knows!' I snap. 'Maybe you should stop looking at what everyone knows and pay more attention to what *you* know. Cos face it, how much do you know?'

She averts her eyes.

'Huh? I don't hear you.'

Naturally, then Raquel invites herself into the conversation. She glances between the two of us and instantly assumes that I'm the problem. 'You running your mouth again?'

Some attitude coming from the girl who was just asking if she could be in my next video. Luckily Raquel is saved from my snarky retort by Dayan, who rolls into the confrontation on his hoverboard, twists and falls off into me in the true Lips style, nearly sprawling across my lap. He uses my shoulder to right himself, dusting off his jumper with a hurried, 'Sorry ladies, sorry, sorry, sorry. Man had a little spincident.' As in his videos, he collects his snapback from Tia's lap without cracking even a hint of a smile, and extends his hand to me as if he hasn't said anything. 'Let's go grab something to eat, yeah?'

I smile mischievously and let Dayan pull me to my feet. Raquel sucks her teeth, which makes me suppress the urge to grin harder. She's a hard one to read, Raquel, but something's telling me she likes to come across cheesed off when she's not sure what else she's feeling. I can practically feel her and

Tia watching us go and I'm so caught up in the feeling that we're already off down the street, being overtaken by Junior's bicycle cousins departing, before I realise that we've just ditched everyone.

'They'll catch us up,' Dayan says, in his normal voice.

We walk for a minute in silence, him carrying his hoverboard as if it's lost its appeal. We pass a small block of flats where someone's washing is hanging out the window and then we're on a big main street where the road opens out and fast-food restaurant signs glow enticingly. The sudden desire to hit Morley's unfolds in my stomach as a KFC sign looms not far ahead. Mummy started a tradition of taking me there on my birthday and since then whenever I was in a placement down that way I'd try and make an annual visit. But to my knowledge you won't find no Morley's north of the river, so into the brightly-lit KFC it is. Dayan squints and pulls his cap further down his forehead.

'You okay?' I ask him, as we queue behind a group of young Goan boys.

He shrugs. 'Just tired.' But he looks away from me as he says it, as if I can't cope with the idea. Or maybe it's the fact that I'm still bouncing from the video shoot, giving off the strongest happy vibes I've had in months. There's so much I want to say about the afternoon, things I want to ask, but something about the hunch of his shoulder stops me.

Dayan's just collecting his order when AMD and the girls plough through the door, all smiles and banter. Junior tells me again that he's so proud of me, which genuinely makes me want to melt, and even Raquel thanks me for including her. Our group's not that big but we're pretty loud and I notice a few others casting looks our way. Oh well. Perks of being popular.

Dayan picks a window spot and we sit down to wait for the others. He's only ordered himself a small portion of fries and chicken nuggets, much like me.

'I'm holding out for my mum's chicken pie,' he says, upon catching me looking.

I twist a chip until it breaks. That must be nice, to be able to go home knowing your mum is cooking the same pie she's cooked all your life. The thought sends a pang of sadness through my body. Charmaine's a great cook – don't get me wrong – but she's not my mum or any of the other foster mums whose cooking I've craved.

And she might just join that long list of past foster mums, says the pessimistic voice in the back of my mind.

My appetite takes a nosedive. I drop the chips back in the packet.

'Not hungry?' Dayan reaches for my box of food. 'What you got? Ooh, chicken wings! How are you not digging in?'

He picks up one of our plastic forks and spikes a chip from his own packet. 'Here. No effort needed.' He makes plane noises and flies the chip towards my mouth. I sit back and look at it, vexed by his genuineness. He makes a second attempt, this time with intergalactic space rocket noises. The chip hovers about an inch from my mouth. Dayan props his elbow up on the table, raising his eyebrows expectantly. 'I can stay here all day, you know.'

I roll my eyes and bite the chip off the fork.

'Ayyy! That's too cute, you know!' Michael, who's at the very back of the queue, has been filming the whole incident. 'You gonna wipe her mouth as well?'

Dayan spikes another chip and offers it to him. 'Are you feeling left out?' Michael dissolves into mischievous laughter and turns around, showing the video to the others.

'They're your fam,' I say to Dayan. He shakes his head, no words for the foolishness of his bredrin.

Once the others have their food, we catch a double-decker bus back to our ends. This one is packed on the lower level so we tramp up the narrow stairs and spread ourselves out at the front.

Tia and Raquel are really clocking me while I eat and it's putting me off my food. Even Reuben and Shadavia are smirking at whatever they're whispering about and judging by their body language, it's probably me. I pop my air pods in as a decoy and glance around. Lips had inhaled his food on the way to the stop and is pretending to cat nap beside me, while the rest of AMD seem to be trying to chat up the girls.

If I listen hard, I can make out snippets of conversation over the bus engine. *Care for ages. So . . .*

Hair . . . naturally that . . .

Colour of gold . . . I didn't . . .

184

Come off it . . . nickname come from . . . that odd . . .

Tia pretends to brush her hair back as if she's about to tell a lie. 'True . . .'

I give them a pointed look. 'You gonna share the joke?'

Tia just looks at Raquel and bursts out laughing. I grind my teeth hard into the end of a chicken bone and the cartilage cracks. Instinct says spit the piece of bone at Tia's head and tell her to stop making fun of me. Instinct also says that, based on the bonds between Tia and Shadavia/AMD, I will be unpopular if I do this.

Three stops later, I hit the red button.

'Hey, where are you going?' Michael calls.

'Away from them gyal.'

'But this isn't the stop—'

'She knows it isn't the right stop,' Junior interrupts.

'Lips, man, what are you doing?' – Reuben.

'Going with Kadie.' And so he is.

'For what?'

'To keep her company.'

I step off the bus then and I can't hear them anymore, although I can see Michael gesturing from the upstairs window, his eyebrows narrowed at the sight of Dayan following. Thirty seconds later, the two of us are standing on the pavement watching the bus pull away with our friends on it.

'Well, now how do we get home?' Dayan asks me.

I start walking, following the way the bus went. It would be smarter to just wait for the next bus, but right now I'm too vexed. Really, I just need some space – it's been a long day, it's late, and I'm mentally and physically exhausted. For this reason, it's actually kind of irking me that Dayan has followed me. Then I kick myself mentally. He must have a good reason for ditching. He came because he *cared*.

Still.

Dayan cruises alongside me, matching my pace easily on his hoverboard.

'Why did you come?' I demand. 'Seriously?'

'To make sure you get home safe, innit.' But he's using his Lips voice, the hard and sharp rudeboy tone. I step in front of his hoverboard, putting out one foot and a hand on his chest to stop him rolling into me. 'For real. Why did you get off the bus?'

Dayan purses his lips, then shrugs. 'Dunno,' he mumbles to the road.

I start walking again.

'I guess sometimes I just feel less embarrassed around you.'

I'm confused. 'Embarrassed about what?'

'To be myself.'

I roll my eyes a little insensitively. 'Bruv, you're such a drama king.'

'No, I'm sick of being the butt of everyone's jokes.'

His words are striking a nerve in me and he looks pretty glum. I give an exaggerated flick of my hair and say flirtatiously, 'Or *maybe* you just like the smell of my perfume.'

'Eau de toilet?' he shoots back. 'No thanks.'

And then, for a short minute, we're both smiling again.

I search my pockets aimlessly for something to touch. Emerson is safely at home. There is, however, a little bag of green that I'd forgotten about. As soon as we reach the next bus stop, I crouch at the bench and get down to business.

'You're gonna get high just before you go home?' Dayan asks.

'Yup.'

'You know there are better things to do while we wait . . .' He checks the timetable. 'Eleven minutes.'

'Yup.'

He tries again. 'Put it away and I'll teach you how to ride the hoverboard. And I'll call my uber. We might even get home before the others.' He's already got his phone out.

I shield my zoot from the wind. 'I'm not setting foot on that thing,' I tell him. 'Don't care how much swag it gives you.' I've wasted precious time watching fail videos and heard a few stories which have illustrated just how disastrous getting on a hoverboard can be for a small percentage of people. I'd rather not be that small percentage.

Dayan turns away to make his phone call as if I haven't said a word. He's softly spoken on the phone, lots of pleases and thank-yous – none of this roadman ting he does for so many of us. It's almost as if he can't decide which Dayan to be at any one time. I listen to his conversation as I assemble my zoot, fumbling as the sound of his voice brings a smile to my face. The wind whips my hair around, throwing the curls in front of my face and yanking them back again. (Note to self: next time check the weather forecast before wearing hair in full natural mode.)

Back from his phone call, Dayan gives me a beautiful-big-brown-eyes look. 'I'll hold your hand?'

'I don't want to hold your hand.'

'Come on!' He pouts. 'Pweeez?' Then, in his Ghanaian accent, 'Make a brudda happy?'

Wow, he's in an insistent mood today. I stick my zoot behind my ear and stand up. 'Fine!'

He pumps his fist. 'Yesss! Bet you a kiss that you'll be able to ride it by the time my uber gets here. Ten minutes.'

'Is that where your nickname is from?' I ask. 'You're always trying to get kisses off of the girldem?'

Dayan pulls a face. 'Nah. It's because I used to rub things on my lips to explore them.' He puts the hoverboard down in front of me and holds out one hand. 'I'm here for you to fall on like a damsel in distress, if you so wish.'

I look at the hand. He holds out the other hand.

'One foot at a time,' he says. 'Trust me. You'll get it. I have the worst sense of balance ever and I got it, so you can too.'

He grips my hands hard as ever. I put my right foot on first, then change my mind and put my left foot on. I transfer my weight. The hoverboard moves suddenly. I put my right foot back on the floor.

'Don't lean forward yet,' Dayan advises.

'I wasn't.'

'Don't lean back, then.'

'But what if—'

'I've got you.'

I lift my right foot. The hoverboard twists to the left. I get my foot on and it wobbles like mad.

'Just stay upright,' Dayan says, my fingers still tightly wrapped in his fists. 'Stay upright and it shouldn't move.'

'I am upright.' I sound more stressed than I need to be over a stupid machine with wheels. His hand is so warm, squeezing mine so hard there's no time for the tingles of discomfort. His other hand brushes my lower back.

'Good. Now lean towards me.'

I lean. The hoverboard shoots forward.

'Not too much!'

I stop, overbalance and step off.

We go again. And again. And again. I get frustrated. It should be easy. I've watched so many tutorials and could never figure out why I couldn't do it. Everybody had such a good go on my hoverboard when I got it – everyone but me.

Maybe that was more because of who it was from. I always remember that red rage when it came in the post – like he didn't know. I told him through the letter box almost every year – *I can't ride a bike. Don't get me one.* He got me roller skates. I used them once and ended up grazing myself in about six different places. I didn't bother trying to ride anything much after that.

Am I being over-dramatic? Maybe I'm just deluding myself about myself.

It takes me a while to get the hang of going forward. Dayan makes me try it between two lampposts and I somehow manage it, the hoverboard inching forward uncertainly. Our bus comes and goes, but I'm so focused on the hoverboard that I don't really notice.

I try to turn to come back towards him, but I must be doing something wrong, because the hoverboard decides to do a one-eighty twist and I suddenly find myself toppling off the back into Dayan, who catches me as if I weigh nothing.

He looks at me. 'That wasn't so bad.'

I suck my teeth. 'If you think so.'

'So you won the bet. Your call.' He puckers his lips and leans forward, eyes closed.

Ideally, I would lean further forward, and there would be a nice light drizzle, and tomorrow we would go official after a perfect Hollywood kiss. But I'm having flashbacks to the night at Kelly's party. To Josh, who wasn't what I thought he was. And the rules. There are the rules, and then there are a million other reasons why I can't – starting with the voice in the back of my head telling me there is no point. *Follow the rules.*

I say, 'I never agreed to that bet.'

Dayan opens his eyes. 'I suppose you're right there.' He pretends to wipe away a tear. 'I guess I'll just go find another girl.'

Follow the rules, comes the whisper.

I squeeze my eyes shut and exhale. Then I grab him by the jacket and give him a quick peck on the cheek.

'You missed,' he says. I can't even tell if he's joking or not, and in that moment my tiredness rears its ugly head.

I groan. 'So? You're not Josh, bruv, you're not getting a snog.'

His eyebrows narrow. 'Why are you bringing Josh into it?'

'I'm not. I'm just saying – if that's what you were looking for, you're not getting it, because I'm not drunk and Josh turned out to be a giant wasteman.'

He crosses his arms. 'Something's really not right with you.'

'Have a gold star.'

'One day you're moving to one of us, the next you're holding back. Then you're flirting again, and the very next second you just "need space". Half of your music is about guys but you don't wanna link up with anyone. What's going on?'

I put one hand on my hip and fake a smirk. 'Are you vexed, g?'

'No.'

'You're vexed.' I shove him playfully.

He scowls. 'I'm vexed because you're acting all weird.'

'Yeah? And you're not?'

'At least I know *why* I'm weird!' Dayan half-throws, half-flaps his arms. 'You're just a mess.'

Again with the digging at my weirdness! Why won't he leave it alone?

I grit my teeth. 'Is it a crime to want to be boyfriend-free?'

'Having a little fling at a party is not "boyfriend-free".'

'That was just a mistake.'

He flings his hands out again. 'So if he was a mistake, what am I?'

Good question.

I press my lips together and look away. 'You're precious.'

Can't take that back now.

'Should I be insulted?' Dayan asks bitterly.

'No.' I'm sure of it once it's out. 'You're not like Josh.'

'News flash.'

I sigh. Why does it always come out like that?

I don't get to clear that up right away, because Dayan turns to the road and flags down a black taxi. This must be the uber.

'Hey, Omar.' Dayan waves at the driver and opens the door for me. I slide across the back seat and stare out the window, fighting the burning tears and waiting for this Omar guy to make some comment. Thankfully he just takes the cash and the directions from Dayan and turns up the radio a little.

Dayan and I endure silence for a few minutes before I manage to say, 'I just meant that our friendship is different. It's not something I'm risking for a little bit of lust.'

Dayan raises one eyebrow. 'Are you suggesting that there's some lust going on?'

192

'No.' *Well, maybe a bit.* 'Bruh, I'm just trying to say I don't wanna hurt you.'

Dayan says nothing. Maybe because he's angry. Maybe because he understands.

Probably not the latter.

I press the cuff of my hoodie against my eyes, soaking up the beginnings of tears. They're angry tears, I tell myself. He's vexing me. They're angry tears.

But at the back of my mind, I know he was poking at the truth – the truth that I've been ignoring for a long while, because there's nothing I can do.

As the taxi drops me outside my house, Dayan says gently, 'Everyone already knows you're odd. There's nothing more to come out, d'you hear me?'

I stop, one hand on the door. 'Excuse me?'

'Nothing. Goodnight.' He slams the door and the cab pulls away.

EIGHTEEN

I must have broken a record. Five months I've been here and I'm sitting in Pastoral for the third time this week. Everyone keeps telling me I'm being uncooperative. That's a difficult one really, but my head of year – Mr Fishwick – seems to think he can help, so Charmaine is in his office having a nice chat with him about the fifty billion reasons why I'm failing my post-exclusion report.

I flip over the Chemistry worksheet Miss Pigeon gave me and continue with my doodle of Lips. It's slightly exaggerated, especially his lips, but it's the best thing I can get my mind to do at the moment. Concentrating with bits of the blazer rubbing on my arms has been a nightmare. This frustrates me no end, but the teachers never notice that because they're too busy focusing on my report, or that I don't write a lot down. It's always *write it down, write it down* – never mind whether or not I can tell them the answers. They want physical proof that I'm working hard enough to catch up and they keep reminding me of this. *You're quite far behind. You have a lot of work to do. Make sure there's something to mark your progress.* Blah, blah, blah, in front of everyone on my desk – like I want the whole class to know the ins and outs of my progress. Drives me up the wall.

This week I've just about had it – I'm so far up the wall I'd rather doodle and make mini paper dolls than look like an idiot in front of all my classes. Add to that the fact that I usually get bored of the work to start with, and what do we have? Kadie in lots of detentions. Or rather, Kadie *not* in lots of detentions, because I never go. I've learned that I can avoid being collected at three o'clock by riding out last period in the library, tucked in a corner with a few good books.

Dayan and I haven't spoken a whole lot since the awkward situation at the bus stop. It has helped that homework and revision has reduced the amount of time we've been spending together, but at the same time it hasn't – I just end up thinking about him more when I'm stuck in Pastoral. Wondering if I've made a huge mistake.

One of the other year leaders breezes by and taps a finger on the desk pointedly. I flip the worksheet over in bored silence and wait for him to return to his desk, shifting uncomfortably in my blazer. I'd love to take it off, but that would mean wearing a hoodie to cover my arms or putting on my arm warmers. I'd get slaughtered for doing either.

I cut out my doodle and chuck the rubbish at the bin. I've been doing a lot of throwing stuff this week – the last object being another Year Eleven girl's bag that went bye-bye down a stairwell after she called me a sket. My reaction was uncalled for, but I felt better afterwards, and now I get to go home.

Charmaine's 'nice mum' act is pristine until we get in the car. She switches on the engine and gives me a long look. 'So what's with all this rule-breaking?'

'Hm?' I pick my head up off the window. 'Rule breaking?' I want to laugh. *I've been following the rules perfectly. What are you on about?*

'Yes. The stuff of my meeting with Mr Fishwick. He's extremely concerned.'

I shrug.

'There must be a decent reason.'

'Does there have to be a reason?'

She coaxes the car onto the road. 'There should be. We talked about communicating when you first came, didn't we?'

'We did?' I ask, even though I distinctly remember.

She gives me a side-eye. 'Like you saying something if you're having problems . . .' She pauses to check the road. 'I just . . . I'm amazed at how many rules you've managed to break. I mean, throwing stuff? I genuinely didn't think you would stoop that low. I'm actually embarrassed on your behalf, since you clearly aren't.'

I twirl a curl. She obviously hasn't spoken to any of my past carers, counsellors or teachers.

'I wanted to believe that what I was told wasn't all true,' she replies, as if reading my mind.

'Deluded much.'

'Everyone has a good streak, you know. Just because you have a bad reputation doesn't mean it isn't there.'

'Yeaaah.'

'Well, it's all out now. Mr Fishwick gave me a monologue about all of your "concerning behaviours", so we need to do something about them.'

'A monologue?' I glance at her. 'Why you tryna make this sound like a joke?'

'On the contrary,' Charmaine says, 'it's you who's never serious.'

'I beg to differ.'

She remains unperturbed. 'Look, I want to help you,' she declares. 'But I can't do it if you're not going to be straight with me about things.'

'What things?'

'Like smoking.'

'Don't get it twisted. I never said I didn't smoke.'

'No, but you tried everything under the sun to get around your clothes stinking of it. I know for a fact that none of Shadavia's friends smoke weed.'

'Not my fault you believed me.'

'I took your word,' she corrects. 'I trusted that you respected me enough to tell the truth.'

'Nobody wants the truth.'

'Okay.' Red light; we come to a halt. 'Well, I want the truth now. About everything.'

'Everything?'

'Everything. For example, the non-uniform.' She gestures to my brown Doc Martens. 'You're not just breaking the rules; you're deliberately flouting them. Yes, I know you wear a different pair of shoes every day. I'm not stupid or blind.'

It's not a different pair *every* day. Just when I feel like it. The selections are very deliberate – but to be fair, I usually always wear black shoes. And the blazer? Don't even get me started. Let's just say, there is only one set of rules that I like and they are the rules that keep my life in check. School rules are trivial and the people who make them enforce the pettiest parts of them because they think they know everything.

Charmaine seems to be the only person who chooses words that make me go on a proper guilt-trip.

My face prickles hotly. I only *sometimes* flout the uniform rules for the sake of it. Nobody's ever bothered to assume that there's any other reason why my shirt is always untucked. I mean, there isn't, but what if there was?

'It's not hurting anyone,' I mutter.

'You're wrong. It's hurting you.'

'It's not hurting me,' I argue. 'I'm comfy. I wasn't learning nothing there anyway. Wasn't even in class. Apparently wearing brown shoes is going to disturb my learning.'

'It is! And whose fault is that?'

I grit my teeth, but I'm not quite strong enough to hold it all back so I end up booting the glove compartment really hard instead. Charmaine pretends not to see.

There are a few minutes of silence. I feel worse by the second, until I feel forced to ask, 'Are you vexed?'

Charmaine sighs. 'Yes. Yes, I am.'

I harden my heart. *Not guilty not caring not guilty not caring*.

Then she says, 'But I'm also really concerned. I'm worried that there's something we're overlooking.'

My heart jumps around in my chest. 'Why?'

'Well, non-attendance aside, there seems to be a common concern from your teachers that something's not quite right. It's not just the laziness – it's everything. You're a very smart girl, which we've deduced from the occasional bouts of effort that you do put in. But since you spend most lessons talking, or getting up or doodling or whatever else it is that you do, you're not achieving your full potential. And one or two of your teachers seemed to think that it's only partly because of your choices.' She pauses, her eyes scanning my expression as she steers us onto a roundabout. 'Your PE teacher was also one of them. The fact that several of them have flagged this up says to me that there's definitely something we're missing.'

Teachers being *concerned* about Kadie Hunte? That's a first.

'Also, GCSEs are frighteningly close,' she adds. 'That's one of the things I discussed with Mr Fishwick. Based on what I heard from your teachers, I thought maybe some form of cognitive therapy might help you to settle down a bit.'

'I don't even know what cognitive therapy is.'

'Well, it wouldn't hurt for us to look into it.'

'Really?' I pretend to perk up. 'Or why don't they just diagnose me with Conduct Disorder or something, because labels magically take away all your problems. At least then I'd be a certified brat.'

Charmaine ignores me. 'I'm not saying you need a label. I'm saying I'm speaking to everyone who could possibly help us out because I'm not going to sit back and let you go on like this.'

'What if I don't want help?'

She smiles a little. 'I'll get back to you on that one.'

The rest of the drive back is silent apart from my fingers, tapping out a song on the window. On the front drive, Charmaine cuts the engine and looks at me. 'How do you feel about the therapy idea?'

I can't help squirming in my seat. 'Cognitive therapy?'

'Yes. We need to do something. Your education is taking a huge hit.' She pauses. 'And other things.'

I groan. 'School is a time waster.'

Charmaine twirls the keys in her fingers. 'You need school to make yourself a future. And we both know you have a lot of potential.'

I shrug.

She adds pointedly, 'Wasted potential.'

She's trying to make me feel bad. I slouch in my seat and scowl. 'Ain't my fault teachers don't like me.'

'They don't like your behaviour,' Charmaine corrects me.

'You're very likeable, when we see the right side. Either way, we still need to do something about it. I don't want you to get expelled and I'm sure you don't either.'

'I don't care.'

'Not even for Music?' She's really playing me now.

'I don't give a fudge, I really don't.' I really want to cuss for real, just to spite her – I've discovered a certain rebellious satisfaction with spitting out rude words in front of foster parents – but that would be like shooting myself in the foot. Because I know she'll just give me that sad look, the same sad look that my mum gave me when I let fly words no eight-year-old should know. The look that aches my heart and makes the edges of my eyes burn with memories. And then I'll sit there crumbling inside and hating myself.

'I know a visit to a therapist is not on your list of fun things to do,' Charmaine says. 'But I really think—'

'What? That they might be able to save me from my plight? Tch.'

'I need you to trust me.'

'You said that already.'

'That's because I mean it.'

'It's a cliché.'

'I still mean it.'

I tut and lean on the window. This conversation is irking me. 'What does it matter? At the end of the day, what does it really matter?'

'It matters because you matter.'

'Now you're just being cheesy.'

'I'm being cheesy because I care,' she says dryly. 'I know I don't need to spell out to you what "things" have got your teachers worried about your progress. I'm just asking you to think about how those things affect your life and how they make you feel.'

I suck my teeth. 'You don't get it.'

'There are always going to be times when you have to straight-up tell me how it is,' she points out.

But I can't.

Because that would be breaking the rules.

I get out of the car and slam the door hard. This conversation has unpeeled something cold in my chest and I'm struggling to pinpoint what it is. Or maybe it's just that I don't want to acknowledge it. The last thing I want to do is go back to another white-walled, brightly-lit building where some person with a degree of some kind in something-or-other can tell me this is what they *think* my problem is and what *they* think will help.

In the porch, Charmaine changes the subject. 'Is everything okay with you and Shadavia?' she asks. 'You two have been frosty around each other lately.'

I roll my eyes. 'It's nothing.'

'Nothing?' Charmaine raises her eyebrows. 'You're sure there isn't something you wouldn't mind telling me?'

There is nothing I want to tell her. There are things I could – *should* – tell her. Nothing I want to. Why would I want to tell her about this week's barrage of messages on Snapchat? Picture after picture after picture with refreshing captions:

Me and Michael with French Fry fangs. *We all know why your "with" AMD*

Me and Junior chilling in Dayan's studio. *They only like you cos your peng*

A snap of my back in the corridor. *Fat*

Dayan and Michael both leaning on me in the playground. *sket*

Every time I post a picture with any skin showing (including my face), somebody reposts it labelled #butters. Sometimes a battle between the supporters and the haters then ensues in the comments section. The last post I made, I covered my face with one hand. It was just a stupid pose. Guess what comes up in the comments? *You finally caught on then #butters*

Why would Charmaine want to know about any of that? She has enough on her mind. I have enough on my mind.

Halfway through changing out of my school uniform, I stand in front of my bedroom mirror in a Kadie-friendly sports bra and football shorts, and glare at myself. No, I'm not skinny. No, I'm not fat. Yeah, I get the munchies, and I'm pretty sure smoking weed makes you lose bare weight – but there's no body image thing going on here. Eating makes me feel good. That doesn't make me fat. And don't everybody's thighs touch?

Maybe it's just me.

Maybe I'm just weird.

I wipe the tears away with the heel of my hand. More come. I shut my eyes so I don't have to watch myself fall apart.

It's got to be me. I know it is. I've seen it when my hands wreck rooms and my screams of frustration rattle the windows. Whatever the cause, I know the consequence, and until somebody shows me how to fix all my quirks for good, there is only one way out.

I go to my wardrobe and fumble around until I find the hoodie with Emerson in it. Then, once the bedroom door is closed and accidentally-on-purpose barricaded with a heap of miscellaneous items, I stick my iPhone on the dock and open a playlist for the darkest days. 67, AM and Skengdo, Loski.

Drill gives you chills down your spine, especially when you turn the bass up and listen to the vibe. If you pick the right songs, you get a pure kick-the-doors-in vibe. I close my eyes and listen to the lyrics, pressing one hand into the floor so that I can feel the beat until I'm really in the zone. I sit, back to my bed, Emerson in hand. I'm running out of room in inconspicuous places, but at the end of the day all scars become visible.

It will hurt. Of course it will hurt – but not for a while. Not like I know it should.

I press the tissue on. I will wear my gold. The marks will stay, just like the messages always go, but if there's one thing I'm sure of, it's that everything is culled just for a little bit.

NINETEEN

I could write a chapter book detailing all the reasons that
family dinners aren't my thing.

Chapter One: Idle Talk About Your Day.

Anything interesting happen?

The end of the day.

How was the test in English?

Fine. (Rubbish.)

Did you hand in that History homework?

Yeah. Mr Tucker wouldn't grade it because it was crumpled
and ink-stained and a bit wet. *Ahmad said he thought it was
an eight.*

Blah, blah, blah. It's all fake. Do they really care? Who
wants to listen to Vince drone on about angle grinders and
the obnoxious wasteman he sits next to? Maybe a different
Kadie, in a different world, would. But this one doesn't. The
Kadie I am knows that it's all short lived, that I can't afford
to get attached to his woeful stories about the lameness of
his class.

'Kadie, you're shaking the table again,' says Shadavia,
interrupting my thoughts.

'I'm not.'

'Yes you are.'

'Not.'

'You flipping are!'

'Girls!' Charmaine puts a gentle hand on my knee to stop it jerking about. 'No need to get in an argument.'

Shadavia casts a cold look in my direction.

'You two are gonna start a civil war, you know,' Vince says. 'I dread having to choose a side.'

Silence falls again. Relative silence, that is. Today is a rubbish day for sitting still. Another reason why I don't do family dinners. And since bad things come in threes, the icy front between Shadavia and I is so thick it's practically a blizzard. I suspect it's got something to do with Instagram.

Two days ago, Dayan posted another YouTube video. Turns out his channel's quite popular locally – mostly for the music. This video featured me – just a jokey *guess the meaning of these Ghanaian words* thing. Nothing serious. But, as usual, the haters flocked to it like it was water in the middle of the desert. The promo picture he posted on Instagram was picked apart so much that the positive comments were almost drowned by things like

Mr_J05HIE! *a "special" couple how cute*

dizzy_14 *freak fleek at its finest*

theonlysuperT *@dizzy_14 ugly duckling and the gruffalo more like*

shayshaytheplug **@dizzy_14** *or princess and the frog*

mr_J05HIE! **@shayshaytheplug** *except the frog ain't no prince*

I'd stopped when I saw those ones.

Josh and Shadavia. I recognised the usernames. Josh I could understand – he'd clearly shown himself to be a wasteman in the past four months. But Shadavia? I don't get what she doesn't like about Lips and I. Fine, so she tried to smooch the guy and ended up humiliating herself. But who cares? She's Miss Popularity. I'm The Weird Girl Who Makes Music with Super Cool AMD.

And it wasn't just the one comment. Each of Dayan's posts seemed to have up to a few hundred comments in total, and I spotted Shadavia's Instagram name popping up multiple times, chucking in comments like *Lips cute in pictures but in real life can't stand him.*

And everyone's revelling in it. It's as if someone's started a game. Curious and a bit vexed, I had perused the last month's worth of pictures and noticed names from the Kelly crew right through to other irrelevant people from school and all over. I'd never even noticed this before – I'm more about Snap than commenting on Insta – but some of the comments really made me bristle.

Same with both of them actually steer clear in real life, weirdo alert

Sket alert

Goldilocks spends too much time with dem boys, wouldn't touch her with a barge pole

#butters

That was the last straw. I took it to Snapchat. 'Some people think it's jokes to be saying all these things about my guy Lips, yeah, so let me just set things straight. It's like a Beauty and the Beast thing. You ain't beauty enough – in the heart or the head – and you don't bring out the handsome prince in the beast. Keep that in mind. You man are all butters, butters, butters in your hearts if you think it's okay to talk about other people like that. And I know I'm not perfect, but you won't see me saying none of that trite about anyone.'

I put it on my story.

A lot of people saw it. A lot of people liked it.

Hence the frosty atmosphere between Shadavia and I.

I drum my fingers, crack my knuckles, stop, and kick Shadavia under the table by accident. My leg has been bouncing nonstop as a beautiful distraction to the things on my mind.

'Ow!' Shadavia protests. 'Mum! Domestic violence!' And she stamps on my foot.

I stab my elbow into her side. She shoves me away by my face.

'Am I going to be like this when I become a teenager?' Beverly asks.

Amando rests his chin on his hands and watches us

with concern. 'You two suddenly seem very incapable of getting on.'

Shadavia kisses her teeth and scrapes her fork deliberately loudly around the rim of her plate. I try not to wince noticeably.

'You used to be best friends,' Beverly points out with her usual naivety.

'We were never best friends,' Shadavia mutters.

'We're being like normal sisters,' I say in my best angelic voice.

'Okay, well, enough is enough,' Amando replies. 'If you're not able to at least tolerate each others' existence, we'll have to find a way for you to spend more time together until you can get on.'

I collect up some plates and head to the dishwasher. Amando clears his throat as if about to tell me off, but Charmaine speaks first. 'Thank you, Kadie.'

A warm feeling spreads through me. It feels like she's thanking me for my resilience and self-control, not just my usefulness.

It's mine and Shadavia's turn to do the dishes today. It's been a quick dinner, no leftovers and no mess on the floor, so everybody else clears out extremely fast. Beverly skips off to play, Vince to his computer, and Amando to his desk.

Charmaine leans on the counter and watches me and Shadavia. 'What's going on with you two?'

'Nothing,' we say simultaneously.

But Charmaine shakes her head adamantly. 'Stop trying to pull the wool over my eyes. It is not this "nothing" that you both keep speaking of.'

Shadavia peeks at me out of the corner of her eye.

'What happened to the two happy girls who went off to Kelly's birthday party together?' she asks, giving us both a pointed look in the eye. 'Or the girls who used to walk to and from school together every day? Don't try to kid me. A month ago you two were joking about like any two sisters and now you keep throwing these screw-faces when you think nobody's looking.'

Because *someone* decided I had the plague.

'That was actually more like three months ago,' Shadavia says flatly.

'No excuse.' Charmaine looks at me. 'Kadie? Want to enlighten me?'

'Enlighten you how?'

'Okay. You two are obviously enjoying playing dumb.' She sighs. 'Let me just get this straight: if you two continue to act the way you have been this week, there is going to be trouble. Alright? Any more fighting, shouting, cussing, et cetera – there will be consequences for both of you. So make sure you work out whatever is causing friction.'

And with that, she leaves the two of us with a pile of dirty pots and pans.

There are about two minutes of silence, bar her slamming the dishes into the drainer, before Shadavia says, 'You're going to regret that thing you put on your Snapchat story.'

I look up from struggling to manoeuvre a heavy pan in my hands. 'Because you weren't right there dropping comments on my Instagram as well.'

'It wasn't just me.'

She's right there. And maybe I should be less angry at her – after all, if we didn't live together, she'd be irrelevant. But we do live together. I know what she's like at home – she used to joke around with me and actually act like I was okay back in that first month or so. I promised myself I wouldn't do what I always do – get delusional, mistakenly thinking it might stay that way – but I did. And that's why it hurt. I expected more of her.

'No, it wasn't just you,' I agree finally. 'But it was personal. To me and to Dayan.'

Shadavia sighs irritably. 'The irony is that it's you that's the problem. It's always you. You're a pain to live with, you're cocky online, and you seem to think linking up AMD somehow makes you a better person.'

I heave the pan into the oven as docilely as possible. 'So far AMD are being a lot friendlier than your lot were.'

'Yeah? Well, it's hard when you're being like you are most of the time.'

'And how is that?' I ask.

She says nothing for a while. 'Just . . . weird.'

211

I want to know but I don't want to know. 'Define weird.'

She sighs. 'You're just not normal, okay? Call it what you want, but you're not like everyone else.'

If those words had come out of Kelly's mouth, they would've got me vexed, or really hurt my feelings. But coming from Shadavia, they don't have the same punch. She's refusing to turn my way, but I can see her side profile and she just looks like she's struggling to actually find the right words. Her lip doesn't curl like Kelly's does, and even her usual scowl is replaced with a frown.

'I can't help it,' I admit. 'Seriously. If I could be normal, I would. You have no idea.'

Her voice is soft. 'Well, you'd better try and straighten out before things kick off with Mum.'

'What's that meant to mean?' I demand.

She ignores me and adds, 'Because it would be pretty bad if your home life started to mimic your school life.'

'Is that a threat?'

'It was a statement.'

'Good.' My mind flips to fight mode suddenly. Logic flies out the window. 'Cos I wouldn't want you to be jealous that I'm running with AMD making sick tunes while some people are running round acting like clones.'

Shadavia stops. 'Excuse me? I'm not a clone!'

'I didn't say you were.'

'You might as well have.'

212

'Then stop following Kelly's lead and hating for no reason!' I wrestle a handful of plates into the cupboard. 'I know you're not like her. She's a beg, and you've got a brain.'

'Stop ordering me around!'

'I'm not. I'm suggesting.'

'Then stop suggesting! I don't need you, okay? Butt out.' She bangs a pot down in the drainer and the crash resonates. 'Stay out of my way.'

'I can't stay out of your way. We live in the same house.'

'Just *stay out of my way*.' Shadavia peels off the washing gloves and flicks water. 'Stay out of my way as much as possible and we're cool. Okay?'

'Whatever.'

'Deal?' She sticks out one hand. I reluctantly take it. She grips and shakes and I can feel the slimy specks of dirt from the grimy water squishing up against my palm. I snatch back my hand and wipe it on my bum hard. Shadavia doesn't even notice. She's so desperate to get away from me that she's already gone.

TWENTY

It kicks off on one of those days. I went to bed early and spent the night stuck in recurring dreams of running towards Megz, but being sucked towards the hands of the people who slapped and pushed and shouted. My alarm clock goes. I hit snooze. My phone goes. I hurl it across the room. Charmaine rolls me out of bed over half an hour late, grumpy as, and grumpier still after I've forced down breakfast. I've missed meeting Dayan to walk to school, so Charmaine offers to drop me in the car. Vince, being a lazy lump, immediately jumps on the opportunity for a lift.

When I lumber into class, I'm half aware of people glancing at me. But maybe it's just me. After all, I am barely awake and my head feels like a breeze block.

Then one of the boys on my table says, 'Alright, Baby Girl?' and the other boys and girls smother their sniggers. He keeps saying it at intervals throughout the whole lesson.

I don't make the link until I check Snapchat between first and second period. The first message I open on is me in one of my oversized baseball jerseys that looks like a shirt-dress. The caption?

she wears these so no one can see her nappy

It disappears.

I try to catch my breath. It's just a troll. Just a stupid troll.

Moving on, I check a few people's stories. My mood lifts a few notches.

Then I open a message that stays just long enough for me to take in the picture and recognise the bed, the blankets – the person sprawled on the bed. On one of those notorious wet patches.

The humiliation is the same every night that it happens – which, when I'm going through a difficult patch, feels like more often than not.

Somebody managed to capture the moment before the humiliation. And they've sent it back as a reminder.

No one likes a big baby grow up

All morning, people are poking fun out of the corners of their mouths. If it's not, 'Alright, Baby Girl?', it's making noises, or asking if I need a toilet break. Stuff like, 'You look sad, Kadie. You need Huggies?' Really menial, terrible jokes. But people still laugh. And I still get hot fists.

I leave second period fuming.

At break, Junior holds open the door to Mr Driver's room for me. I storm through without a hello. Junior raises one eyebrow. 'You on your period?' he asks with his usual indifference.

I slump in the nearest chair and slam my backpack down on the table.

Junior seats himself opposite me. 'No sleep?'

'None.'

'Here.' He pops a Guava Rubicon, and slides it across the table towards me.

The door bangs open and Dayan comes in, Reuben and Michael on his tail. Their chatter dies almost as soon as they see me.

'Alright, Kadie?' Reuben says with his usual jauntiness.

'I'm gonna strangle the next person that says "alright" to me,' I growl.

Junior clears his throat.

The boys make themselves comfy, politely ignoring my screw-face. Dayan sits on his chair backwards and gives me a light shove. 'What's the matter, rude gyal?'

I grit my teeth. 'Is there something I don't know?'

Michael and Junior exchange a look.

'Like what?' Reuben asks.

It's taking all my self-restraint not to crush the Rubicon can in my hand. 'Everyone's been laughing at me all morning.'

Nobody says a word.

'Are you serious?' I down some Rubicon desperately. 'You man have nothing to say?'

'I don't know where it's all come from,' Michael says apologetically.

'It's probably just some stupid rumour someone made up,' Junior agrees.

'It's *what*?' I demand.

216

After a long moment of silence, Dayan says gently, 'Apparently you wet the bed.'

And there it is, for all to hear.

Reuben is taking a lot of interest in his phone. Michael looks embarrassed, as if he's the one being trolled, while Junior is just studying me inquisitively, as if waiting for confirmation. Dayan sits back in his chair.

The Rubicon turns sour in my mouth. I slam the can on the table and push it away. 'Rumours aren't always true, you know.'

'Right!' Michael agrees, way too enthusiastically.

Junior looks at his phone. 'You're not going to, like, confirm?'

'Bruv!' Dayan scolds him.

'It's private,' I say tightly.

'Sort of,' Reuben adds.

I clench the edges of my chair and shut my eyes, trying to compose myself and fight the sick feeling developing in my stomach. Discussing this would be horrible enough with a group of girls, but with guys – especially *these* guys – it's even more awkward than that time I walked in on them discussing the finer details of wet dreams. Oddly, my mind throws up a sudden fear that they won't think I'm peng anymore.

'Do you care?' I ask tentatively. 'Would it change whether you would hang out with me or not?'

Junior shifts uncomfortably and smirks. I glare.

'No way,' Michael says quickly.

'Is it true, though?' Reuben asks absently. 'I've heard so many stories I don't even know what the real deal is.'

I study him. It's impossible to tell if he's being genuine or not.

'It's private,' I say again. 'And it's been proper exaggerated.' But they're all still looking at me like I need to give a legit explanation – even Dayan.

My face burns all over and I shift my eyes to Reuben's muddy school shoes, the table legs, my school bag – anything to avoid eye contact. This is harder than I thought it would be. I never *thought* about it. I never thought that it would get out. And the mandem are supposed to be my acquaintances. Maybe even friends. They're not supposed to make me feel this small.

Michael tries to reassure me. 'We don't really care if it's true or not, you know. It doesn't change who you are or anything.'

I can tell by his voice that he's trying to be comforting, but the silence that follows only makes the atmosphere more awkward. I'm fully wishing I hadn't bothered coming here today. The boys are used to me randomly avoiding them every few weeks or so, when I need a moment to myself to get my head straight. Sometimes I go to Pastoral at break time and just sit with the other kids who are in trouble or getting through their own problems. The staff who work in there don't mind. They don't judge. They know nobody's perfect.

'We're digressing.' I force myself to look each one of them

in the eye. 'I asked you all a question, and no one's answered it so I'm gonna say it again. Is there something I don't know?'

Reuben acts like he didn't hear me.

Junior looks at me. 'That *was* the something.'

Michael clears his throat nervously and says, 'I thought it was just some madness off Snapchat.'

On my left, Dayan sucks his teeth and swipes aggressively at his phone screen. So far, Mr Driver has been pretty lax about the phone rule in his classroom, so long as we're not being blatant about it. Must be a favouritism thing.

'What's with you?' Junior asks Dayan.

'Nothing.' But Dayan's screw-face is nearly searing a hole in the carpet.

Junior stares into space for a long moment. I'm just considering leaving to find a quiet, solitary spot to disappear when he sits up and says, 'I don't think you want to know.'

I blink, shocked that I got an answer. 'You don't think I want to know?'

'What it is that you're missing.'

'I'm sick of being laughed at!'

'Telling you what it is won't change anything.'

'How would you know?'

Junior sags slightly under my glare. He tugs at his hat uncomfortably and glances at the others for help. No one says a word.

'And what am I gonna gain from staying oblivious?' I ask.

'More than from seeing what they're laughing at.'

'Tch. Just tell me what it is.'

Now Michael's watching me too. 'You sure?'

My voice nearly breaks. 'Yes, I'm sure! You don't understand!'

'She has a right to know,' Dayan says softly, but he's looking at the floor.

Junior tuts. 'Just because you have a right doesn't mean it's going to settle you.'

'She asked,' Dayan says tightly. 'If you don't tell her, I will.'

So they tell me about the source of the rumours: a fake Instagram account: the_real_gold!locks.

I search it up. Junior rubs his face. Michael busies himself opening a Müller yoghurt.

It's blocked: I'm not allowed to view it from my Goldilocks profile. Someone is definitely out for me.

I cuss and look to Dayan for help. 'Bruv, I need your phone.'

He hands it over silently.

The moment the page loads, I know they were right.

The first of the two most recent posts follow on from the one I got on Snapchat this morning. The picture isn't even related – what's me sitting on Michael's bed got to do with wet sheets? – but the caption doesn't care. *No wonder she wanna get in other people's beds*

The pictures of me that I got on Snapchat this morning

are both up there. I've seen the pictures, but some of the words have been modified so it looks like I wrote them.

I wear these so no one can see my nappy

Didn't wear my huggies one time

Then after that, it's a picture of Dayan and I, the mandem chilling in the background.

AMD obvs don't support him smh they letting him roll with the no#1 sket

And a photo shopped picture of me the one time I've actually worn some makeup since being here.

contour gone wrong

The amount of likes and comments on each picture is sickening.

And so it goes on. Phone snaps, screenshots, Snapchats, the lot – somebody has been keeping tabs on me and posting regularly. People are *following* this fake Goldilocks account. Half of the comments are from people who follow me.

The captions have a thing for my hair.

couldn't even straighten my hair properly smh

Only freaks have natural highlights

Straight or curly, it's still a mess

What exactly is a brush?

When you're too stupid for a YouTube tutorial

The video of my classroom 'meltdown' is on there, captioned *Crazy Beg*. I knew everyone thought it was a joke, but to see the comments going on and on and on under the video makes me dizzy. And someone's been taking all my

Snaps from my story and reposting them with a *Caption this* title. I skip the captions. First glance tells me they're very harsh.

Towards the bottom of the page, the very first selfie I took with Beverly, Shadavia and Vince is on there – from when I first moved in during the summer. We look happy. They didn't really know me back then, but I tried so hard to behave normally in those first few weeks, and they look like they love me. Our faces glow. But that doesn't matter. It's doubled up with another picture. The caption says *The fake vs the real thing* and the following picture is a screenshot of a jokey snap that I posted on my story some time back. In context – with the caption *school makes me feel so* – a picture of me sitting backwards on my desk chair, obscene fingers raised, tie loose and hair wild, looks perfectly reasonable. Here, squashed up next door to the other picture, it makes me look demonic.

Something crushes my heart.

Dayan reaches over and snatches the phone out of my hand. 'That's enough.'

My hands are trembling. 'How long has this been a thing?'

None of them look at me.

Fine. I'll find out myself. I seize the phone from Dayan and open the page again.

'Don't!' He grabs my wrist. 'Close it.'

He looks so distressed that I close the page that very second.

222

'It's been hovering about pretty much since September,' Reuben says quietly.

'And none of you said anything?'

Junior tries to look me in the eye. 'We were trying to protect you.'

'Protect me? You weren't protecting me from nothing! People have been laughing at me from day one!'

'You were happy,' he argues. 'Most days you were coming to school off your face, chatting about music and media and joking around. It was great! We've seen you when you're upset. You think we wanted to kill your good moods?'

'So no one even has the guts to drop a few supportive comments?' I fight to keep my voice steady. How do I manage to do this every time – pick friends that don't have the backbone to stick up for one of their own? It always happens. I shack up with people who smile and open their arms, welcoming me into their houses, their studios, inviting me to parties and sleepovers, oblivious to the fear that lives inside me and remaining so even when things turn sour; people who see my flaws and see my tears but jump on the trolling bandwagon anyway, almost relishing it when I blow my top – how are these always the ones who seemed like the best bet to start with?

'Comments do nothing,' Reuben says. 'That Snap you posted about Beauty and the Beast got everyone talking, you know. Some people probably think you started it.'

The first time I saw my friends for who they really were

was when I was ten. A sleepover I'd been dying to go to ended abruptly when one of the girls singled me out. Every time, I tell myself I'll do better. And the cycle starts again and the bad bits just keep on reoccurring, a cruel repeating pattern.

The thought of all those betrayals rakes up more anger. 'Whose side are you on?' I shout.

Across the room, Mr Driver looks up from his laptop. 'Excuse me!' he says pointedly.

'I'm neutral,' Reuben says, managing not to look me in the eye.

'Bruv,' Junior warns.

Dayan gets up abruptly, crosses the room in four strides and is out the door without a word. The room shakes with the force of the door banging shut.

Reuben peers after him. 'He's always on his man period these days.'

I suck my teeth and grab my bag to leave the room with a curt, 'You man are actually a waste of space.'

Reuben starts to reply. Junior kicks him. They let me go without a word. The silence follows me like a shadow.

Dayan's mooching his way down the corridor, lingering like he's not sure where he's going.

I jab him in the belly with my elbow. 'Got something on your mind?'

'I always have something on my mind.'

'You're grumpier than normal.'

'I'm not normally grumpy.'

'On your man period?'

'Yes.'

'Seriously.'

'It doesn't matter.'

'It does.'

He sighs, rolls his eyes, and brings up a screenshot on a Snap message on his phone.

none of them really like you, just wait when push comes to shove none of them will back you

From some next man called the_stitch_uno20.

I curl my lip in disgust. 'What's that meant to mean?'

Dayan shrugs. 'You saw the guys today. They're not backing anyone. You or me.'

I sigh raggedly. 'News flash. So what are we meant to do?'

A water bottle slams into the windows to our left and jeering erupts from around the corner as Ellis, followed by Aidan, comes our way.

Ellis picks up the water bottle from the floor and bops both of us on the head with it. 'Alright, Crazy Legs?' he says, grinning at Dayan.

'Shut your mouth,' I blurt out.

'Keep your hair on. He's a big boy. He can handle himself.'

Kelly snorts as she swans past with Josh. She doesn't have to say anything. The snort is enough. Eisha gives me a little smile as she passes, but it's covert enough that nobody else sees. As for Shadavia, she just takes half a second out of her conversation with Raquel to shoot me a smug expression. I'm pretty sure I hear *crazy beg* uttered under somebody's breath.

I want to yell something cocky. I want to throw a chair. I want to cuss them out, scream, wave Emerson – but for once my words have vanished.

That smirk. I've never seen Shadavia clock me like that before, and I can only think of one reason why she might.

'I thought "crazy legs" was a private joke,' I mutter, once they're gone.

'It was.' Dayan sighs. 'It got out somehow and now we're Crazy Legs and Crazy Beg. Catchy, huh?'

I grit my teeth. 'We're gonna have to fight back one day, you know that, right?'

He shrugs. 'Fight back how?'

'Somehow.'

'A retaliation will just make it worse.' He peers at me. 'I like how you tried to defend us with that fancy Beauty and the Beast analogy, but if we're up against them, we're dead. Plus, we're not in a relationship.'

I ignore the last part. 'Bruv, you roll with the likes of AMD. What are you on about?'

'I "roll" at their heels,' Dayan says, making aggressive quotation marks. He pulls his hood up and hides behind the fluff. 'More time they're chilling with Ellis and that. They want to play footy half the time. We're friends, yeah, but we're low key friends. They're not there for me, and if they're not backing me, don't wait for them to back you.'

'What are you saying?' I demand. 'Someone needs to do something.'

'I know!' he growls. Then, in a calmer voice, he adds, 'You'd believe me if I told you about the origin of our friendship.'

I peep at him. 'You were friends from young?'

'I wish.' He laughs bitterly. 'They heard that my uncle owned a studio – the one where we now do our proper recordings. We must've been about thirteen.' He's staring dreamily into the distance. 'I don't know how they found out. Junior and Michael never paid me no mind before, not until they conveniently stumbled upon me playing the guitar one time. Then suddenly they were all, "Wow, you're sick, bro!" And then, "So your uncle's got a studio, yeah? Can we use it?" And the only reason I ended up in the group was because the deal we cut with them was that I got to record with them if they got free studio time – because my uncle knew I was a Larry Loner most of the time and took the opportunity to set me up with some friends. The fact that I'm doing well is beside the point.' He turns his attention to me. 'Do you see where I'm coming from? We were never just friends because they just wanted to be my friend. They're awesome guys, but they're really quite shallow sometimes.'

'That sounds a bit harsh.'

'Believe what you will. They don't seem to care much anymore, since they've struck a nice deal with my uncle over paid-for studio time that doesn't include me.'

'So are we gonna do something?' I ask.

'Course we're gonna do something.' Dayan smiles mischievously. 'I've got plenty of tricks up my sleeve. Just you wait.'

TWENTY-ONE

I stand waiting for the three o'clock crowds, bunning a zoot guiltily. Vince is basically the reason I've been able to have a daily smoke these past few weeks. He doesn't know. That's the problem. I didn't have any money, and he did.

Do I really need this stuff? If I wanted to be all rainbows and flowers about things, I would say that I can get by without it. I shouldn't take Vince's money. But I'm hardly the notorious Kadie Hunte without a little weed, am I? That's all I've got to hold onto. The notorious Kadie Hunte, and Emerson. I only dream of a Kadie Lucas, or a Kadie anything. I think I can only dream of being somebody else.

Charmaine's doing her best to slowly undo the knots that I've carefully tied in the tales I tell. Since our awkward chat in the car, she's been making me do things differently. Helping with dinner, taking the rubbish out, doing my homework essays under strict supervision in dead silence – random things, some of which I get rewards for – which is nice. But I still waste hours tossing and turning at night at the thought of what will happen when she realises what she's up against. Everyone bails when they realise they're excavating a bottomless pit. I can delude myself, but not for long. The very least that I can do is set things up so that when it all goes to pot, I'll be the incorrigible girl who probably was going to wind up that way anyway.

So I barged out of class first and lit up a zoot by the gate. Courtesy of Vince.

'Kadie! What you saying?'

I heard Reuben coming way before he got to me, but I give him a suspicious nod anyway. To my surprise, he stops by my side without cutting his eye at me. 'Alright?'

'Been better.'

'Yeah.'

I eye him. 'Not gonna make some dig? No relevant jokes?'

Reuben stares at his toes. 'Why would I?'

'None of you have said a word about the whole Instagram ting.'

'We all unfollowed the page.'

I snort out a mouthful of smoke. 'Oh, wow! You *unfollowed* the page!' I clap sarcastically. 'Thanks! You're such a great friend.'

'I don't think you get it,' he says.

'Get what?'

'You were popular once, you should know what everyone's like.'

That strikes a nerve. *Once.*

'People are expecting us to jump on certain things,' he adds.

'So? You have your own brain!'

'You obviously haven't tried reasoning with Josh and that.'

I inhale and watch the smoke billow out of my nose so I don't have to answer.

Reuben shifts awkwardly and changes the subject. 'D'you know what's up with Dayan?'

I grind out the end of my zoot on the floor, half-snigger, half-kiss my teeth. 'Are you stupid?'

Reuben cuts his eye at me. 'I was only asking. I thought maybe you could sort him out.'

I'd love to say I know what's up with him – why he's been slouching around, throwing quiet screw-faces and being monosyllabic – but I don't. Not really. I've been trying to survive the week of trolling from the entire year group without getting excluded.

'I don't know what's up with Dayan,' I tell him. 'Maybe you should talk to him and find out.'

'Talk to him?' Reuben snorts. 'He doesn't tell me stuff.'

'Have you ever asked him?'

'He's never in one place long enough for that.'

'Long enough for what?'

I jump at the sound of Dayan's voice. Reuben recoils and moves away from him. 'To have a proper conversation.'

Dayan cuts his eye at Reuben. 'What are you chatting on? You've been acting like I've got the plague since Kadie came around.'

231

'That doesn't explain why you've been moving funny this past week.'

Dayan shakes his head a little, like he doesn't understand. 'Funny how?'

'Like the rest of us have done you wrong.'

Dayan curls his lip and glances at me. What am I supposed to say? I don't know why he's acting.

'I thought you were my friends,' he says eventually.

Reuben looks unconvinced. 'Aren't we?'

'Are you? Then why ain't any of you got my back?'

'What are you on about?' Reuben demands. 'If this is about standing up for Kadie, I don't know what you want us to do.'

'Why you bringing me into this?' I protest.

'Oi, oi, oi. What's going on?' Junior busts his way into the face-off. 'Why you all looking so vexed?'

Reuben tries to hide his scowl. 'My man's telling me how we don't have his back.'

Junior locks eyes with Dayan. 'Don't we?'

'The fact that you're asking says it all.'

'You want to explain?'

Dayan presses his lips together so hard that they pale in colour and, after a few beats, mutters, 'You probably wouldn't get it.'

Junior's poker face cracks then. 'How wouldn't I?'

Dayan stares him down for a tense moment. He screws up his face, but he's not finding the words. He glances at me.

I shrug. 'Show them the message.'

As Dayan pulls out his phone, I hear Josh's boisterous voice drawing closer. It's like he has a special ability to make his laugh carry across the heads of the other students.

I get a Snapchat message. All my instincts scream *do not open!!!!!*

I open it.

ugly sket get your dirty vibes away from junior

And another one.

Brush your hair you scatty ting

A second later, Josh makes his presence known by hollering, 'Oi, Junior? You man coming out later?'

Dayan's head jerks up. He stops scrolling his screen and his whole body stiffens. Junior and Reuben seem to miss this, despite the fact that they're stood right next to him.

Josh dribbles his football up to us and toe-flicks it up into his hands. He curls his lip in my direction and addresses the mandem. 'Why are you still entertaining the freak show?'

Junior raises one eyebrow. Knowing him, he's probably about to drop some cool response to make Josh back off – but whatever he was going to say is cut off as Dayan launches himself straight at Josh. And he would've got there too, if Reuben didn't step in the way.

There's a struggle for a good few seconds as Junior and Reuben fight to hold Dayan back. Dayan really wants to get a punch in, and Josh isn't quite sure if he should be scared or be mocking. He settles with mocking.

'What are you doing, man?' he demands. 'Control yourself!

I wasn't even talking about you, but if you want in on that, be my guest.'

Dayan tries to fight off the boys, but the two of them put together are stronger and they eventually manage to wrestle him away from Josh, giving him a good shove straight back into me.

Michael emerges out of the crowd. 'You okay?'

'Don't call me a freak!' Dayan is breathing very heavily. He's adopted my screw-face and his fists are clenched so tight that the brown of his skin is paling around the knuckles.

Reuben tries to laugh. 'Be easy, man. He didn't call you a freak.'

'He was talking about her,' Aidan says helpfully, jabbing a finger at me from behind Josh. I scowl. He gives me an almost apologetic smile.

Josh smirks. 'Listen to your bredrin, Lips.'

Dayan makes for him again, but this time Josh is ready and he throws his muddy football at him, rebounding it directly off his face. Dayan lurches back to the sound of jeering from some Year Nines watching from a few feet away. Actually, there are quite a few students starting to linger. Oblivious, Dayan steps right up into Josh's face. 'What is your problem? Seriously?'

Josh squares up to him. 'What's *your* problem?'

I look to the mandem for a response. Thankfully, Michael moves in and punches Josh hard on the arm. 'Hey, allow it. Leave my man alone.'

'Me leave *him* alone?' Josh snorts, pulling an offended expression. 'This sideman was the one trying to start something.' He cuts his eye at Dayan. 'Weren't you?'

Dayan screws up his face and glances between Michael and Josh desperately, his lips pouting and parted slightly. He blinks hard like he's about to either cry or explode. An obnoxious group of Year Eight boys shout, 'Fight! Fight! Fight!' as they roll their bikes past.

Just like that, Dayan turns and runs. Like a roadman-cross-toddler.

Junior reaches after him. 'Bruv, wait—' But he doesn't move. The only thing that follows Dayan is laughter from the audience – and five seconds later he's disappeared in the mass of blazers, through the gate and out of sight. The boys stare after him, agape, as if that was the last thing they expected.

Josh smacks a high-five with Aidan. 'Wow, man, what an anti-climax.'

That sends me over the edge. 'You're an idiot!' One smack for Josh's football. It flies out of his hands. One smack for Josh's face. I hear the collective gasp that comes with the sting of my skin on his. The crowd is watching again as I round on the mandem. 'And you're a disgrace!'

Then I bolt after Dayan.

The main road is chock-a-block with cars inching along between the ones doing pick-ups from the school. The three-fifteen bus manages to crawl away from the bus stop, crammed with blue blazers.

235

I stand up on an old tree stump for some extra height and spot Dayan in the distance down the road, stomping with his hood up, fists balled, towards the swarms of young kids coming from the junior school. I sprint to reach him and end up puffing and panting by the time I get there.

I call his name about six times and eventually have to thump him to get his attention. 'It's Goldilocks.'

He pulls his hood far over his face and keeps walking.

'You should have told him,' I say.

'Told him what?'

'About the message.'

'What? For them all to brush it off like they did the Instagram thing?'

I start to reply and stop. He's kind of right. It stinks, but it looks like that's exactly what they'd do at this point.

'Hold up, man!' Panting, I grab for Dayan's arm, miss, and end up seizing his hand instead. I snatch my hand back as soon as our palms touch, but I've got his attention.

'It doesn't matter,' he says, his voice empty. He looks at the hand which I touched and twinkles his fingers. 'None of it matters.'

'Why?' I demand.

'They'll get what's coming to them.'

'How?'

'They just will. I'm going to do something.'

'Something like what? You know you can't touch them man.' Like I can't touch Kelly.

After a moment, Dayan gives me a long, sad look. He lifts his shoulders. 'I dunno yet. But whatever it is, it'll be big.'

'Yeah.' I hold back a snort of disdain. 'Something big. Like what? You gonna set their knickers alight?'

'I don't see you doing anything.' His face is hidden behind his hood, but I can practically hear the scowl in his voice.

'Tch. I'm not wasting my time and energy on them gyal.'

'You're not?' Dayan turns to look at me now. 'Are you for real? One of "them gyal" is living in the same house as you, and you're not going to settle the score?'

'What am I supposed to do?' I demand. 'They got me on ropes.'

'You need to talk to Shadavia.'

'That girl doesn't listen to me no more. You know that.'

'Yeah? Well, make her listen. She's at the heart of this Snapchat thing.'

Logic says this is right. Vince isn't that way inclined. Beverly doesn't have a phone. Shadavia is the only person who could have taken such a close range picture.

I turn cold inside. 'Don't wanna talk about that.'

'Don't talk all you want. Everyone else is talking.'

I watch my feet go one in front of the other. Everyone will always be talking. It doesn't matter what I do – there will always be something for them to talk about. Especially with that fake Goldilocks account.

'It was her,' Dayan adds, matter-of-factly. 'It was Shadavia that baited it out. She's the person who can get attention diverted away from it. You need to stand up to her, or what's gonna come next?'

'What can possibly be worse than a fake account distorting just about everything about me?' I mutter. The possibilities flood my head. 'Tch. Don't answer that.'

'You need to do something.' Dayan is firm, determined in the same way he was when he got me into the duet. He's steered things away from his own situation, and he's not backing down on this. 'Someone needs to set her straight before she ends up as bad as the others.'

I glance over my shoulder and glimpse Shadavia with her friends just as we turn the corner – she's sharing ear buds with Kelly, chatting animatedly as usual. He's right. She's not quite as bad as the others. Not yet.

Maybe she's my hope.

Shadavia gets home around four. When she jogs up the stairs, skipping every other step, I'm right there by her bedroom door, waiting for her. And my fingers are crossed behind my back, because I'm seriously hoping that she's going to react the way I need her to – in a way that shows me she's not like the others. Or that she's so indifferent because they're her friends, and she's supposed to be loyal. Or – even better – that it wasn't her.

I am literally praying that it's the latter. My heart's pounding up a storm inside, and I have to keep reminding myself how it works.

Don't count on anyone.

Act. Always act.

Be prepared to lose everything.

So I have to stand there reminding myself I've got to look like I couldn't care less (for the most part anyway), like it's all just a joke as usual. And I think I deserve a gold star, because this is no easy feat with the fear churning and whispering, *what if it was her? What if she's just like Kelly? Like everyone else?*

Shadavia gives me a funny look. 'What's up?' she asks, attempting to step around me.

I shift so that I'm blocking the doorway. 'I know it was you who started it.'

She frowns. 'What are you on about?'

I'm burning up all over my cheeks but I rein it in as best as I can, proper resisting the temptation to step into her personal space and get aggro. 'The bedwetting thing – Snap. Everyone's talking about it. Everyone's seen the pictures.'

Shadavia blinks slowly. 'Um . . . what makes you think it was me?'

'I *know* it was you.'

'Great.' She shrugs, not looking me in the eye. 'I'm so glad you trust me.'

I grit my teeth. 'Is that all you have to say?'

She groans. 'So you think it was me. So what?'

'So what?' My hands curl into fists. 'So . . . it hurts! You *know* you don't have to jump on the bandwagon. That was private stuff and now it's out there for everyone to laugh at!'

She shakes her head slowly. For a moment, a naive part of me wonders if this is a sign that she's about to make an uncharacteristic apology. Instead she says, 'You're chatting rubbish.'

My naive hope is shot down and crashes ungracefully.

I rub my hands across my face. 'We need to just stop this, you know. If you're gonna treat me like E. coli, course I'm gonna feel like sending shots for you back, so why don't we just call it quits? I don't wanna be at odds forever. I'm tired of fighting with you.'

Shadavia mutters, 'I'm tired of living with you.'

'What?' A chill spirals down my body.

'You heard me.'

So that's it.

She doesn't care. She doesn't even have enough respect to admit that she's done me dirty.

Amando's words bob to the surface of my mind. *I expect you to have some respect when you're talking to other members of this family.*

You've got to use respect if you want to be respected.

Well, apparently that only applies to me. All I'm getting from Shadavia is blatant signs that I'm not worth the effort.

The rage fireballs out into my face and my fingertips. I clench my fists. 'You think you're so big, don't you? Ooh, bad-a-man Shadavia, chilling on a podium—'

'Calm yourself.' She pushes past me into her room, making my shoulder slam into the door frame.

I barrel on. 'You don't have to try and make my life a misery just cos the others do it. It's not a fashion ting.'

Shadavia tosses her handbag on the floor by the bunk bed she shares with Beverly. Then, turning her back to me, she slips off her blazer and kicks off her shoes as if I never spoke.

So this is how we're playing it.

She wants no respect? I can do that.

'Is it a jealousy ting?' I call from the doorway. 'I don't understand. Is it cos I've got Lips and AMD checking me?'

Shadavia snorts. 'What, Shrek? No way, fam. That boy's so butters even Cruella De Vil wouldn't have him on her toast.'

Wow. Now we get bad puns as well.

'Yeah? Well, Shrek's Instagram has more followers than you and me put together. Maybe that's what you don't like? That the boy you lot are out here calling weird is popping off more than the lot of you?'

Shadavia ignores me and hangs her blazer up. Either she's letting this go because of what she's done, or she's gearing up for a sassy comeback. I wait for a moment, pretending to pick my nails, focusing on getting air into my lungs.

Nope. Not even a sassy comeback.

My fingers curl into fists again. I want more than this from her. I know she can do better. Where's the banter about where to buy pyjamas, and the quality of Morrison's doughnuts, and the lunch snacks we accidentally leave in our bags for days on end? Where's the girl who flounced into my room, put

241

her feet up on my bed on day one and asked if I was into Post Malone?

I just don't know where she's put that Shadavia . . . or if she's ever coming back.

You're breaking the rules.

Yep.

I barrel on, thinking too fast to stop. 'Or . . . is it that I've got your mum wound round my little finger?' My voice twists into a sneer. It doesn't do it often, but it's easy peasy. 'That I can do what I like because I'm a foster kid and you're just the goody-two-shoes in the corner? I bet your mum doesn't even care that much. She's too busy doling out hugs to kids who missed out.'

Shadavia is visibly annoyed now. 'Kadie, go away.'

'No, I know what it is.' I position myself in the doorway like I'm comfy. 'I've been here like five months, and everyone at school is pretty much always looking at my Insta. Even if they just wanna hate. They're still watching, aren't they? I'm hitting double your amount of views since AMD took me in. Face, it, that's what's bothering you, innit? Cos I'm racking my brain now, for real . . . I honestly don't have a clue what I've done to cheese you off that much. I'm out of guesses.'

Shadavia groans and stamps to the door, moving to close it hard. 'If you say one more word—'

'What?' Now I move into her face, all patience burned out. 'What are you gonna do that could *possibly* make my life any more painful?'

Her voice is a screech. 'It's always about you, isn't it?'

Always about me?

Yeah . . . Sudden moves in the middle of the school year, those were about me, were they? Being squeezed into the corner of somebody else's bedroom time and again, starting with the two girls I was supposed to call half-sisters: that was about me? The hours and hours spent inside the four white walls of a room filled with machines and wires while watching my only family deteriorate – that wasn't even slightly about me. I might have been a kid then, but I knew it was about Mummy and I made my time with her special. I tried to learn new things every day so that when Jacinta – the foster lady and friend of Mummy who looked after me – took me there, I could make the most of the time. I screamed when Jacinta said she would take me home during the last days, because I knew Mummy couldn't stand being alone.

Shadavia is dead wrong. Not that she would know, having lived her cush little life in her nice big house with her mum and dad.

But she's still wrong. The only time it's all about me is when—

WHACK.

My fist hits Shadavia cleanly across the jaw. She doesn't reel back far, seeing as my other fist is clamped around her tie. Neither of us saw that coming.

But she's back like a jack-in-the-box and her fist catches me hard in the same spot – and scratches, thanks to those sparkly rings she wears on her index finger. 'Shut up!' she yells. 'Give me a break!'

'Give *you* a break?' The anger explodes, dizzying like a head rush gone wrong. Next thing I know, I'm head-butting Shadavia in the face. *Crack!*

Shadavia shouts and stumbles back. I dart for my room, but she grabs my shirt and puts her fist hard into my lower lip. That girl certainly packs a punch.

'Stop it!' A little blur rushes between us. Beverly stretches her arms as wide as they'll go. 'StopitstopitstopitMUMMYCOMEHERE!'

Shadavia barges her little sister into the wall. 'Sorry, Bev. She's taking the mick.'

She manages to shove me off my feet before Vince bursts out of his room and bellows, 'Oi, allow it!' before putting himself directly in front of Shadavia, who looks like she's about to go for the kill. Literally. Charmaine flies up the stairs a second later. She takes in the scene and demands, 'What's going on?'

Vince casts me a cold look. 'By the sounds of it, Kadie started another fight. I heard everything.'

I squeeze my hands under my armpits. 'I did not!'

'Then why did I hear your voice doing most of the provoking?' he asks. 'I might not be anybody's bio brother, but everything I heard was totally out of line.'

I bare my teeth. 'It was her as well!'

Vince gives me half-mast eyes. 'No excuse.'

'Come on, you know it was. I tried to make a truce! She started the fight.'

'I started the fight?' Shadavia is incredulous. 'You punched me first!'

'You said—'

Vince groans. 'It was both of you. But mostly Kadie.'

'Hope you're happy. You broke my glasses when you head-butted me,' says Shadavia. She holds them up delicately so that everyone can see the crack in the nose piece. Her lip is bleeding too, but apparently this isn't important.

Charmaine's attention snaps straight to me. 'Is this true?'

'I—'

'You know what? I don't care.' She jabs a finger at the stairs. 'Go and sit in the kitchen.'

'But I didn't—'

'Don't test my patience!'

I cuss under my breath and stamp down the stairs. I tried. Now I'm getting done for it.

This is exactly why I never should have stopped following the rules.

TWENTY-TWO

I'm chilling in my room, touching up the last verse to a new song on my MacBook which I just got back, when Vince bursts in. Vince is known for bulldozing up the stairs and slamming into the kitchen, so naturally I ignore the loud bang of my bedroom door and carry on until he marches straight up to me and bats the headphones off my ears.

'Watch it!' I protest.

'You're a snake!' he replies. 'Where's my money?'

I know exactly what he's talking about. It's been on my mind for nearly four weeks now – since Charmaine took my smartcard off me. But I play dumb. 'Your money?'

'Yes, my money. I know you've been taking money from me.'

I've been taking money from Vince for three weeks precisely, so he has obviously only noticed recently. Why did he have to notice now? I was going to give it back tomorrow.

When I don't say a thing, Vince adds, 'If you needed money couldn't you just ask Charmaine or Amando?'

I count to five and bite my lip hard.

'Ignoring me isn't going to make everything magically

better,' Vince says. 'I know it was you, and I want it back now.'

'I've only been in your room, like, once,' I mutter.

He snatches my phone out of my hand and tosses it on the bed. 'Liar! Pay up!'

'What, you think I just have it lying around on the floor?'

His eyebrows dance as he thinks. 'Dirty sket. So that's how you can afford to smoke.' His voice rises. 'You've been stealing off the rest of us!'

I press my lips together and mentally push some guilt down. The bandage covering Emerson's most recent cuts on my arm itches and I distract myself by rubbing the plaster back down onto my skin. It's not that bad. It's going to blow over. Everything will be fine. The heat is not coming.

Inhaling, I put on my Goldilocks act, and spin one-eighty degrees on my chair to face him. 'I'll get you your money by tomorrow.'

'So that's it? After everything?' Several veins in Vince's forehead are visible. He's that vexed.

'Everything like what?'

'Since the day you first stepped through that front door, all I've tried to do is be a supportive big brother,' he growls. 'And this is always how you repay me! With snarky comments and screw-faces and stealing.'

I fold my arms tightly. 'I'm sorry. Since when does calling me a sket and a waste of space and saying my family is messed up count as being supportive?'

'That was just one time, and don't change the subject. You need to get my money back to me by tonight.'

I roll my eyes. 'I don't have my smartcard, genius. I can't just go withdraw a bunch of p's.'

Vince seethes quietly. 'What if I needed that?' he demands. 'Did you ever think of that, huh? What if I was saving up for something important? Now I've got to wait for the most untrustworthy girl I've ever known to get my money back before I can pay for my thing.'

'You work,' I say dryly, gesturing to the Subway shirt that he's still wearing. 'Isn't payday, like, tomorrow?'

'That's irrelevant!' Vince pushes me back by my chin, making me spin a full circle.

'I told you—' I turn back in time to receive another push that nearly sends me off the chair.

'Shadavia's right. You're just a waste of space. Maybe you *should* go get kicked out of school and move somewhere else. Because if this is how you're gonna treat us, we won't miss you.'

I let the rage flood me. I know I shouldn't – I'm the one at fault, after all – but it just happens. I've been holding it in all day every day for the sake of that stupid behaviour report – for Charmaine – and the flood gates just give.

The nearest heavy object – my Physics text book – finds its way into my hands. I swing it at Vince's shoulder, miss, and catch him hard in the jaw.

Vince roars. He drags me straight off the chair by the

scruff of my neck and shakes me hard, yelling something about getting him his money by tonight. The jumper pulls taut on my arms and I squirm in a wave of discomfort, crying out. *Why now? I only needed one more day.*

Fight mode hits me like a sugar rush.

Vince is still growling, but his anger turns into shock as I grab an ear and a clump of hair and stamp in the general direction of his foot. He howls and loses his balance, stumbling back into the bed. My free hand swipes and claws and my voice fills my ears with the sound of my own desperation, my own silent plea – *go away. Give me one more day.*

Then there's another pair of hands and another voice – 'Woah, woah, hey! Enough! Break it up!' – and we're yanked apart. Charmaine has to stand in front of Vince and physically block him from jumping on me again.

'You're a thief!' shouts Vince. 'And a liar! Is that all you know how to do? Ruin everything?' He stops pushing Charmaine. 'Are you seriously going to sit here and let her ruin our family? All of us versus her? Is that how it is?'

'No, and—'

'I've been here three years and I've watched some crazy kids come in this house,' he fumes, 'but no one has ever, *ever* stolen money from me. No one!' He yells over Charmaine's shoulder. 'I tried to be nice to you, Kadie! You're just scum!'

'Cool it!' Charmaine lifts one hand, but instead of trying

249

to comfort him, she restrains herself from cuffing him around the ear. 'You're out of line! Go to your room and calm yourself down and then we'll talk.'

Vince growls and storms off.

All of Charmaine's attention falls on me then. 'Stealing? Is this true?'

My eyes find something shiny on the floor to fix on.

'Kadie, I asked you a question.'

'Maybe.'

'Don't play games with me. Have you been stealing money, yes or no?'

'Umm . . . maybe a bit.'

She looks daggers at me.

The pumping heat of the fight in my chest thickens into something like remorse. My fingers dance on the side of the chair and I know it looks obnoxious but I can't stop. I can practically feel myself falling back into the Notorious Kadie Hunte slot. But that's what I wanted, wasn't it? I didn't *have* to smoke. I could've raided Beverly's piggy bank and she wouldn't have known for about two months. I could've skipped the weed altogether. But I have made my move.

Charmaine uses a strained nice voice. 'Go and sit at the kitchen table and don't talk to anyone. I'll be down in a minute to deal with you.'

I pick up my phone and head for the door.

She holds her hand out. 'I'll take that.'

'But—'

She stares me down. 'You don't deserve it. You'll be lucky if you get it back by tomorrow.'

I smack the phone in her palm and turn to go but she grabs me so suddenly that I start violently at her touch and almost pull away.

Charmaine pulls back my hoodie sleeve to reveal a plaster covering one of the latest, a quick morning one that I did for luck even though I don't believe in luck. 'What is this?' she asks, rotating my wrist to the sky.

My breath catches. 'I—a paper cut.' Yes, #followtherules. 'I got a paper cut when I was doing my homework. It's nothing serious.' But I'm straining to stop my hand from trembling violently, because I know that if she chooses to pry further and pushes back the whole sleeve, and the bracelets, she will see the rest of the no man's land between my palm and my shoulder. And I can't have that.

I snatch my arm back, covering the ugly pink plaster, and glare. 'Don't look at me like that. It's just a stupid paper cut, and I'm not a baby.'

I stamp to the kitchen. Yes, nobody can act like me.

Beverly comes in, post-scolding, to find me sitting there cracking pistachios to eat with my third slice of toast. Eating usually makes me feel better, but today it's not helping at all – and it's got nothing to do with the guilt I'm feeling because Charmaine has been trying to get me to stick to a meal timetable which does not include huge snacks.

It doesn't matter how hard I try; my relationships always get shot to pieces somewhere along the line. There's almost no point. That's what keeps going round in my head. No point. No point. No point.

'Wow.' Beverly looks at the aftermath of my eating spree. 'You must be really hungry.'

'I'm not hungry.'

'Then why are you eating all the bread?'

'I don't know.'

Beverly leans on the counter and tries to look casual. 'Is it because you broke Shadavia's glasses?'

'No.' I crack a pistachio and the shell goes flying.

'She's really mad at you, by the way.'

'News flash.'

'So is Vince.'

'Well.'

'So is Mummy.'

'What do you want?' I demand.

Beverly blinks. I wait for her to say something childish and naive.

'Well?'

'Are you upset?' she asks in a tiny voice.

'Upset about what?'

'You eat when you're upset. Like Kung Fu Panda.' Beverly pokes the pile of orange skins by my plate. 'Last Saturday, you ate four slices of bread, and three big chicken wings. Daddy was a bit disappointed because he didn't get one.'

Last Saturday. Shortly after the Instagram incident. I'd blotted that out. 'I don't eat when I'm sad.'

Beverly sits down next to me and grabs a handful of pistachios. 'I don't believe you. I eat peanuts when I've had a bad day. Lots and lots of peanuts.'

'If I did that, there would be no peanuts left.'

She giggles.

'If I just ate and ate when I was sad, there'd never be any food in the house.'

Which is why I do other things when I'm sad.

Beverly giggles some more. 'Would you like a hug?'

'No.'

'I like hugs when I've done a bad thing. They make me feel less naughty.'

'A hug isn't going to solve anything,' I say flatly.

'Can I still give you one?'

'Why would you want to do that?'

She turns her big brown eyes up to mine. 'I like how you smell.'

'I smell like body spray and weed.'

'You smell like Kadie.'

I clench my fists and press them into my eyeballs.

'Don't cry,' Beverly says softly.

'I'm not!'

'Vince doesn't really hate you.' Beverly leans into me and gives me a gentle-but-not-too-gentle hug. 'Neither does Shadavia.'

'How do you know?'

'Because she doesn't. She was humming one of your songs the other day.'

'Then you don't know anything. If she liked me, she would stop hating on me on Instagram.'

Beverly is quiet for a moment. 'Why don't you tell Mummy?'

'She wouldn't understand. *You* don't understand.'

'But you told me,' she points out.

'You're special.'

'So are you.'

I catch my breath. Nobody has called me special for about six years.

I crack another pistachio. 'Doesn't it annoy you that your mum and dad bring random kids home all the time?'

'It's not all the time,' Beverly says matter-of-factly.

'It's not the same as having one set of bio siblings.'

'But Vince has been here for years, and you've been here like . . .' she counts. 'Five months?' She shrugs. 'This is my normal.'

Random kids, random families. Her normal. My normal.

'Don't you ever wish it could just stay the same?' I ask.

'Yeah! Sometimes I forget that my foster siblings aren't my real siblings.' Then she grins mischievously. 'And sometimes I secretly wish Shadavia could move away and take her sweary attitudes and weird music with her.'

'No way!'

'Yes way.'

'Don't say that.'

Beverly shrugs. 'Everyone is like family once you get to know them. I forget quickly.' She hops off her stool, grabbing a pistachio. 'I don't like it when people leave. Like Alyssa, and Tianna, and Francesco, and . . .' She trails off. 'You're not going to leave, are you?'

I fix my attention on the pile of dirt in the corner of the floor. 'Don't ever ask me that again.'

A look of shock hits her as she registers the cold in my tone. I feel a pang of guilt, but then the expression passes. She nods slowly and takes one last pistachio. 'Leave some for Vince.'

Then she prances off as if we just had a conversation about normal stuff. Which I suppose we did, in a way.

*

After dinner, Amando and Charmaine sit me down for a talk. I know it's going to be serious because Charmaine takes out this metallic pink fidget spinner, flower-shaped, and pushes it at me even though I'm already fumbling around with Homo Sapiens Rubber Butt in my lap.

'Thought you might like one,' she says, as if it wasn't once a major fad. 'Keep those restless fingers of yours busy.'

I sit Homo Sapiens Rubber Butt in my lap and pick up the spinner. The bearings run smooth, the frame seems to change colour. Whoop. It's the thought that counts, but I bet she doesn't know that the bearings probably don't have a seal and so would quickly stop working if I was spinning it constantly.

'So, I know everything's been a bit crazy recently,' Charmaine begins.

This is code speak for *you've been an absolute incessant pain in the backside these past few weeks.*

'. . . But, to put it simply, we were thinking it might be good for you to get away from here for a little.'

'Away from here?' I can't stop myself rubbing the spinner's smooth bits on my lips. The feeling is such bliss, I actually shudder.

'Yes. Not for long,' Amando puts in. 'Just a weekend or so. You wouldn't miss school.'

I frown, suspicious. 'Wait. What do you mean, away from here?'

'Away from this house,' Amando replies. 'Give yourself a break from us.'

'Away from this house,' I repeat, my scepticism increasing by the second.

'It would literally just be for the weekend,' Charmaine adds. 'Pop somewhere else, chill, pop back. How's that sound?'

Everything falls into place suddenly.

'A respite placement,' I say, teeth gritted. 'You're asking me if I want to go to a respite placement for the weekend.'

'I suppose one could call it that,' Amando agrees, after a second.

'Respite isn't supposed to be for foster families,' I say.

This is a joke. Tell me this is a joke.

I look at Charmaine. She smiles weakly and says nothing.

'We won't let you go far away,' Amando goes on. 'Just down the road. We know a couple who'd be happy to house you, and they're experienced with children who have challenges like yours, which is an added bonus.'

'A couple?' I feel like I'm choking. They've already chosen a family. They *know* them.

They've already chosen a family.

It doesn't matter what I say.

They've chosen a family.

They've already made their minds up.

I turn on Charmaine. 'You said no weekend placements!'

She looks distressed. 'Actually, I—'

'You promised!' I jump off my bar stool. There's only one coherent thought in my head and I scream it at her. 'You promised me you wouldn't send me away!'

'We're not sending you away,' she insists.

'You said! You pinky promised!' I shout.

'Pinky promised?' Amando asks.

'None of you foster people know how to keep a promise! All you know how to do is shoot somebody down.'

I use my whole body to yank the kitchen door shut. It slams so hard that the wall shakes and two picture frames slip onto the floor. On the other side, Amando bellows after me. 'KADIE. COME BACK HERE RIGHT NOW.'

I run to my room, screaming swear words as I go. My mum

would be ashamed of me. She'd smack me. She'd confiscate my favourite things and skip on that month's pocket money. But what does it matter? She's not here.

At least she didn't give me false hope. Propped up in her hospital bed, she told it how it was. 'It's gonna be hard, sweet pea. It's gonna be hard. You just have to keep your head up. Show fate your stubbornness.'

Except you can't be stubborn forever. How can you keep your head up when people keep punching you in the face? You eventually learn that there's no such thing as progress. There's no such thing as improvement. There's just me, sobbing into my bed sheets, hugging Emerson.

TWENTY-THREE

'You're proper wound up today, aren't you?' Dayan replays the last thirty-two bars that I've just recorded. My angry voice fills the studio.

I spin on my chair and carefully pick a few onion rings out of the bag he's left on the side. He has orange dust on his upper lip and I'm not telling him. He looks cute.

He stops the recording. 'Clean bars. Can I ask you something?'

'Fire away.'

'Why are you on about your "squad" getting your enemies? You don't have a squad.'

I roll my eyes. 'Your squad is my squad.'

'I'm starting to wonder if they actually are my squad.' He looks at me pointedly.

'Does it matter? It's just entertainment. Who cares if it's a bunch of lies?'

'Because what's the point in making music that's not true to you?'

I snort and roll my eyes. 'Because *your* talk about having bare girls and money is *so* true.'

'I do have bare girls,' he retorts. 'They're mostly YouTube subscribers. The ones in real life don't pay much attention to me. And for the record, I actually do make some money off the music and that. Where do you think I got my hoverboard?'

'KMT.'

'Excuse me? That's got nothing on your talk about boys.' He folds his arms. 'You practically go Naruto on people whenever someone randomly touches you. Tch, I don't even know what's going on between you and me, so you can low all that talk about close contact.'

I wave him away. 'Hush your mouth. No one wants to hear the truth anyways.'

'What makes you say that?'

I shoot him a cold look. 'Look at what's trending, bruv. You wanna blow, you can't make real talk music. When did you last hear Not3s going on about depression and mental health stuff?'

He sits and stares at the computer screen. He knows it's true. I know it's true, because I've tried dropping the gritty stuff, and no one cares. Okay, Stormzy fessed up to having problems with depression, but you don't see him hitting a couple million views with whole songs about his dark days.

'There's no point in putting out the truth,' I say softly. 'No one listens.'

'Sometimes somebody needs to know.'

'I don't trust anyone enough for that.'

Dayan raises his head. 'Not even me?'

I shrug and look at the onion rings. 'Not even you.'

'I thought we were going somewhere.'

'We are.'

'Are we? You don't trust me. Come on, it's been ages.' He doesn't bother hiding the hurt in his voice.

I swallow hard and delicately munch another onion ring. Normally I'd probably give him a cocky reply, but today I just spin and listen to the pulsing anger in my chest. Charmaine and Amando went along and finalised the whole weekend placement thing, despite the fact that I clearly didn't agree to it. They were going to set it up regardless.

I want to tell Dayan this. I *know* I should. I need to get it off my chest – I'm losing sleep over it and it's making me more and more vexed by the day. Today I just want to hit something and it's coming out in my bars. The tune I'm trying to record – by the name of 'No Yard' – is about always moving, never becoming a permanent part of things, and in all honesty it should be an angry song because that is how moving makes me feel. But sometimes you have to take into account what the masses like, so instead of it being angry, it's more like a joke. Lazy vibes, not finishing nothing sort of thing. Either way, it's clear that today no amount of rapping is going to drain all the emotion out of my heart.

'I'm not feeling this tune no more.' My voice is shaking. There are tears on the brink of falling and I can't do that here, I really can't. 'Can we do something else?'

'You don't want to go home?' he asks. We have been here

all day, after all. Michael and Junior and Reuben left a few hours ago because they had tons of homework to finish before tomorrow, leaving Dayan and I to do what we like. I consider the option of going home and lounging about with my feet up or being made to scrub potatoes by Charmaine. Studio wins.

I give Dayan a mischievous smile. 'I want to do something mad. You and me. I got pure anger I need to express.'

'Like what?'

I grind my teeth and think. Something mad.

I sit up straight and drop the bag of onion rings on the floor. 'Let's do a diss track.'

*

It's dusk by the time we leave the studio. We grab fish and chips for dinner and ride the bus in relative silence, until Dayan says, 'Tell me a secret.'

I arch one eyebrow. 'Is this a bonding exercise? Cos I'm not telling you nothing.'

'I'll tell you a secret, then.'

'Go ahead.'

'It's probably gonna sound stupid. Promise you won't make fun?'

'I'm not that kind of joker.' I offer my pinky. 'I solemnly pinky promise.'

He rolls his eyes, but we hook pinkies.

Dayan swallows a large chip in two bites. 'I collect snapback caps.'

I raise one eyebrow, surprised. I'd been expecting something slightly deeper or more heart-wrenching than that. 'That's not stupid at all.'

He slips off the cap he's wearing right now so that I can see the front (he's been wearing it backwards). 'Chicago Bulls. My brother got me this one from the States.'

'Surely you can get any hat online,' I say teasingly.

Dayan positions his cap again. 'Say what you like. This one's been in real-life Chicago air. It's one of twenty in my growing collection.' He crunches another chip and smiles nervously, as if he's afraid that such a tiny thing could be unimpressive.

Snapback caps. Who'd have thought it?

'Your turn,' Dayan prompts with that half-smile.

I sigh over-dramatically. 'Don't pressure me.'

'I'm curious.' He pouts cutely, the kind of pout he does for Snapchat when the mandem aren't looking.

I pick at the edge of the seat. Part of me doesn't want to. I don't do secret-telling. But Dayan's watching me and waiting with conviction and it doesn't feel fair. What's the worst that could happen? No one's had my back more than him in these past two months. Does anyone deserve to know a sliver of something more than him?

I take a deep breath and go for it. The thing that feels like the biggest something nobody knows, and probably is something he deserves to know if he's going to take me seriously. If he's going to know the real Kadie, and not the Kadie from the rumours. 'I've never had a real boyfriend.'

Dayan blinks in slow-mo. 'You what?'

'You heard me.'

He drags his last chip through some sauce. 'But . . . you flirt with, like, everyone.'

And there go the rumours. 'I don't.'

'You do.'

'I don't!'

'You obviously haven't seen yourself.' He flicks some imaginary hair over his shoulder and does a terrible imitation of a girly giggle. 'That's you whenever you get within a mile of something male.'

I flick his ear. 'I'm not flirting.'

'Then what are you?'

'Not flirting, bruv. Just being me, and I ain't no sket.' I eyeball him. 'Don't tell me you believe that.'

Dayan looks guilty. 'I did at first.'

Of course he did.

Everyone did.

Everyone does, no matter how hard I work.

'I don't anymore,' he adds, trying to sound decided, but I'm sure I pick up a tiny degree of uncertainty. Maybe it's my imagination – my perception of the way our friendship sort of fell together – but the way I see it, if he wanted to make me his girl, he would have tried it out a long time ago. He's keeping me at arm's length for some reason. Whether that bothers me or not is something I haven't quite figured out. I'm not that experienced with relationships. What I have picked up is from messing around with boys and it's left me pretty dubious of the whole palaver. And Mummy left me with some pretty blunt advice when I was about seven and she was sprawled on the sofa after some man who said he was my dad spent fifteen minutes banging on the door.

People are melodramatic, sweetie, and young people are stupid and melodramatic.

When you grow up, remember not to waste your energy with relationships until you're at least seventeen. Babies are no fun if you don't want them.

Still, I find myself getting a bit vexed. 'You better not believe it. You know how it is with me.'

'Do I?'

He's playing with me, wearing that cheeky smirk, but this time it just gets under my skin. 'You don't get it. I just . . .' I kick the seat in front and struggle to find the right words. 'I just wanna be that girl, innit.'

'What girl?'

'That girl that everyone loves. Talk of the town.'

'You are talk of the town.'

'In a good way. If people are gonna throw shade, I want them to do it because they're jealous, not because they think I'm weird.'

'You want people to be jealous?'

I flick him upside the head. 'No! I just wanna be successful. No bad vibes, just good energy.'

There's a moment of silence which is broken abruptly when the bus windows rattle loudly as a large tree scrapes against the glass. My fingers jump to plug my ears before I can stop myself. It's one of those days. I'm bussing in the most comfortable jersey shirt I have and some pricey Nike leggings and I'm still fidgety and on edge.

'You gonna tell me your second secret?' I ask, in an attempt to distract myself.

'Okay.' Dayan shifts in his seat. 'I . . . sometimes just wish I could be myself. You know, Dayan. Just Dayan. Not Lips.'

'Just Dayan?' I narrow my eyes. 'There's a difference?'

He half curls his lip. 'Yeah. There's a big difference.'

I mull over all those times we've been alone together. When the pout dropped, when his legs danced that bit more. He tones it down at school a lot. Mostly he just slumps around looking zoned out all the time, sometimes squeezing a lump of Blu Tack with one hand. The only time I've seen him – with AMD – without the permanent pout was the few days we'd gathered at his house. Where he was free to wear his chains and do crazy legs as he pleased.

I study him. 'I knew it.'

'You did?'

'I knew you acted different around me.'

He slumps in his seat. 'Everyone likes Lips, you know.'

I reckon I already know the answer, but I ask anyway. 'How come?'

'Dayan . . .' He pauses, as if registering the fact that he's referring to himself in the third person. 'Dayan's just weird, by general standards.'

That sounds familiar. 'Define general standards.'

'Do I need to?'

'Probably not.'

'Just think about it. The knee-jiggling and the humming and all those bad habits? There's more. It's just a subconscious thing that happens because I concentrate better that way, because it helps me feel right. But people get so tired of me tapping and humming and all that, and there's only so much I can play off as Lips being a joker, you know?' He glances at me to see if I'm following. 'You probably know what I'm on about, don't you? I've seen you nuff times in Science swinging your legs for ages.'

I'm speechless.

'That's why they call me Crazy Legs,' he continues. 'It's not attractive, so I have to hold it in all day – all this humming, jumping, running, touching . . . everything my body wants to do. It's like being two different people.'

I hold my breath and admit it. 'Yeah. I know what you mean.'

'It's hard, isn't it?'

I blow my hair off my face. 'Can't even describe it. Like corking a shook-up bottle of champagne.'

'Exactly. The perfect metaphor.'

'So what's the real difference between Lips and Dayan?'

'If I had my way,' he says, 'Dayan would be allowed to do crazy legs and be clumsy without being made fun of. Lips gets around all the things Dayan can't do by being super cool about it. Like, "Oh yeah, man's not doing footy cos man's got his good Nikes on."'

I giggle. A smile flickers across Dayan's face as he gazes out the window at a group of boys hovering outside the entrance to Maccy's.

'It would be nice if I didn't have to worry about these kinds of things,' he muses. 'If I could just play footy with two left feet and, you know, be tolerated. I don't like having two left feet, but it would be a hundred times less painful if people didn't laugh at me.'

We lapse into silence again while the bus winds its way through the dark streets, passing the school and continuing on towards the places we call home. Usually we would both get off at different stops, but we dismount a few stops before the point where Dayan gets off and wander through the houses, enjoying the relative silence. To the east, the giant Asda looms. That will be the point at which we go our separate ways, and I'm already slowing my pace inadvertently.

'You still thinking about that Insta-relationship offer?' Dayan asks, out of the blue.

'Nope.'

'Why not?'

'It's a no,' I say firmly. 'We're not in a relationship.' The words feel like some sort of betrayal and I have to remind myself that they're not. Being in a relationship is not a requirement for sixteen-year-olds, is it? You don't get extra life points or anything. But Dayan looks like he's on the brink of pouting, so I add my lingering thought. 'I've told nuff lies already. I don't wanna lie about you.'

'Right.'

Is it me, or does his voice sound a little deflated?

'That's the truth,' I tell him. 'A hundred per cent.'

After a beat, he asks, 'Why don't you want to lie about me?'

Because I don't want to hurt you.

And I know it's going to happen eventually.

It always does.

'Is that the only reason?' he presses.

I force out a tiny breath. 'No. I also don't want you to get hurt.'

Dayan watches a Range Rover cruise past, soul oozing out of the open window. 'You know what? I'm kinda hurt that you can't just say "I want to keep you in the friend zone".'

'Is that a crime?' I challenge.

'No, but you're always so . . . so flirty! It sounds bad, but there isn't another way of putting it. I know I'm not Michael or Junior or Josh, but if you're not girlfriend material, why are you always acting like you're head over heels in love?'

That strikes a nerve. Maybe I'm a biased thinker, but

when have I ever acted like that? 'So now I'm not allowed to love someone?'

'Not if we're not in a relationship!'

'We're not *in* one,' I say, 'but we *have* one. We have a friendship, right? A thrown-together pariah sort of thing, but it's a bond. It's just not romantic.' My words are speeding up with emotion, and it's a struggle to remind myself that this is Dayan. There's no point in getting angry. I shouldn't get angry at him. He doesn't deserve it. But the anger is still collecting in the pit of my stomach, ready to go off like a volcano, and I've got to sling it somewhere, haven't I? I can't take this baggage back to school. Can't throw it around at home. 'Am I not allowed to love that? Can I not appreciate how well it's been working – how you support me? Am I not allowed to love that just because I don't want to kiss you?'

He doesn't deserve this, but it's kind of still bothering me because part of my mind is like *why shouldn't I have a boyfriend?*

Because you know why.

And I do. Fate's set me up in this situation and that's the vexing part. There's always this heart-wrenching desperation to tell someone I love them versus the logic whisper-whispering at the forefront of my mind – *you haven't known him long enough. According to your record, this is doomed.*

The logic keeps on at me, digging its nails in. *You know what the dads are like. Why would this boy here, now, be any different?*

Dayan lets an awkward silence hover. 'I guess you save the kissing for eediots like Josh.'

'Yeah.' I laugh weakly despite myself. 'Because they don't understand what it is to be attached, and then to be cut off. They can play with hearts like it's poker because there's another stupid girl waiting in line after me. And unfortunately my heart isn't expendable. I learned that much from my mum.' The tears are gathering now, ready to fall. I tilt my head up at the stars blocked out by pollution and clouds, begging myself not to break cover in front of him.

I still dream about those days when things weren't working out. Mummy would shut the bedroom door between us, but I could still hear the edge in her voice, the rise and fall of her tone as she fought to keep things together over the phone. A lot of her men dumped her like that. Three, four dates and then they were just done. And then there were the ones who were about for longer, who knew my life too, sometimes staying in our flat like it was their own.

I still relive echoes of the time after Elton left us after two years. We came home from the child minder's one day to find the front door unlocked. Elton had gutted the flat of everything that was his while we were gone. Amongst more things than we'd expected were the cups and plates he'd bought at their one-year anniversary and the cute stuffed dog he bought me for my birthday five months before. We sat on our ragged sofa and cried, Mummy hugging me like it was the end of the world. We cried all our pain out onto each other so that when he bumped into us in the street two weeks later and returned his door key, all he got from either of us was a poker face. Which was just as well, because he didn't seem to notice that I was there.

After that, every time there was a new man I wondered why Mummy kept giving her all to every single man, as if her heart was going to regenerate every time.

I say it again. 'My heart isn't expendable.'

Dayan's voice is soft. 'Neither is mine.'

'Like I said before. You're precious.' I squeeze my eyes shut, willing the tears to stay put. 'I just don't want you to get hurt. You've heard all the rumours about my track record.'

'We could save a lot of pain if we had an Insta-relationship,' he says pointedly.

No we couldn't.

Someone would find out. No lie is fool proof.

Clearly he doesn't understand. He doesn't understand because although he's got it hard, he hasn't been pushed as far as me. He's so desperate to be accepted that he would lie about something that should be about more than just acceptance by a bunch of other kids. Maybe some time ago I would have done what he wants, but now I know how it ends. And I don't want that for either of us.

I shake my head, trying and failing to smile. 'You're worth more than that, bruv.' My smile wobbles and crumples and a tear escapes, followed by another and another. What am I crying for? Oh yeah. Everything.

I duck my head self-consciously as somebody walks by, but it's just a businessman engrossed in his phone. I wipe the tears away quickly, but I've started now and the flood gates won't close against the torrent of things plaguing me from the back of my mind.

Dayan takes my arm, stopping me dead, and gently reaches up to wipe the tears from my cheek with a tissue.

'Don't smear my makeup,' I say jokingly. My voice breaks, my shoulders jumping with each sob that works its way out.

'Why not? You look better without it,' he says bitterly. 'All girls look better without filters and makeup.'

A fresh wave of tears rolls down my face. Patient as ever, Dayan catches each one and dries my cheeks and even though I'm still bristling from our conversation, I let him. I let him because nobody asked him to, because he does it so delicately, his other hand hovering just beside my ear.

'You're too cute, you know,' I sniff.

'You can't say stuff like that.'

'But it's true. You're cute and gentlemanly and you're not afraid to be.'

'Um, thank you?' He folds the tissue and stuffs it in his jacket pocket, but doesn't move back. His other hand is still at my cheek, one thumb just touching my chin. Somehow, in the light of the streetlamps, he has even more of a baby face. Obviously I spend a second too long looking, because the next thing I know he's giving me a gentle kiss. Kisses.

Gentle, delicate kisses, even though neither of us is gentle or delicate.

Our noses somehow collide. His finger is brushing my jaw a little too much, making me squirm. I pull away, shutting my eyes so I don't have to see the look of betrayal I will get. His hand falls.

I whisper, 'I need you in the friend zone.'

Five seconds pass. A bus chugs by. I can still feel Dayan's breath on my face.

I open my eyes. He's watching me, his dark eyes openly sad.

'For now,' I add, as an afterthought. 'Friend zone for now.'

He steps back a little, nodding, and shrugs. 'It's okay.'

But the way he averts his eyes says it's not.

Of course it's not.

He needed me.

He needed me to back him like I needed him to back me, and I stamped on his cry for help.

'It's okay,' Dayan says again. His mouth quirks upwards for a second. 'You owed me one anyway.'

But it's not okay. That much is obvious as he turns and slowly continues walking. The slouch of his shoulders; the hood pulled far over his face; the way he won't look at me – it says a lot. And the lips. Oh, the lips. I haven't seen him pout that way since the party.

I've ruined it.

I've ruined everything.

Just when I think Dayan is never going to talk to me again, he says to the ground, 'Hey, you never told me your second secret.'

'Do I have to?'

He considers. 'I told you mine.'

I sigh. 'You have to promise not to snitch.'

He shrugs.

'No, like, really promise.'

'You don't trust me?'

'I . . .' I want to. Of course I want to. I'm breaking the rules left right and centre so why not just carry on?

'I promise.' Dayan turns and looks me in the eye firms. 'Floss my heart and hope to fly.' He makes flossing motions in front of his chest.

I smirk.

'I'm not going to regret this, am I?' he asks. 'You're not going to tell me that you want to die, or that you're planning to set the school on fire?'

'Nah. It's a bit more low key than that.' I close my eyes, hope with all my heart that I'm not going to regret what I'm about to do, and go for my hoodie pocket. For Emerson. We're still on the main road, approaching the point where the two of us have to go our separate ways, but nobody is really about so I take a deep breath and pull out the black blade. 'His name is Emerson.'

Dayan steps back abruptly, into the road. 'Is that a knife?'

'Yeah.'

'Why are you carrying a . . .?'

'I don't have to tell you. That wasn't part of the game.' I slide Emerson back in my pocket.

'I don't know what to say.' Dayan spreads his hands. 'Why?'

'It gives me courage. Plus, you buss that and nobody's bothering you.'

'Courage?' Dayan sounds disgusted.

He's not going to understand. Just like everyone else.

I carry on walking. 'Let's go home.' And forget we ever played this stupid game.

'I can't believe you!' he mutters, shaking his head.

'Believe it.'

'I thought you were better than that!'

'Better than what?' I turn so fast that he walks straight into me. 'Everyone already thinks I'm that crazy girl who attacked someone at her last school. It's not like I'm going any lower. And besides, I'm not out to hurt no one. I'm out to protect myself. Which I wouldn't need to do if people weren't constantly sending for me.'

'What kind of excuse is that?'

'It's not an excuse.'

'What is it then?'

'Let's just forget about it.'

'I can't just forget about it!' Dayan raises his voice. 'You . . . keep surprising me.'

I put one hand on his chest. 'Promise you won't tell.'

He looks down at the hand and steps away. 'I can't promise anything.'

'Promise. It's not to hurt anyone.'

'I can't promise.'

'Wasteman!' I stamp off across the next road. 'What happened to all that trust stuff?'

'Fine. I won't tell, so long as you leave it under your pillow.'

'That's not a promise.'

'I'm not promising, because if you turn around and do something with that . . .'

'Just be my friend,' I plead. 'It was a secret. You asked me to tell. You asked me to trust you and I did.'

He plays with his zips and toggles for a few moments. 'Fine. Your secret is safe with me.'

'Mm-hm?'

'That's as close to a promise as you're gonna get.'

I check his face. He nods curtly.

'One day,' I say, 'I might tell you another secret.'

'Yeah? How about now?'

'No. Time's not right.'

He snorts. 'Is it ever?'

'The time's not right for a lot of things,' I say, but I don't know if that's reassuring.

Dayan looks at his watch. 'It *is* about time I get home and go to bed, though.'

'Cool. See you tomorrow?'

He shrugs. 'If you're going to school, I'll be there.'

He holds out his fist. I bump.

Nobody fist bumps anymore. But then we don't care what anybody thinks.

I stand at the corner and watch Dayan walk off towards the path that cuts behind the Asda car park. He swings his arms absently at his sides as he goes; his low-riding belt glints as he passes through a sliver of white light, and I can't help smiling. I look at his empty fingers and wish I could hold them and tell him I'm sorry, that it's not his fault – that everyone says it's going to be okay so maybe, for once, it actually will.

Head says follow the rules. Heart says bun the rules.

I don't know which to follow anymore.

TWENTY-FOUR

On Friday afternoon, Beverly helps me pack. I use the blue sports bag that carried all my essentials the day I came to the Lucas' house. Beverly doesn't see the connection. Unaware of the reason for my bad mood, she quietly flits about folding up my clothes as I shove them in the bag, asking no questions about the extra pairs of underwear that I put in, or the waterproof bed mat that I found in the airing cupboard. Instead she colour coordinates my small collection of items, nestles my iPad on top, and tucks in the current *TV Times*, which is already dog-eared and graffitied. 'Just in case you want to watch TV,' she says, beaming.

Then Charmaine comes in and politely undoes all of Beverly's work as she scours for paraphernalia, while I slouch on my chair, eyes shut, and spin. If this is my feeble attempt to forget, it fails miserably, but it definitely gets Charmaine to stop asking me about school and music.

Just before we head, I sneak into Vince's room while no one's around and stick an envelope full of cash on his dresser. He'll no doubt count it, count it again, and assume that the extra tenner I put in there was just money I took that he didn't notice. I don't know what he'll do when he reads the note, if he can even decipher it. I wrote it by hand – not because I didn't care about its tidiness, but because I thought he deserved a heartfelt effort.

> *Vince, sorry about the money thing. Here's the missing p's. Hopefully maybe one day u can forgive me but I guess I don't blame u if u don't cos no one really does. Goldilocks*
> *p.s. I'm a try and quit smoking too* ☺

I thought I'd feel better once I got that off my shoulders. The feeling only lasts about twenty seconds – until we're heading and it really hits me that no one seems to care.

Vince shouts, 'Bye Goldilocks!' from in front of the TV. Shadavia yells, 'Enjoy your weekend!' – but only because I tell her I'm off as I pass her room. Beverly gives me a big hug on the landing and runs off to do her homework.

That's it. Nobody comes to the door. Nobody even asks where I'm going or when I'll be back. Probably none of them even know.

Amando makes the effort to see us out, and I'm pretty sure he looks smug. I just look daggers at him and tuck my shoelaces under the tongue. I'm not having the shoelace battle in front of him.

The atmosphere in the car is pure tension, mostly on my part. I sit in my seat like a rod and stare straight ahead and

Charmaine isn't bubbly like she usually is. She says, 'Got everything?' but she sounds like her voice is about to wither away.

As we head east out of the borough, I count red buses to distract myself from my cramping stomach. It's not even that late but traffic's already piling up. A double decker cruises by, followed closely by two others. I learned how to count by red buses, because the block where I grew up overlooked a main road. Terrible view, but not so bad for learning numbers.

Charmaine is a patient driver, never in much of a hurry. She switches on the radio – thumping it a few times to get it into sync – but I don't miss the fact that we've gone at least a mile or two and are still going. So much for 'close by'. I suppose a lie is the first step to the roots of Rule #3.

They all have their different ways. Some like to really butter you up, give you presents for "being good" or whatever. Others don't tell you until a day or two before it's going to happen, knowing you'll kick off. Often they're the ones that don't care how you feel – they'll tell you whenever it suits them. Of course, some of them are decent and try to break it to you nicely, as if it's nobody's fault, but what difference does that make? Leaving is leaving. Every new start is harder than the one before.

Leaving always reminds me of that year when the hospital practically became my home. It took too long for me to realise that this was it for the foreseeable future: in and out of the hospital, drop-ins at home, randomly staying the night at Mummy's friend's place, late nights at the child minder's, my very first foster home with Jacinta. Afternoons sitting by Mummy's bedside and reading to her, writing raps and learning songs to perform to her. Every day waving goodbye and knowing that walking out that door was a sign that I was going to lose something soon.

This could be a warning. A *get back to the rules*. *Put your guard up*. I'm already wondering what an evening by myself will be like – an evening without Vince farting on Shadavia, and Beverly asking me to brush her hair, and Charmaine checking on me at bedtime. I've gotten used to the way she comes into the room, her footsteps muffled by her slippers, to ask if I'm okay. It really vexed me when I first arrived because she'd stick her head around the door regardless of whether or not I told her to go away – even if it was just for a moment. I thought it was just a show, but then it continued after a month, two months. She pushed the boundaries until one day we were sitting a few feet away from each other. That was when I realised I was going to have a hard time not breaking the rules at this placement.

I watch two buses trundle in the opposite direction, both advertising vapes and local sixth forms, and swallow back a surge of nausea.

We drive until we're well out of the borough. My stomach turns over and over and my knees, which I can usually keep fairly still if I concentrate, have gone into jiggle overdrive.

We wind through street after street of parallel-parked cars and brown-brick houses. I squeeze the bridge of my nose. I am not going to sleep tonight.

Charmaine pulls up on the pavement suddenly. 'Here we are.'

I stare through the window, hardly taking it all in. Quaint little house. One car on the drive. Looks like someone tries to keep the garden aesthetically pleasing, but after the winter the flowers have shrivelled into nothing. There are just a few daffodils poking their heads up, unaware that sunshine doesn't mean spring.

'They're really lovely,' Charmaine says. 'They're very experienced with all sorts of children. I've talked to them and explained about your situation.'

Sure she has.

'You'll be okay, won't you?' It's almost as if she's pleading with me, saying it just to convince herself.

I look at the floor.

Gina answers the door before we even ring the doorbell. Her face lights up. 'Hello hello! Come on in!' She stands aside, already giving off no-nonsense vibes. 'Aha! The famous Kadie!'

I blow a bubble with my gum.

'Say hello,' Charmaine prompts.

'Hi,' I tell the floor.

Charmaine smiles tightly. 'She's in a bit of a difficult mood.'

I pull my hood further over my face and resist the urge to roll my eyes.

We kick off our shoes in the porch and Gina leads us through the house. It's a spick and span place, with that kind of spaciousness that houses seem to get when all the kids grow up and move away. The smell of air freshener tickles my nose.

Gina gives me a full tour, chattering the whole time. She recently let go of three girls that she'd long-term fostered and now she and her husband mostly do short-term.

'My' room looks out over the front drive. It's smaller than my room at the Lucas' house, but kind of cosier in a neat way. A bookshelf sits in the corner by the bed, stacked with films and books and magazines. I try not to notice the picture tucked on the wall outside the door: three sisters, climbing/ hanging off each other, their laughter practically bursting out of the frame. Not what I want to see right now.

I stare at the floor.

Gina spreads her arms majestically, either ignoring or totally missing my sad vibes. 'Do make yourself at home.' She winks. 'Charmaine and I will be downstairs if you need us, okay?'

I try to make myself at home, I really do. I put my iPad and phone on the desk and my bag by the wardrobe, wire up my speakers and get some music on. Once I've got some good old J Hus filling the room, I pull on my indoor shoes and sprinkle a few more of my things around the room half-heartedly.

I collapse onto the bed and rebound with more bounce than a basketball as that poisonous Snap flashes into my head.

Baby girl couldn't even take a nap without peeing herself.

I squeeze my head with both hands. I can run as much as I like. Something will always, always follow me.

Charmaine stays for half an hour, talking downstairs with Gina. I switch J Hus for some angry grime music – Kano and Ghetts are the best for that – and slouch at the desk, craving weed, alcohol, Red Bull, coffee, sugar.

I am not going to cry. Tears don't do anything except make your eyes sting and your head hurt.

'Kadie, I'm going now.'

When I don't respond, Charmaine knocks gently on the open door. I press my face further into my forearms and wish everything would just disappear.

'Just go.' My voice is weak.

Her hand materialises on my back. Firm, the way she knows I like. 'Look, I—'

I shake her off, jerking out of the chair so hard that it nearly topples into her. 'Just go already! You're a snake and you obviously don't get it, so just leave me alone! Go chill with your *real* family.' My voice rises until I'm nearly screaming.

'I—'

'Go away!'

Charmaine goes.

I slam the bedroom door after her. Then, just to make a point, I turn up my music as loud as I dare. I hope she can hear Kano's voice loud and clear.

A minute later, Charmaine steps out from under the porch, her head ducked. Within two minutes, she's gone. I watch her drive away, clutching Emerson in my pocket with one hand. Even after she's disappeared, I stay there with my head resting on the glass, trying to kid myself that I didn't want a hug.

*

Ten minutes after Charmaine's gone, I test the waters. Hoodie and jacket on, bum bag up under my arm, I stop at the hall mirror to check that my curls are still contained by the scrunchie and then I call, 'I'm going out,' and proceed to get my Converse on.

Gina emerges from the kitchen, her eyebrows furrowed. 'I'd prefer if you didn't,' she says.

I stuff my laces down inside the shoes and try the door handle, which seems to be slightly stained with black finger prints. Of course, it's locked.

'A lot of kids have been through this house,' Gina says, her voice so level that I'm irritated just listening. 'I don't make it an easy task to get out. And like I said, I'd prefer if you stayed here.'

'So I'm locked in?' I ask.

'No. I just don't want you to go wandering off right now.

However,' she adds, turning to the back of the house, 'you're welcome to explore the back garden.'

What's the use of going outside if I can't walk around aimlessly? If I wanted to go out the back, I'd go out the back. Anyway, for some reason I still find myself slamming Gina's back door behind me before stepping forward into a small yard, decorated with leaves of all colours, a decrepit swing set in the far corner, and a trampoline growing something green up one side. I always wanted a trampoline when I was a kid. I never got a back garden until after Mummy died, and by then I wasn't really interested anymore.

My phone rings quietly. The screen lights up with Shadavia's profile picture in which she's wearing a hat that says NERD. Do I want to talk to her? Doesn't matter. My thumb's swiping before I've thought about it.

'Oh . . . hey. Sorry.' Shadavia sounds bewildered. 'Stupid phone doing its own thing again.'

I manage not to tut. 'Oh. Okay.' Of course. She wouldn't be calling because she actually *cared*, would she?

Then she demands, 'Where are you anyway?'

I raise my eyebrows in disgust. 'No one told you?'

'Mum just said you were going away for the weekend.'

I splutter. 'Wow! Oh, yeah, I'm living it up in a five-star hotel for good behaviour!' I pause, hoping for a reaction, and carry on in disgust when I don't get one. 'Nah, bruv, your parents couldn't stand me being around and shunted me off to a respite placement for two days so you lot can get a rest.'

Silence on Shadavia's end.

And more silence.

'You're not serious,' she says, after a good fifteen seconds.

'One hundred per cent. I'll Snap you as soon as we get off this call.'

'Yeah, do.' Shadavia sounds grave, as if she's just been informed that she failed all her exams. 'Beverly wants to know where you are.' She hangs up. I take a video and send it to her straight away. She doesn't reply. I shove my phone in my pocket and stand there staring at the garden, wishing I had a genuine desire to jump on the trampoline.

The door opens behind me and Gina orders me back inside in that no-nonsense way that she seems to have. I step in and kick my shoes off stiffly. The whole exchange with Shadavia has confused me a little bit. Did she really want to know where I am? And if Charmaine and Amando seriously didn't tell any of them, why did they do that? Maybe they thought they wouldn't care.

I screw up my face and exhale through my teeth. Nah. Beverly knew. She sniffed out the whole state of play with one look into my room. That girl's got a sixth sense, I'm sure of it.

Gina asks me if I want to help her make dinner – macaroni and cheese – and I don't really. In fact, I'd rather be upstairs doing revision than down here in this neat kitchen, looking at the assortment of fridge magnets and cringing inwardly at the memory of the clatter of Mummy's fridge magnets as Saul threw the bin bag into the box of her things. He put that box up in the loft. I never saw it again. One of his daughters said that he burned it, but then they told me lots of lies in the short time that I was there.

I tell Gina no way on this earth and go upstairs to do some revision. Yeah, *revision*. Insert canned laughter.

Ten minutes later I'm back downstairs sitting at the kitchen table, staring vacantly at those fridge magnets while my hand grates Red Leicester cheese without any thought required. There are probably a thousand reasons why I sat upstairs struggling to concentrate on my English Lit. But the one sticking in my mind is hanging on the wall in the hallway, filled with innocent faces. I can't get it off my mind, and suddenly I'm asking, 'What's with that big picture frame in the hall?'

Gina stops chopping pepper. 'You mean the collage of faces?'

'Whatever you want to call it.'

'My husband and I have done a lot of fostering for a long time. Anybody who has stayed with us for more than a few hours gets to go in there, if they wish.' She glances at me. 'That would include yourself.'

I snicker. 'Are you mad?' Why would I want to be in that? People are clueless. People like Charmaine and Amando who didn't even tell their own kids, my foster siblings – however short-term – where I was going. They meant well – didn't they? – but meaning well isn't enough sometimes.

'Why would you want to remember all of them?' I demand. 'Surely they weren't all nice. I can vouch for that.'

'Hmm.' Gina scrapes the pepper into a bowl. 'I agree with you there. But there's always a reason for the not-nice children. I can vouch for that.'

'Do you seriously think they'll remember you?'

'No,' Gina admits, 'but it's important that they know that they're not going to just be forgotten. A lot of children I've looked after have already been neglected by the people who are supposed to look after them, so if I can show them love just for a month, or a week, or even a day, and show them that I'm not going to forget them, then I think that has an effect, however tiny.'

I tut and go back to grating cheese. This actually sounds like some nonsense. Never thought I'd hear it come out of someone's mouth in real life. Who sits down and thinks about how much love they're giving out?

'You think I'm funny, don't you?' Gina asks.

'You're too enthusiastic, bruv,' is all I can manage without cringing.

'I've got to be,' she replies. 'Some kids haven't had a lot of sunshine in their lives.'

That's true. True enough that I suck my teeth hard to express the build-up of what I don't know how to say. Some places the sun just doesn't shine, right? And by the looks of the weather outside, my life is one of those places. I always knew I wasn't the only one – years in the system gives you the chance to meet other kids more and less fortunate than yourself – and I'm not the one with the worst story, but that doesn't exactly make it any less painful, does it?

'Do you want to be in the collage?' Gina asks, peering over her shoulder.

'Pfft! Nah, man.' I sneer. 'I don't even want to recall a second of being here. I didn't want to come here. I made that clear as crystal, yeah, and Charmaine went back on the promise she made.' I scowl from under my hood. 'Did she tell you that?'

'In a rather round-about way.' Gina pauses. 'This *is* only temporary, though.'

I respond by sucking my teeth.

'Trust me. I was a foster child once,' she adds. 'I know what I'm talking about.'

'So you know that more time people don't expect much from a brat who's been around the world in eighty days,' I say bitterly. I'm kicking myself inwardly with all this backchat, thinking of my mum again and her thing about respecting your elders. But she's gone. And I'm vexed.

Gina's watching me, the look in her eyes akin to the one Andi gets when she's really listening. 'May I ask you something?'

I shrug.

'Do you expect anything of the people whom you say expect nothing from you?'

I watch my fingers do a Mexican wave on the table. She's thinking too deep. Why would she even ask that?

'I'm just giving you food for thought.' She tilts her head at me. 'Because if you don't open your heart to others, how are they going to fill it with love?'

It takes a lot of restraint not to suck my teeth again. 'If I don't open my heart, then no one can fill it with gravel. And you should stop trying to stick up for Charmaine. She did me dirty.' I can't get that out of my head. She *did*. She *promised*. She made that promise on a day when I was at the end of my tether. I might play class clown at every opportunity, but I'm not stupid. I don't mention things like that for a joke.

'I'm not taking sides,' Gina says, interrupting my whirlwind of thoughts. 'Charmaine is human. Humans make mistakes. *I* make mistakes. I've been fostering for twelve years and I still make mistakes.' She beckons me with one finger and I reluctantly follow her out into the hall, to the collage. She points at a massive gash in the plaster. 'That was one repercussion of a mistake I made,' she explains, her voice grave. She leaves that thought with me and returns to the kitchen.

Charmaine is human. Humans make mistakes.

She's got a point.

She's actually kind of right and I don't want her to be.

I sit down on the floor and lean against the wall, closing my eyes. Why do I feel so alone when everybody thinks they're doing their best to help me out? The mandem, keeping hush about the Instagram page. Charmaine and Amando, removing me for the weekend. So many people I can't even count them all on my fingers and toes. And yet I'm always on my own.

My phone pops softly in my pocket – Michael and Dayan have been Snapping me non-stop since I told them about my situation – but I don't move to check it. They're too far away for any message to make a difference right now.

A new lyric starts to unfold in my head.

I'm always on my own.

Bredrin right here but they on my phone.

I put on some Afro swing style instrumental, open Snapchat and attempt to lose myself in a freestyle. It's a good freestyle, but I don't quite lose myself. I toss the phone along the floor and stare at it.

The kitchen door is open and I can hear the oven purring away, Gina clattering around as she tidies up. The smell of chocolate cookies baking is beginning to spread from the kitchen to the other rooms. Against my will, my mouth waters, as if the cookies are calling me.

Gina comes out into the hall, drying her hands on a tea towel and stops when she sees me. 'Oh. I wondered where you were.'

'Yep.' I get up, inclining my head slightly to look at her. The collage of faces is right at my head height, hovering in my peripheral like a notification, the question forming strongly in the back of my mind. *Do I want to be a part of that collage?*

I realise I'm staring at the collage again and so is Gina, as if she's sensed the cyclone of doubt going round in my head and is waiting for an answer to inch its way out.

'I wish . . .' I begin, but I don't know where it's going so the words trail off. 'I wish . . . I don't know.' And then, for some reason, I look at Gina and our eyes meet for a few seconds – just a few seconds, but it's enough. I know that she knows.

'When's dinner?' I ask, after a moment.

'Forty-five minutes,' she answers. 'Would you mind setting the table for me?'

I shrug. 'Sure, whatever.'

And once I've done my good deed, I go up to my room to pump my music as loudly as I dare, so that if I sit on the floor and close my eyes, I can pretend I'm at the place I call home.

TWENTY-FIVE

The weekend is surreal. Snapchat's constantly going off so that eventually I just put my phone on silent, my interest in communicating dead. The night is mostly sleepless, the bed too different to be comfortable even with the towel that I brought just in case. Except when I wake up tangled in that wet prickly thing, there is nothing I can do because I'm not at home. It's my worst nightmare.

On the plus side, Gina offers to make me breakfast in the morning and I scoff a pile of waffles like it's nothing, trying to forget the stomach cramps and the tossing and turning of the night. Like a good girl, I dig out the revision stuff I brought at Charmaine's forceful suggestion, but nothing happens. My mind is too distracted, legs and fingers on hyperactive overdrive. Just being here is making me lose the will to live. I can't even smoke because I had to leave everything behind, lest I run the risk of having Charmaine find something on me. In the end, I wander out into the garden at intervals and sit on the swing set in the cold spring sunshine, listening to music and waiting for Gina to call me inside to do something productive.

I'm on the swing, gently swaying back and forth, when Charmaine comes for me on Sunday afternoon. Apart from hoovering up all the food Gina's put in front of me and occasionally helping her out with things, I have done nothing but sleep and watch TV all weekend – if you discount doodling all over my revision homework sheets, that is. And I don't regret it one bit. In fact, maybe I'm even a little bit sad to leave – to go back to the world that never lets me go.

I feel like I've *almost* pulled myself together. Almost. Not in a way that means things are going to change, though – in a way that means I've learned my lesson. Break the rules, *you* break. Simple as that. We need to get back to them.

'You look happier,' Charmaine notes.

Wrong.

'Did you have a good chill out? Recharge?'

I shrug.

'I know you're angry with me,' she says quietly.

I shrug and go to get out of the car.

'I'm sorry. It wasn't a totally mutual decision.' She runs a hand through her hair and looks everywhere but me. 'I'm not making excuses; I had my part to play. I had what I thought were good reasons. I was just . . . so stressed out. And confused.'

I open the car door and get out. Slowly, Charmaine lets herself face me and I can see it in her eyes, the stuff she's trying to articulate. But I don't know what to say. She shattered the bridge we built.

I'm expecting to step inside the house and find life continuing as if I never existed. Just the thought of it is making my stomach cramp the way it tends to when I get overly flustered.

The front door opens unexpectedly and Amando pokes his head out. 'Well, look who it is!'

I hide behind my screw-face.

He steps out onto the front step, gives Charmaine a kiss and turns to me. 'Shall I take your bag?'

I cut my eye at him. Amando takes this as a yes and slides my sports bag off my shoulder, glancing between me and Charmaine as we move into the house.

I'm wedging my trainers on the shelf when Amando asks, 'So how are you?'

I curl my lip and shrug. Tired? Angry?

Amando doesn't press any further. He takes my bag upstairs for me and holds it out to me at the doorway to my room. 'Alright?'

I snatch the bag from him.

'I know this weekend's been really hard for you,' he says, as I drag myself into my room. The urge to be cocky rears in my throat but I'm too tired to act. I toss the sports bag on the bed and give him a dry look.

Amando tries not to wilt. He rubs his face. 'I've been

talking with Charmaine about everything, but it's just taking me a little while to understand how it all works.'

It what? He makes it sound like I'm some sort of rare intricate machine. 'So?'

'So . . .' Amando wets his lips and attempts to look me in the eye. He leans on the wall. 'It . . . I need a bit more time to get how the puzzles go together, but maybe when I really understand, we can start moving forward.'

'Moving forward? Tch.' I fold my arms. 'Yeah, then three steps back?'

'That's not the plan.'

'Things don't always go to plan.'

Amando swallows. He tries to adjust his posture to look casual and only comes across more nervous. 'Kadie . . . I was really hoping that . . . we could try and make things work.'

I genuinely don't know what to make of this. What comes out is a curt, 'Hope away.'

'I want to be a good dad to you, you know. I want to, but I just need to work out how. You have slightly different needs to the others—'

'Uh huh?'

Amando breathes out slowly. 'Things are going to change.'

'Oh yeah? You think?' I've just come back from exile, and he's coming talking to me about change?

'In time, yes.' He imitates the cocky tilt of my head. 'I want them to. If you want them to, I'm sure we can make it happen sooner than you think.'

He closes the bedroom door softly after him.

I roll my eyes.

Amando thinks things are going to change.

He wants to be a good dad. For real. Well, I guess that's a start. Unfortunately, a 'start' is the basis of Rule #1.

I collapse in my desk chair. People are tearing up my rules left right and centre. It's like Gina said – like Charmaine said. I'm supposed to let down my shields for them. If I'm not straight about things, no one will ever get it. And I'd like to think I'm strong enough to do it – to just live, no rules, taking each day as it comes. That's how everybody else lives, isn't it? They look to the future. They believe in it.

I sigh and reach for my speakers, ready to blast my emotions away.

The bedroom door swings open and Beverly skips in. 'Kadie!'

She throws herself on my lap so hard that I nearly fall off the chair. 'It was so dead without you! It was too quiet.'

'It was too quiet?'

'Yeah. Nobody was pumping loud bass or anything. Vince was playing lots of trap, or whatever he calls it, but I like Clean Bandit better. And there was nobody talking nonstop at dinner. Nobody else can talk nonstop like you.' She hops back and gives me a salute. 'I'm glad you're back home.'

Once she's gone, I turn up my music as loud as I dare, just to remind the others that I'm back, and set about unpacking my bag. My room hasn't been touched since I left on Friday evening, but I neaten things up anyway, put things back where they belong.

I'm rooting through my school bag, sorting stuff out for Monday, when I find it. A little pile of red, buried under the corner of a text book.

I empty the bag out. The pile of red tumbles out amongst dust and paper and pens. Snipped pieces of rubber band?

I rifle through the rubbish. A body. A rubber band body.

Homo Sapiens Rubber Butt, who was linked onto my zip, has had his looped arms and legs snipped so they dangle in two limp pieces and his head has been severed. Someone has taken the effort to disembody my little token of friendship and shove it between two text books.

I put Homo Sapiens Rubber Butt's dead body on the dresser and take a picture for Snapchat.

Then I delete the picture. No more beef. Let no one know I found anything. Let no one know I hurt.

I stuff Homo Sapiens Rubber Butt's corpse in one of my jewellery boxes and head downstairs to get something to eat. Everything is okay. My hands are not shaking.

On the stairs, Vince double takes. 'Huh. You're back.'

I stop. 'Yeah. Problem?'

He exhales dramatically. 'What did I do now?'

'Don't look at me like that, man.'

'What did I do?' he demands. 'Look, don't be accusing me of throwing screw-faces. You're practically trying to melt my face off.'

I grit my teeth.

'Are you mad at me because you got moved?' His voice softens a little, but I'm already hot in the face. I ignore him and skip into the kitchen, singing to distract myself, and go straight for the juice in the fridge.

Shadavia watches me from where she's perched at the kitchen table, surrounded by perfectly colour-coordinated revision posters.

'Good weekend?' she asks.

I snort. 'Ha. Maybe.'

'Mediocre? The garden looked pretty.'

'Like you care.'

She clicks her pen. 'I'm just trying to be nice.'

She does 'nice' now? Okay. I rummage in the fridge for something to eat. 'I got as far as attempting to get some revision done. Did some good doodling. Does that count as good?'

She snickers. 'I thought you didn't *do* revision.'

'This was a one-off.'

There's silence for a hot minute. I find some couscous, add a piece of homemade naan bread and a couple of fat salt-fish fritters, and prepare to head back upstairs.

'That picture wasn't meant to go viral, you know.'

I stop. 'What?'

301

Shadavia swallows. 'That picture. It wasn't meant to blow up like that.'

I already know what's coming next, but I ask anyway. 'What picture?'

The look of discomfort on her face almost makes me feel good. 'The one of you . . . on your bed.'

'Yeah? I thought you said you had nothing to do with that.'

'I was just talking about it to Raquel.'

'Talking about what?'

'About . . . living with you.'

I kiss my teeth and turn to leave. She's taking the mick. Next thing I know she'll be calling me names again, or making dumb jokes, or posting some next madness on Snapchat.

'I wasn't saying bad stuff.' Shadavia clicks her pen nervously. 'I was just stressing and I just told her the facts—'

'You were stressing about *living* with me?'

Shadavia scowls. 'I have feelings too, you know.'

For a moment I'm silent. Generally speaking, Kadie Hunte doesn't *do* other people's feelings. But Shadavia is sitting there looking at me as if she's just said something really important.

It's hardly my fault that Charmaine is constantly chasing me around for bad behaviour. I mean, I don't *try* to take up people's time; it kind of just happens. But that should hardly affect Shadavia, should it?

Should it?

A speck of doubt starts to grow in the corner of my mind. I push it aside and get back to the indignation. 'But seriously?

We don't even share a room. What have I ever done to make your life hard?'

She ignores that. 'The point is, I was chatting to Raquel about the state of things, but she didn't believe me.'

'So you sent her proof.'

'It wasn't even a good picture. I thought she'd just let it disappear.' Shadavia stares at her revision sheets. 'But I guess she didn't.'

'You guess?' My voice is shrill. 'You *guess?*'

'It wasn't meant to go viral! I never meant it to get so big. I never meant it to get big at all.' She rubs her face. 'Raquel's proper into all of the stuff Kelly says, you know. She honestly thinks everything weird about you is just an attention-seeking thing and I told her it's not, that there's actual stuff going on. I wasn't trying to get at you or anything. I just . . . had a moment.' She actually sounds halfway apologetic and slightly guilty. 'I told her not to share it. I *told* her bare times. I said, "This is private. This is between you and me." I told her so many times; I said you had enough on your plate without everyone getting hold of that too – that it was just so she could see I wasn't making things up. But then . . .'

But then.

I stand stock still, clutching my pile of food. This is the last thing I expected from the girl who's stepped back and watched me go through hell from her squad. Part of me doesn't want to believe it, but looking closer, I can't deny that she's wearing a genuinely apologetic expression. I smirk slightly and Shadavia drops her gaze back to her text books. Yep, that looks like legitimate guilt.

There's just one problem: she still hangs out with *them*. And if she's still hanging out with them, she's still going to go along with them, because that's how cliques work. So how am I supposed to know whose side she's really on?

I set my bowl down on the table and give Shadavia a cold look. 'You know that stuff was personal, right?'

Shadavia runs her fingers through her hair and looks decidedly uncomfortable. I continue, 'And you know you didn't even get the facts correct either? Did you mention that to Raquel?'

Shadavia shades in the corner of one of her revision sheets and shrugs, refusing to look at me. I let the silence hang, listening to the analogue clock in the hall tick five long seconds. I don't really need to do this. Shadavia's not like Kelly, but she's not like Eisha either. She's a difficult middle-ground sort of person – which, if anything, is almost worse. I tell myself I have to keep testing her loyalties – don't I? – or I'm never going to know where she stands in regard to me.

I dredge up some smugness. 'Ain't got no lip for me?'

Shadavia sucks her teeth, but she pretends to go back to her revision, starting a new mind map on a fresh piece of paper. No lip for me. She won't give me any hint of her being any sorrier than five minutes ago, as if to do so would be far too embarrassing. Maybe that's something that needs nursing out of her – the confidence to just say 'bun you' and go for it even if the squad doesn't. But as for her apology . . . That feels like it could be real.

Couldn't it?

I take in a deep breath. Can't believe I'm actually saying this. 'Apology accepted.'

Shadavia lifts her head slowly. 'Seriously?'

'Seriously.' I scoop up my bowl to go. 'You're not off the hook, though.'

'What hook?'

I sigh and stop at the door. How to say this without starting something? 'You'll know when you know it.'

And of course Shadavia pulls a face and goes, 'What's that supposed to mean?'

But I'm already gone, leaving her confused. She's still clueless, and there's nothing I can do to change that. I can only prepare myself for if that never changes.

TWENTY-SIX

Since I got back from Gina's, things have been very different. The kind of different where I'm struggling to find my feet and holding onto Emerson for confidence. It's hard in a busy house, especially with Charmaine practically keeping one eye trained on me. Every time I wash the blade, I feel guilty. Then I get vexed that I'm feeling guilty. I'm not shedding anyone else's blood, am I? Only mine. Only mine seems to have the power to diffuse things.

Despite this, I'm still losing my hold on my act. Charmaine has been systematically cutting into my secrets. First it was the food chart so that we could have a visual of my junk food intake. Then she got a hold of the smoking. I'd already been down to the dregs of my supply, but she forced me to turn my room inside out and she confiscated all the paraphernalia she could find. My anxiety seems willing to take a break, but the emotions? I can only pin them down for so long. And every time I feel the back of my neck get warm, I wonder if it's going to turn into something else.

Lunch break rolls around and I rock up late from a ten-minute detention, ready to start on the Rubicon. Detentions are still to be the bane of my life.

The boys are sprawled on a bench under a sheltered area by the field, watching a bunch of Year Nine girls and boys milling around and predicting which of the girls are going to be the most what in a few years' time. Someone's Bluetooth speaker is playing some popular tunes, but the summery Afro beat vibes are no match for the February winds. Technically this is breaking the rules, but as Year Elevens with a sixth former in the midst, we can get away with things like this if we perch in a clever place where no teachers will see.

I shiver and plonk myself down in the only empty spot – on the end, beside Dayan. 'Man, it's freezing. Why you lot out here?'

Junior looks up at the sun, which is shining brightly despite the breeze. 'It's not that cold.'

'The breeze, though.'

He adjusts his hat. 'It might just be you.'

The wind whips down the side of the building again, chilling my back. I rub my ears violently and curse myself for getting my hoodie confiscated.

Michael shudders and zips up his coat. 'Uh huh. Just you,' he says sarcastically.

'Get a coat, sister. It pays,' says Dayan. He catches my eye as he says it, grinning mischievously.

The boys go on rating the fourteen-year-olds, deciding

who will wear the least makeup, the shortest skirt, and carry the most books. When they've been through all the girls they turn to me for my opinion on who will be the most peng. I snigger and give them loud-mouth, truthful answers because I'm a bit hyper and lesson's just fried my brain. Michael screws up his face at some of my choices, but beauty is in the eyes of the beholder, right?

The music comes to an end, dropping us into silence. Reuben glances our way. 'There's still ten minutes left of break, DJ.'

Dayan sighs the way he does when he's been in his own world. He looks tired, like he's been holding back all day. He's definitely been quieter since I went to Gina's.

He slips out his phone and hands it to me. 'Here, you're the queen of music. Sort it out.'

I swipe Dayan's pass code in, well aware that Michael's watching me like a hawk, trying to suss out our relationship status. As if it's not enough for me to know his pass code, the screen background is a snap of the two of us, chains and tongues out. It's pictures like that that have got people thinking we're together, when really and truly even we don't know what's going on between us. Neither of us has dared bring up that evening when it all went down, but that never stopped us Snapping like mad every day.

I open Spotify, but I can't ignore the number of notifications on his Snapchat. Thirty-eight. He posts daily just like me, so there's no way he hasn't seen them.

I glance around. The boys are chatting. Dayan's in his own world again.

I open his Snapchat. Twenty of the notifications are from people he follows and all that. The other eighteen? DMs.

I open one.

Everyone knows you slits your wrists the long sleeves don't fool anyone

It disappears.

Stop trying to move like real donnys you ain't one of AMD

Gone. But they just keep coming.

Your girl is a sket

Nothing from AMD them man obviously not your friends

No bredrin

Even your girl doesn't want you she all up on Michael

You ain't not3s go home to your mum

And they go on.

And on.

Okay, so they're not all recent – I can see that some of them have been sitting around for weeks now.

'Are you putting on a playlist or taking selfies?' Michael demands.

I straighten my face, running one hand through my half-curly bun to distract myself. 'Calm yourself, bruv. Hardy Caprio coming up.' I choose a playlist and put the phone down. My hands are shaking so I squeeze them under my armpits.

His Snapchat messages have unearthed exactly what I

used to spend precious time smoking to forget about. The whole bedwetting thing has died down somewhat since last week, but the other stuff keeps rolling in. The worst part is, I can ignore the messages and the stupid pictures, but I can't ignore the way people treat me – the snide comments, the allusions, whispers, exclusions. And it leaves this shame and humiliation sitting on my chest every day, a weight that no amount of weed can lift. It gives me this kind of lethargy that makes it hard to concentrate. The kind of heaviness that's been making me take Emerson in my fist more often than usual, spreading the tally of pain from my arms down to my legs.

And I'm not even the only one getting trolled.

I swallow and rock absently. Dayan bops to Hardy Caprio singing about a girl who wants a baller, a trapper. 'You alright?' He peers at me.

I crack my knuckles and dare to look him in the eye. 'You need to tell someone.'

He blinks. 'Tell someone?'

'About Snapchat.'

His confusion clears. He sniggers. 'What are you chatting on? You're still high. Hush.' He presses a fingertip on my lips.

'Are you for real?' I mean to sound disgusted, but it comes out as a whisper.

'Yes. I'm for real.' He leans and bops. 'Real talk.'

'I don't see you doing no real talk.'

'I don't need to.' He touches my chin. 'You're already

listening.' And I want to protest – why is he being like this? – but then he smiles that smile, like he did that time we met in the corridor and I melt a little bit inside.

Head says follow the rules, always.

Heart says I've already broken them all, in every which way possible.

Michael groans. 'Just wifey her already, man!' Then he shoves Dayan into me, nearly knocking me off the bench. Dayan starts scrapping with him and the rest of us turf them off the bench and egg them on, laughing and jeering while Hardy Caprio sings. And then the bell rings and the chaos goes on and for a little while, I forget that I thought things would never change.

TWENTY-SEVEN

A fortnight later, we release 'Crazy' – the 'diss track' which, after a couple of freestyles, became more of a song than a rap. It gets one hundred thousand views in two days, even with a music video thrown together by Dayan, Reuben and I in less than a week. *And many people hate me, same way, couple hunna thousand rate me.* I keep singing that line, because I know it's true.

It was Reuben's idea to slip in short video clips from Insta and Snapchat. It made for a disjointed, two-tone sort of video, but at least it was original – there's nothing that irks me more than a video that just has guys and girls bopping around expensive cars in expensive clothes with no originality. So although it's a vibezy song, it's got a sort of mismatched music video. I thought it wasn't going to cut it, but by the end of another fortnight the video is pushing four hundred thousand views on YouTube alone. And by then, people who know us are starting to realise who the indirect insults are for.

They're subtle; somehow what I thought was going to be a pure diss track ended up being a summer vibes sort of tune, with way more singing than rapping and a beat that makes you want to bop, not punch someone. *Haters making jokes at the back of the class, starting plenty beef cah my bros are in charge* . . . It's got a lot more views because of that, and the indirects are now out there for the world to stream at its leisure. Of course, by now it's too late to regret my logic, but whatevs.

Lips and I, we did that tune for the sake of telling everyone what we think, what they shouldn't think, and how it is. I'm expecting reactions. There always will be, especially when you've been chosen to be troll central. But there's only one person I'm really looking to see a reaction from. My guard's up – I'm ready and waiting for it all to kick off, because for me, that's what the song was about. Putting the state of play out there. Taking a risk. I don't care anymore. Rule #3.

To my disappointment, Shadavia's not been acting any different towards me, even since her 'apology'. Charmaine might have stopped nagging us about our lack of sisterly bonding, but I'm still pretending like we're not mortal enemies at school. Until Shadavia stops worshipping Kelly, nothing is going to change between us – so excuse me for instantly being sceptical when she slides into the chair opposite me at breakfast and actually looks me in the eye.

I lick a piece of strawberry off my spoon. 'What?'

She glances left and right. We're alone. 'Lips is gonna get beaten up, you know.'

I stir the remains of my fruit salad. I don't even know what to expect from this girl anymore. Is she on my side? Their side? Telling the truth, sticking up for me, or weaving more beef? Chances are she's on about Josh and that. More than likely, they're vexed about something on Snapchat. But it could be 'Crazy'. There may have been one or two indirects tailored just for them. *Proto swag, man I'm not like you* . . . In your face, Josh. Ellis. Kelly.

It's taken Shadavia a while to get used to the fact that I often mishear or partially lose people's words stuff in the midst of other things, but today she seems kind of offended at my lack of response.

'Did you hear me?' She leans forward. 'Lips is gonna get boxed up.'

There's a touch of heat in my face. I grit my teeth. 'Can't your lot just stay off our backs for one week?'

'I'm just saying—'

'I know, I heard. Can't you do something about it?'

'Um . . . well. You know how they are.'

'They?' I push my bowl away, my appetite swallowed by the fire spreading down the back of my neck. 'Bruv, you're one of them! You're as bad as the rest. It doesn't matter how many times you apologise: if you're a bystander, you are just as bad as the rest of them.'

Now Shadavia's on the edge of her seat too. 'Bad as the rest, yeah? Then why is your man all up in my DMs?'

I'm getting up, about to run before the heat spreads, but that stops me cold. 'What?'

Shadavia holds back a smirk. 'I said, if I'm as bad as the rest, why is your man in my DMs?'

'He's not in your DMs.' He would tell me if he was DMing Shadavia, surely. We might not be on the whole girlfriend-boyfriend ting, but we're still friends.

Shadavia's got her phone out now. She clicks, scrolls, and turns the phone to face me. Dayan's face smiles out from his profile picture at the top and underneath – yes. Messages. Emoji.

Shadavia scrolls down and down so I can't read what the DMs say, then puts the phone face-down on the table when she's sure I've seen enough. She's full on smirking now, tipping oats into her bowl like she's just won a round of poker. Like she's not just dropped a proper low blow.

I grip the chair hard. My knee dances as the back of my neck prickles. 'You just don't know when to stop with the mind games, do you?'

Shadavia moistens her lips. 'There're no mind games going on. I'm just telling you how it is. Just like you did. I quote, *I'm just telling you now so you know, air me I'll run up on the bridge of your nose.*'

That line is from one of my Instagram freestyles. I'm surprised she remembers it at all.

Shadavia floats about, throwing herself together a lunch she won't eat in front of her friends. Nuts (probably for during History), pineapple sticks and a few pepper slices from the pile of assorted veg. Mostly stuff from what Charmaine left on the table, before she hurried out to drop Beverly at school on the way to some help course for foster mums. She didn't say a whole lot about it – only that she'd be back by two-thirty (fingers crossed, since she had to go *all* the way to the next borough).

Our phones ping simultaneously. Suddenly Shadavia's right back at the table, her lunch forgotten. Technically we're not supposed to have phones at the breakfast table – one of the many ground rules that Amando and Charmaine always emphasise – but nobody is about to tell us off, so I spear a lump of mango and check my Snapchat as well. It's Dayan. Phew – something worth reading.

The caption stretches across the middle of the photo.

You need to tell or I will

I nearly drop my phone.

There I am, standing with my back to the camera at Dayan's kitchen counter, reaching up to one of the high shelves. I'd taken my hoodie off – it was just me and him and Michael there, and they were in the studio so I didn't have to worry about my arms being seen. Or so I thought. Someone saw, and someone took a snap, and thanks to the angle and the lighting, the scars zigzagging down my inner arm and past my elbow are nicely illuminated. You can't miss them.

The picture stays for a full eight seconds. I spend that eight seconds choking on my mango.

Opposite me, Shadavia gapes at her phone and then screenshots deftly with a double-tap of her knuckle.

I slam my phone down on the table and sit back.

He knows.

If Dayan knows, how many more people know? How many more people are about to let me down?

Shadavia is staring at me with a look somewhere between disbelief and something else. This expression is not unfamiliar on her, but when I glare and she just keeps studying me with this look on her face, something dark settles in my stomach. I don't know how, or even why, but I know. She has just seen the exact same picture.

My scars ache faintly again, as if asserting themselves, reminding me. *Yes, we're still here. We'll never leave you.*

'Delete that picture.' My voice is so steady and firm that I'm shocked.

Shadavia stares at me. 'What picture?'

'The one you just screen-shotted.' I lift my head so I'm proper scowling at her. 'Delete it now.'

'You don't even know what it is.'

'I do!' I shoot to my feet. 'I know exactly what it is! Get rid of it!'

Vince strides in then, still in his pyjamas, singing a line from *Crazy's* chorus. *'Proto swag, man I'm not like you, don't get it twisted that's just the truth . . .'* He farts loudly. 'Rah, that is rank. What's good?' He stops, seeing Shadavia and I stood glowering at each other. 'Are you two beefing again?'

Shadavia rolls her eyes. 'She wrote a diss track. What do you expect?'

My hands are trembling.

It wasn't a diss track. I just wanted you to see how I feel.

I wanted everyone to see how I feel. The last two lines of the chorus echo in my mind.

I'm tryna be wavey, don't try to faze me,

I got emotions don't call me crazy.

'It wasn't really a diss track.' Vince shrugs. 'I picked up on a few minor shots being sent, but mostly I just heard a wavy tune. Gonna be playing that this summer, you hear me?' He pats my shoulder. I throw his hand off.

'Hey! What's the matter?' Vince tries to peer at me, as if he really needs to see my twisted-up face to put two and two together. I turn away and grip the counter, my teeth clamped together and my shaky breath comes out like a hot pan meeting cold water.

'Let's just give her a moment.' Vince backs towards the kitchen door, beckoning Shadavia. 'We're giving you a minute, okay? Just try and chill.' He pulls the door closed behind me.

Try and chill. Yeah, because it's as easy as that.

I suck in a breath, but it shudders its way into my chest and the next one trembles harder. What would Charmaine say if she were here? Or Dayan – no, Junior? Not Dayan. Dayan has formally declared that he's going to bait out my problems if I don't say something. He thinks he understands. Man doesn't have a clue. You can't just *say* something. You can't just tell everyone about all the stuff spinning around in your head every day. That would be breaking the rules. And yeah, I've broken them time and again, but now is the ultimate time *not* to abolish them. Now, when it's all coming apart at the seams, I need to hold fast to them.

I snatch up my phone and call Dayan. No answer. No surprise there. I call Charmaine. No answer. She probably has her phone on silent, or buried in her bag.

I slam my phone down and slide it across the counter. It flies off the other side and clatters onto the tiled floor. What use is a precious iPhone when the people you need to talk to won't pick up?

Everything in my head is racing: the picture; Dayan. The picture; Shadavia; the mandem. Someone has switched on me and I want to believe it wasn't Dayan.

But what if it was?

What if this is just the cycle completing itself?

The rules are the rules.

Don't count on anyone. Blew that one.

Always act. Kinda blew that too.

Be prepared to lose everything.

The rules have been all but shredded and burned. And now Dayan's switched, Shadavia's still playing pawn, and still nobody knows *anything*.

My breakfast bowl is the first thing that goes aerial. *Smack!* Chunks of fruit tumbling through the air in a wonky pink and white rainbow. Then the snacks on the table – well, they're not on the table anymore. And then, one thing after another, the Lucas' kitchen slowly comes to bits at my hand with crashing and swearing and tears that blur everything so much that I can't see half the damage. The cruel sing-song of cutlery flying across the counter mingles with the hard clatter of old Carte D'Or containers bouncing, Beverly's Winnie the Pooh cup plate spinning along the counter, the upturned cups in the drainer taking flight. A mug turns itself over in my palm before I watch it hit the wall and unfurl like a firework, spraying bits of blue into the air.

How can Dayan ask me to tell? I told him about Emerson. The scars are something else entirely. The scars are my very last rule, so sacred that it's not even official.

Shouting from upstairs finally makes it to my ears as I burst out of the kitchen, dipping down to grab my phone from the floor. One look at my forty seconds of handiwork in the kitchen was just enough to remind me what happens when I don't have time with Emerson.

On my way down the hall I snatch up my bag and collide with Amando as he thunders down the stairs.

'Kadie! What's going on?'

I wrestle my feet into my Nike Airs. No time for laces. *Act. Always act.* 'Nothing!'

More shouting from the kitchen. Shadavia has discovered the mess.

I fumble to get the key in the door and curse, curse, curse, my voice trembling with tears, my hand practically having a seizure.

'Kadie, you need to stop.' Amando's got one hand on the door handle. 'Running away isn't going to make everything better. Take your time, sit down and—'

The key goes in. 'Let me go!' I put my hand over his and wrench the handle down.

'This isn't going to work.'

'Bun you!' A Dr Marten boot comes off the shoe shelf and thumps him in the chest. Shocked, Amando reels back and I take the chance to throw the door open. He tries to come after me and is greeted by a welly: one of Beverly's. Then a pair of misplaced keys, the shoehorn off the wall, a bunch of words Mummy would have whipped my hide for and a multitude of things I can't even recall through the searing rage. Amando is calling, calling my name. I don't hear him over the sound of everything.

TWENTY-EIGHT

I'm so vexed right now I don't even want to talk to anyone, but I need to know. I knock for him even though I'm like fifteen minutes early. Dayan's mum answers the door and patiently tells me that he's already left.

Why on earth would he leave early without telling me?

I want some answers so badly that I'm getting impatient. When he doesn't answer the fourth call, I leave him a rude message. The sound of my own voice seems to echo in my head like a warning bell. I replay what I just said in my head. *Wow, wash your mouth out with soap, Kadie.* The fear bubbles up. I try to trample it and let out a breath I didn't realise I was holding. There's a build-up, build-up, build-up inside me, like a shaken-up champagne bottle. Eventually, the bubbles will power out of the bottle. And right now, the pressure is seriously ramping up.

I call Junior as soon as I'm on the school site, desperate for a distraction from my simmering frustration.

'Yo, Kadie, what you saying?'

I don't bother with a greeting. 'You seen Dayan?'

'Doesn't he walk to school with you?'

'I'm at school already. My guy wouldn't answer his phone.'

'What a grumpy guts.'

'So you don't know where he is?'

'Haven't seen him since yesterday.'

There's a pause. Then Junior says, 'I . . . should tell you something.'

'Yeah?'

'You're not going to like it.'

'Try me.'

He's faltering in a way that both irritates and worries me. 'It's personal. For you.'

'Just get on with it.'

'I sent Dayan something on Snap. A picture of you.'

I catch my breath desperately and stop to close my eyes. 'Wait . . . was it a picture of me in the kitchen at his place?'

'Yeah. It was.'

I exhale loudly. 'Why?' My voice gets big quick. 'Why would you do that? It's none of your business!'

'We . . . were worried.' Junior has never, ever been this lost for words. 'I know you've got everyone fooled, but I've been chatting with Dayan and we were pretty worried after we saw . . . that.'

'So you sent it to my public enemy number one?' A mother walking two children in the King's Manor Lower School uniform glances my way at the volume of my voice. 'Why? WHY?'

'Wait, who?' Junior sounds confused. 'No, I only sent it to Dayan.'

'Well, *somebody* sent it to Shadavia. I'm sure.'

'Maybe he thought she could help.'

'Help? Are you mad – help from *that* girl?' My voice hits a new level of shrill. 'Why are you being such a wasteman? Leave me alone!'

Junior protests. I hang up. Learning Support, here I come.

There isn't a quiet corner in there today; a bunch of other kids are using the beanbag room and the computer suite. I slam the door on my way out and ring Dayan again. And again. He better have a decent excuse for all this.

My school uniform is itching up a storm down the backs of my arms – odd since the sleeve interior is silk. Maybe it's just my anger and my imagination crossing paths. I take my earphones out and turn my locker inside out just in case there might be some hidden weed. At least if I could bun a zoot I'd get caught by a teacher and have someone to yell at. It would make a great distraction. But I find nothing. Nothing but hot palms, hot neck, hot cheeks.

'Oi, Kadie!'

I bang my locker shut and turn around. It's Aidan. Oh, joy. 'What?'

'Found this on the way to school.' I stiffen as he reaches out, but there's no cheek today. He just drops a phone in my hand. An iPhone with one of those fancy shock-absorbent cases.

I take it and press the button. Mine and AMD's faces grin from behind the code pad.

'Where'd you get this?' I demand.

Aidan ruffles his black hair. 'We found it on the way to school. On the floor.'

'When? What time?'

He shrugs. 'I don't know. Like, ten, fifteen minutes ago?'

'And you haven't seen Dayan?'

Aidan hesitates. 'Nope.'

The bell rings.

Aidan hovers for a moment, until I fix him with a steely glare.

I wake up the screen on Dayan's phone, my head reeling. All of my calls are missed. No notifications on Snapchat.

Michael pops out of the bustling crowd with the others, making sure I can see him before he nudges me. 'What's the matter, gold girl?' He stops dead. 'That's Dayan's phone.'

'Yeah.'

'We still haven't seen him,' says Reuben.

'Did you call him?' I study them all, sceptical. 'Any of you? Did anyone check up on him?'

They all shake their heads. Junior's not looking me in the eye.

'So you're playing Save Kadie but you don't care about your own bro? Tch. Look, Aidan just gave me this.' I hold the phone up. 'Don't you think that's a bit weird?'

'They like to play games,' Reuben reminds me. As if I might have just forgotten.

Junior nods. 'They've done that before. Jacked his phone and come to us saying they found it.'

Reuben puffs his chest out a bit and folds his arms. 'I know them man wouldn't do anything deep to Lips. They know how it is. They touch him, they deal with us.'

Is that how it is? Or is that how they want to think it is?

I study their faces. Michael's studying his freshly-polished shoes, Reuben chewing his lip and watching Junior watch me. It's too hard to read what any of them are thinking, but right now their silence speaks volumes. My hands are low key trembling. I punch the nearest locker and stuff my fists in my hoodie pockets. This is pure madness.

'Hey.' Junior catches my arm. 'We'll go find them. We'll get something out of them even if they haven't done anything.'

Michael is nodding in agreement. Reuben looks somewhat doubtful. 'You gonna be okay?' he asks me.

'Like you care.'

'We do!'

'Right. So you took it to Snapchat.' Now I'm glaring at Junior. 'That's your way of caring? You're stupid! Tch. Just leave me alone, man.' I turn towards the scenic route to English.

'English is that way.' Michael tries to spin me by my shoulders. I twist and shove him off.

326

'Whoa! Okay.' He backs off, throwing his hands up in surrender. 'It's a Moody Morning.'

I seethe inside, wishing I could put it all into words, but there are no words for what makes me form fists. Things are falling apart just when I thought they were coming together, and I don't know what to do.

I march off, too tense for goodbye banter, barely registering Junior calling after me that he'll let my teacher know. Beethoven plays from my air pods but I'm not feeling it, not one bit. I clench the prickling heat inside my fists.

The English block isn't far from my locker but I circle around the school deliberately slowly until the corridors are almost empty, one hand curling tightly around Emerson in one pocket, rubbing the smooth metal with my thumb. I close my eyes, regretting that I left home so quickly. Regretting the whirlwind that started all of this off. The anger keeps simmering, refusing to settle down. The memory of the plates flying and ceramics smashing passes fleetingly, enough to make me wince. Surely I'll be out now. Amando will never have me back in with the kitchen totalled.

Footsteps. I open my eyes – but not fast enough to stop myself smacking straight into Raquel as I round the corner.

She elbows me back a step. 'Oi, watch it!'

Kelly points over my shoulder. 'The special needs area is that way, hon. Turn around.'

I try to squeeze in the gap between her and the wall, but Kelly backs up so that there's no way past the four of them.

I grind my teeth. 'You gyal are gonna be late, and none of you have a green card.'

Kelly rolls her eyes. 'Look,' she sneers, 'I don't know what makes you think you're so smart. You're just a little attention-seeker, yeah, and no one cares about you or your stupid diss track.'

'It's not a diss track. It's a wavy tune,' I say tightly. 'And it's got like half a million views, so I think you need to go check the definition of "no one".'

Raquel snorts. 'I heard that loads of people watched it because the visuals are so bad.'

The visuals are not bad. On the contrary, they're pretty sick considering that Reuben and Dayan and I filmed them in one afternoon, no professional help. Reuben is an excellent producer for a guy taking A-Level Media. It'd be easy to just get jealous of his camera skills.

'Innit! Hun, people only watch your stuff because you're slyly peng on Insta.' Kelly flips her hair. 'But, man, your hair is *butters* in real life. What do you straighten it with? A rake?'

I make fists in my pockets and try to squeeze the anger away. 'Let me pass.'

'Make me.'

And I want to tell her that I will make her, but I don't want to make her. I want her to stop insulting me and allowing all this nonsense.

'Let me pass.'

'What's the magic word?' Raquel says. She's low key enjoying this too, I can see it.

'I ain't begging.'

'Okay. Then turn around and get out of our way.' Kelly shoves me back a step. 'The department for the mentally challenged is that way.'

'You're going the right way, then.'

She spits. I feel the lump of saliva splat on my neck. The heat floods me.

'So you *can* shut up!' Raquel exclaims.

Kelly watches me rake my blazer sleeve across the spot. I don't even have a cocky response for her. Somehow I'm shocked – maybe because this moment is taking me back to that night at the party when I spat on her floor. *What goes around comes around.*

Maybe I deserved that.

Their laughter echoes behind me as I run back the way I came, round a corner and another corner. Laughter and heckling. Practically my leitmotif.

I yank out my air pods, stuffing them in a pocket. The calming music is no use. The chaos is rising all around me. I'm filled with the sounds of everything: Beethoven, laughter, heckling, distant voices, muffled teacher-student banter from an open classroom door. I can't take this anymore. If emotions had a three-strikes-and-you're-out policy, I'd be out about fifty times.

I kick the wall and swear loudly. My fists won't go any

tighter. I'm losing the fight and I despise how it feels. Skin prickling, neck burning, desperation, fists curling, then the spread of it down into my face, fingers and feet. I watch myself unfold my greatest weapon in my fist. I watch Emerson tease a line in the paintwork and feel the pressure pushing against me from inside. On an impulse, I use one finger to part off the front of my hair and comb the flat-ironed hair in front of my face.

Kelly is the closest when I round the first corner, so she nearly gets a face-full of Emerson.

'Back up!' I yell.

Kelly backs up so fast that she steps all over Shadavia's toes. Eisha swears. Raquel's got her phone out. Has she had it out all this time? Doesn't matter.

Does it?

Eisha's still swearing and that bothers me, far in the back of my mind. There's real, raw fear in her eyes. Don't care. I've got Emerson in my fist like a sceptre. I'm commander of this standoff. Nobody moves, all of them transfixed by the weapon in my hand. Maybe that's what finally gives me the power to speak.

'Let's make this easy, yeah?' I step closer, brandishing Emerson in a tight grip and gesturing with every word. 'Drop your phones, get out of my way, and leave me alone before I decide to shave your eyebrows off.'

Kelly's smugness has melted into something else. She licks her lips with sudden nervousness. 'You wouldn't.'

I level Emerson at her nose and bark at Raquel. 'Drop the stupid phone!'

Raquel hesitates.

'Drop it!'

Raquel places the phone on the floor without taking her eyes off Emerson. She's transfixed.

'You're just a big act, man.' Kelly sounds a bit weak. 'Allow it. Everyone knows you cut yourself too. Why don't you go make a song about it?'

So now not just the boys know: everyone does.

Everyone knows all my secrets.

It was a long time coming, but it had to reach the climax some time, didn't it?

'Kadie, put the knife down,' Shadavia pleads.

I spit on the floor. 'Why do you care? You're practically next in line to get touched. You hate me.'

'I don't hate you.'

'You said you were sick of living with me!' My voice is small, tight with the effort of holding everything in. I step forward, making them all edge back, and place my heel deliberately on Raquel's phone. 'You gonna make up your mind?'

But there's still a part of me that wants her to give me a decent reason to put Emerson away. After all this, I am still breaking the rules. They've parted slightly, made a path, but that's not enough anymore. I want them gone. Out of sight, out of mind.

331

Inside of me, everything claws and twists. *I just wanted to get past.*

Charging forward, I swing Emerson wildly, catching somebody somewhere as I barge past desperately. By the time the scream hits my ear drums the four of them have flattened themselves against the wall to let me through.

Kelly touches her face and freaks as her fingers come away red. 'You *psycho*!'

She hurls her PE kit at me.

I turn and lunge, slicing the air with Emerson. Kelly is saved by Eisha, who yanks her just out of range.

I can't even see straight anymore, let alone make out the words coming out of my mouth. All I know is that my shout has never been louder. All I know is that my effort to keep things under control – everything I did to protect the people around me – is being undone.

The shouting brings other students running – mostly stragglers, the ones waiting lined up outside classrooms. I stumble down the corridor, half-blinded by tears and the fluorescent light dancing off the floor tiles and display boards. Emerson is right here, right in my fist, and I know if I stop he will gravitate to my arm. Or, worse, to someone else. But then what does it matter? I've already done it. The hubbub following me is proof of that. My thoughts are spinning, my whole mind out of control but for a tiny corner that retains the look on Eisha's face at the sight of Emerson.

She doesn't know – she wouldn't get that Emerson was never meant for this.

But no one would get it.

Even I don't.

I don't understand how the fail-safe failed.

I don't understand what's wrong with me. Why things just explode. A meltdown, Mummy called it. *Anger* certainly doesn't cover it. The swearing at the sky and tearing things off the walls and the way colours blur, and not just with tears, and how all the sounds blend like my brain has forgotten how to filter: a mishmash of names and calls and voices and voices, while the rage bounces back and forth like a tennis ball between Emerson and I. Fist, knife, fist, knife, and an empty classroom comes to bits. Emerson and Kadie: the two of us versus the world, all the evidence written upon my arms like a script, good days and bad days alike in an indecipherable story of my life. It's confusing, but I think it all comes from different places. I see red when I smash things. I don't see red when I'm drawing patterns on my arm with Emerson.

The pressure in my head thins slightly, but there's no chance to simmer down because the teachers come flocking down the corridor, pushing past the students, arriving like knights in shining armour from both sides, radios in hand and calm, calm voices that drive me insane as they usher the audience away and surround me—

Is this what you want?

There's an easy way to do this.

Give us a little cooperation and no one gets hurt.

They catch me with iron fists from behind, clamp my wrists, so hard that my fingers give out. Emerson skitters across the floor. I feel the emptiness of my palm instantly and the shock of it brings a wave of panic that drags me screaming with it. That's good. It's belting out all the sleepless nights and the frustrating, headache-filled days into the air so everyone can hear how I feel. But the harder I scream, the harder they hold me down, until I find myself writhing and cussing too, cussing so creatively that I churn with guilt and then grief. I'm out of breath. Panting, shouting, then clawing for some control and flailing when I can't find it. But I can't tell them *this is what Emerson was for*, because Emerson is in a plastic bag by the nearest door, and my words just keep twisting up like my fists.

The iron grips clamp my shoulders, trying to pin me inside my blazer like a straitjacket. The silky interior of my blazer rubs, yanking the latest plasters loose. Old wounds open and I cry out, hard.

It could get worse. They say it once but the words circle in my head over and over, like an insult chanted by an idle crowd. *Calm down, or it will get worse.*

Really? What could possibly be worse than this moment?

The Lucas' kitchen is totalled.

Everyone knows about my scars.

Dayan's switched on me.

Shadavia's on some rocky middle-ground ting.

The rest of AMD don't have a clue.

334

Emerson's gone and so I must be going for sure.

If I'm going, surely I should go out with a bang? I can make a bang if I want.

Thing is, I don't want to go.

I can't go.

I can't go.

It's sudden. The anger, pressure, the heat in my fists and feet, the hands on my wrists, the barking voices over my head – it clogs my head. The confusion, too much of everything trying to fit itself into my head – there's not enough space in my head or my heart and in a split second, my emotions descend into something else. I have no words. They have no words.

I can hear everything. The sound of stern, upset, concerned voices. The sound of broken rules.

TWENTY-NINE

It was only a matter of time. A social worker turned up to collect me from the police station when they decided to release me on bail. She told me her name, explained that neither Charmaine nor Amando could come, that she'd be taking me to an emergency placement for the time being. *For the time being*. I'd already switched off.

It was like always. They wore their plastic smiles and were excessively kind. Maybe they didn't know. Maybe they couldn't see it written all over my face. Maybe they just saw another foster kid.

I sit in the bedroom against the bed that isn't mine, trying not to breathe in the unfamiliar air freshener and wondering how long I will be here for. Hours? Days? Weeks?

I should be happy. No one who cared about me got hurt. I did what they told me; I let them into my world. Now they have an inkling of what my world is like.

Because I have nothing else to do, I call the mandem one after the other, over and over, until somebody picks up.

'I thought the feds took you away,' Michael says.

'Yeah.'

'Is it true?'

'Is what true?'

'That you backed out a massive knife.'

'Tch. The blade was five inches,' I tell him sharply. 'Tell them to get the facts straight.'

There's a long silence. I could ask him what everyone's saying. But I already know.

Then Michael says, 'They found Dayan.'

I narrow my eyes. 'Who's "they"? And where was he?'

'I don't know who found him.' Michael sounds like he's shrinking away. 'That's all I heard. And apparently he did get beaten up.'

'By Josh and that?'

'Yeah. Bad as well.' He hesitates. 'And then . . . and then he took some pills.'

'Some pills. Rah.' The freshest of my scars throb dully as that sinks in. They're only a day old, but they were aggravated while I was being restrained. The bandages and plasters I had allocated to hold myself together turned out to be useless when I was shoved chin-down on the floor with my arms wrenched back. And the word *pills* . . . I know what that means. I've been there before.

'Is he—'

'He's in hospital. That's all we've heard.'

'Heard?' I bite back a torrent of questions. Of course. They're all still at school. 'Who's the inside source?'

'Shadavia.'

I suck my teeth. 'Nah. No way. Allow it.'

'Yeah.'

'Sorry, bruv, I don't believe that.'

'Believe it.'

'No! D'you know what she told me this morning?' It's tumbling out of me now and I don't even care. 'She comes up to me in the kitchen and tells me that Lips is gonna get boxed up.'

'Raaah,' Michael says in disbelief. 'She said that to you this morning?'

'Yeah. So excuse me if I don't believe you.'

'I promise, bruv, it was! Here. Ask Junior.' There is some muffled chatter as he passes over the phone.

'It was Shadavia,' Junior says. 'Look, she's shaken up too, yanno. Her friends are out here telling bare tales about who started the fight in the corridor and she's still just keeping her head straight, telling the truth. Cut her some slack.'

'Slack? She hates me!' My voice rises. 'She baits out just about everything about me, yeah, so—'

'Listen, if this is about the picture—'

'Kelly *said* to my face that everyone knows I . . . you know.' My voice gets thick. 'The only person who got that Snap who would've told Kelly is Shadavia.'

'How do you know Shadavia got that Snap?' Junior asks softly. 'Did you see it?'

'No. I just know. She screen-shotted it and then looked at me like I needed to be in an asylum.'

Junior is gentle. 'I think – and don't bite my head off – I think Kelly just figured that out by herself. Or maybe she was just spinning tales and didn't realise it was actually true. I don't think Shadavia told her.'

'How do you know?'

'I just do. Trust me.'

'I don't trust anyone.'

'Maybe you should.'

That's when I hang up and throw the phone over my shoulder onto the bed. Who's going to be the next traitor?

The day drags. Downstairs, whatever-her-name-is has the TV on while she cooks something I don't want to eat. I silently gnaw my way through all the food she brings me anyway, listening to my dark-days playlist. All the stuff that makes me want to pull my hood up and go out smashing stuff. There's the horrible tension of waiting, but I don't even know what I'm waiting for. Someone to come and tell me everything's okay? Someone to poke me and wake me up?

Just after midday, the social worker drops off a duffel bag which the foster lady deposits in the doorway of my room. They've packed enough to get me through a few nights. It might be respite, or it might not be. They haven't decided yet, but more than likely, it's just the stepping stone between two placements. They've included just enough to last me until the rest of my stuff is boxed up and moved to a new placement. Whoever packed my bag did it in haste and clearly didn't like the idea of touching my underwear, because my bras and knickers are all inside a basketball vest. They've missed out my MacBook and the picture of my mum, but remembered to put a messy handwritten note in.

I'm sorry. Chin up. You're not crazy.

I bet it was Vince. Amando was out on a plumbing job in south-west London, far out in the suburbs. Charmaine probably had her phone on silent. Even if they got hold of her, what's the chance she'd want to see me after I totalled her kitchen anyway?

Everyone's jumping in my DMs asking me if I'm okay, what's going on, rah rah rah. Vince, Junior, Reuben, Michael – even Shadavia is dropping me messages. I half read them and then post a generic reply on my Snapchat story.

LEAVE ME ALONE.

Then I switch it off.

Shucking my school uniform and flinging it on the bed, I change and slump on the carpet, head on my forearms, waiting for the end of the world. The only time I sit up is when the door opens and food appears. Later, I briefly venture downstairs to say hello to that open bottle of ginger wine sitting in the cupboard. It pays to be observant, and this oh-so-kind foster lady probably thought it was safe there. She didn't realise that I noticed when she was getting beans out. She also makes the mistake of leaving the room for fifty seconds while I'm 'washing the dishes', which is just enough time for me to decant the contents into my water bottle. Then I fill the ginger wine bottle with water, replace the lid, and slip it back into the cupboard. Once the dishes are washed, it's back upstairs to the prison cell.

Afternoon crawls into evening. The social worker doesn't show her face again. The foster lady's husband comes home from work and I stay behind my bedroom door, sipping my ginger wine secretly. My portable phone charger runs out of juice. Fifty per cent left on my phone and nobody put my charging lead in my overnight bag. Tch.

I pull out an old homework sheet and scrawl the answers, then doodle all over the back. On seeing this, the foster lady brings some 'mindfulness' colouring for me. I squint at the tiny shapes and shut the book of psychedelic patterns.

Evening fades into night and my ginger wine goes down until I'm sprawled on the floor half asleep. Next thing I know the foster lady is coming up with a glass of milk to tell me I should get ready for bed as I'm probably staying the night.

Somewhere inside me, something appreciates her effort, and I want to take the milk with a smile but instead I take it was a screw-face because she has no idea about the rules Charmaine and I made together. What I can drink when and how much. She doesn't know that this mug of milk will likely render me sticky and wet tomorrow morning. Charmaine and I sorted out a bed-wetting alarm, but that's at home in my dresser. My dresser which won't be my dresser in forty-eight hours' time.

I look at the glass of milk. Why am I still sat here like I'm waiting for something? I told them I wanted to be left alone and that's exactly what they're doing. What should I expect?

The foster lady leaves me staring at the glass of milk, turning it slowly in my hands like Japanese green tea. It's not her fault that she doesn't know about itchy sheets and heavy blankets and sleep patterns.

Something drips off my cheek and lands in the middle of the liquid. I watch the milk ripple as it receives one, two, three more drops, and then wipe my eyes.

Just drink the stuff. You're staying the night, maybe two nights. Nobody cares anymore. You don't care anymore.

Don't I?

Imagine another repeat of Day One. Dragging the suitcase up the stairs while another Charmaine shows me around; another ice breaker with somebody who's not Shadavia hovering in my doorway, asking me obvious questions: 'You don't like moving, do you?' Them looking at my unpacked suitcase, at me lying on my back on the floor, trying to disappear – waiting, then asking, 'What are you listening to?'

Do I care if I lose the Vince that persuaded me to ride on his handlebars? 'Just lean back. Yeah, like that. And relax. I won't let you fall.' Confidence so brash that he was oblivious to the fact that I went all stiff when he got too close. Up and down the curb we went, bump-bump, swerving around at the corner so quick that I screamed, and speeding back towards where Charmaine was filming, unaware that the boy who isn't really her son was planning to fart big-time as he passed the camera. And his voice, hot in my ear. 'Now do you trust me?' The look his face when I shook my head. I don't need to see that again, do I?

I put the milk aside. There's no dry mat here. No alarm. The only thing I've got to help me out is my brilliant lie complex. And anyway, my head feels like a jar of honey.

Dragging my heavy limbs, I change into a pair of relatively invaluable basketball shorts, plump up a pillow and curl up on the floor.

It's just like Daddy said when he dropped me at school once. *You're on your own, kiddo.*

The door vibrates with five hard knocks. 'Kadie?'

Okay, so I'm not entirely asleep. More like in a drunken daze.

The door vibrates again. 'Hellooo . . . Kadie?'

A sudden cold comes over me. I roll over to face the wall, nearly knocking over the milk. 'Don' wanna see anyone.'

'It's Charmaine.'

Can't be Charmaine. She's out on a conference thingy. With her phone off. Either that or tidying up her kitchen.

I raise my voice. 'Don'twannaseeanyone. Atall.'

'I know. I can see the sign you left on the door.'

'Go away.' Then I contradict myself. 'Why've you come here?'

'If you let me in, I'll tell you,' she says in her most patient foster mum voice.

I let her in. This takes a bit of effort, since I can't stand that well as my feet are apparently numb. Charmaine puts an arm out to steady me as I yank the door open, stumbling into the wall. Her face registers something, but she manages to look pretty unperturbed. She plants herself on the floor, against the wall. 'I came to pick you up,' she says right away. No hello. Not a word about earlier.

'Pick me up for what?' I ask flatly. My head feels like a bubble.

'To take you home.'

'Home?' I glance down at my pyjamas and laugh unexpectedly hard. 'Laugh at Goldilocks, why don't you.'

Charmaine just looks at me.

I curl my lip. 'The social worker said they were finding a different placement.'

'I know. We knew from the start that we were supposed to appeal for help if we needed it, and today a lot of people just tried to point out every reason why you should be moved.' Charmaine moistens her lips. She's *nervous*. Of course she's nervous. I backed out a knife at school today. I overturned tables and threw chairs and bit and swore and screamed. Anyone sane would be nervous around me.

'There was a very heated discussion, but eventually we won. I'd rather have been at home doing ironing than go through that to be honest, but there you go.' She laughs dryly, pushing her hair off her face.

I pull fluff out of the carpet. 'Why didn't you appeal for help?'

She sighs. 'A lot of reasons. I thought we were actually getting somewhere.'

We were.

'And also,' she adds, 'I was saving that for if things really kicked off at home.'

'They did.'

'Yeah, they did.' She shrugs. 'But that's why our plates and cups are mostly plastic.'

She waits for me to laugh or something. I carry on picking fluff out of the carpet for a hot minute, until my voice comes back. 'So what now?'

Charmaine stands, shouldering her bag. 'You can come home with me, and we'll talk tomorrow. Or when you're ready.'

'Is that it?'

'It?' She looks confused. 'Were you expecting a catch?'

'So I'm definitely not moving?'

'Not while I'm alive.'

'One hundred percent?'

'One hundred and twenty percent,' she says firmly. Her mouth twitches as if she might say something else – an 'unless' – but she doesn't.

Charmaine watches me pack the bag that's not mine and carries it for me to the car. She waits until we're nearly home before she breaks the silence. 'I've got some good news for you.'

I peer at her from the corner of my eye. I'm still on guard, half waiting for things to take a sudden turn for the worse.

'Is it about Dayan?'

She puffs out a breath. 'No, sorry. I don't really know much about what's going on with him, except that he's in hospital. They're probably going to keep him there for forty-eight hours.'

I shut my eyes. The thought of the blow-up with Shadavia this morning suddenly makes me feel a bit sick.

'Shadavia knew it was going to happen.' I say it with my eyes closed still, pressing my knuckles into the bridge of my nose.

'I know.' Charmaine doesn't even sound a bit surprised.

'And she didn't do nothing about it.'

'Who told you that?'

I kiss my teeth. 'Are you mad? She said so herself. "You know how they are." And, "Lips is gonna get boxed".'

'Mm? Well, she told me that she'd talked to Dayan recently and warned him.'

I snort, but then she adds, 'And I saw the messages. She wasn't lying.'

'She's a two-faced snake.'

'Please watch your tongue,' Charmaine says. 'Look, I know you're upset, but I'd like you to remember that you don't always know everything. The same way I discovered I don't

346

always know everything. I know you've had an extremely difficult time with friendships, but Shadavia has as well. Not as much as you by far, but more than you know.'

I close my mouth. She could be right there. After all, who was the one who begged me to put the knife away?

Charmaine lets me mull that over for a minute, and then changes the subject. 'The good news is that I've been talking to your year leader again, and your tutor, about what we can do to try and get you some more help.'

She peeks at me. I stare ahead blankly. I'd forgotten about all that, in the midst of the madness. More counselling. Whoohoo!

'Your counsellor, Andi, was agreeing with me about cognitive therapy,' Charmaine says. 'We decided that I would speak to you and then the three of us can meet up to discuss the options. And today has essentially confirmed my thoughts about this. We've nailed most of the things that are holding you back, but there's still . . . something that's not quite right.' She pauses. 'I feel as though I'm missing it.'

You are.

But I'm still feeling raw, emotionless, so instead of speaking that thought, I say, 'Why? You afraid I'm gonna do a Dayan and pop some pills?'

Charmaine wrenches the car onto our road. 'Kadie! How could you say something like that?'

She's right to ask, but there wasn't a hint of humour in my voice. Maybe I haven't done a Dayan, but I've definitely done something else, and I haven't had the guts to stand up and tell someone.

I press my head against the window and watch the houses go by. 24, 26, 28. My fingers clutch the bottom of my hoodie sleeve, my thumb rubbing the inside of my wrist. Around and around and up and down. Around and around and up and down. Number 34, 36, 38, 42. Charmaine pulls the van onto the drive and yanks the handbrake. 'Did you hear what I said?' she demands, giving me a steely look.

'Yeah.' My fingers are trembling. I make myself look at her. 'I'm sorry.'

A flicker of surprise crosses Charmaine's face. She nods.

'I didn't mean it like that,' I say, my voice withering away.

Charmaine stops halfway through opening the door. 'That's not an excuse.'

I reach up and switch on the ceiling light. She's not making this easy. But am I entitled to have it easy?

'It just came out that way because I know how it feels,' I explain. And then I pull back my sleeve and show her the no man's land. She shuts the car door then, turning all her attention back to me. Her expression changes from confusion to horror, her mouth dropping into an O of disbelief and then acceptance as she tilts my arm to the faint light, glancing between the scars and my face.

I wait for her to start interrogating me, for her disappointment in my lack of communication.

Instead she asks, 'How long?'

I shrug. 'Doesn't matter. Emerson's gone now anyway.'

'Emerson,' Charmaine repeats, as it computes in her head. She exhales, clearly trying to calm herself. 'Oh, Kadie, I wish you'd said something.'

'I did. I told you not to touch me.'

Charmaine shakes her head. 'This is why I was constantly hugging Andi and Mr Fishwick. This is exactly why I don't know as much as I would like to or as much as I think I do.'

'Bet you weren't bugging them as much as I do,' I whisper. I try to smile, but it wobbles and crumples and then I'm crying for so many reasons.

I did it – I told my biggest secret.

I also broke the first two rules. I'd broken them before since coming here, but I've broken them again just for good measure.

There goes the little voice in my head. *There's no going back now. It's all downhill from here.*

A pang of fear opens up in my chest and I wrestle to keep it under control, covering my mouth to block the sobs from escaping. Charmaine is out of the van in a flash and for a moment I think she's leaving me. But then she runs around to my side and flings open the door to put her arms around me as I stumble out of the van. For once, I let her – and I'm hyper-aware of her hand, rubbing circles in my back, and my head which just about rests on her shoulder because I'm nearly taller than her, and the fact that for once, I don't want to pull away.

'It's going to be okay,' Charmaine says to my back. 'We're all here for you. We're going to get you sorted.'

I sniff, fumbling to find my composure, and surprise myself. 'I'm scared.'

'Scared of what, honey?'

If she'd said that to me four months ago, I'd have sucked my teeth. But now I'm too worn down to feel demeaned.

I'm scared of breaking the rules.

But I can't say that to her, so I don't say anything.

'You're strong, you know,' Charmaine tells me, as I finally pull away. 'You're stronger than you know.'

'I'm not.'

'You are. What you just told me proves that.'

I frown and drag my overnight bag from the passenger seat of the car. Doesn't what I just told her confirm that I'm *not* strong?

Charmaine seems to read my expression. 'The fact that you told me is the strength,' she explains. 'It might seem small in the grand scheme of things, but right now, it's not.'

I pull my hood tight. 'That sounds like a cheesy motivational quote.'

Charmaine seems to restrain herself and eventually manages a smile. 'Gwaan, cheeky. Let's get inside.'

I turn towards the house. All the lights are off – understandable, since it's, like, ten pm. But then one comes on in the bedroom and the curtains ruffle in one of the front windows as a little brown head appears, her 'fro all wrapped up in her pink scarf for the night. The scream is mostly muffled by the window. The wild knocking on the glass is not. When Beverly pulls off her scarf so that her hair explodes in all its frizzy glory and disappears from the window, a fresh round of tears spills from my eyes. I have to cover my mouth again – this time to stop myself from laughing.

THIRTY

Charmaine tries to keep me busy, but it's hard to be so busy that I forget the state of things. The mandem are keeping me posted while they're at school, but what I really need to know is what's going on with Dayan. The forty-eight hours that he spent in hospital are up now, but when I asked if Charmaine could drop me at his, she told me that he was 'recovering emotionally' still and needed some space. This may or may not be true. What was definitely the truth was that he just wants to be alone. This was a message that came directly from Dayan's mother. And the mandem.

But here I am nonetheless, standing outside my guy's house, driven mad from lack of messages. His family's car is in the drive but I know for a fact that he's started doing half-days back at school, and since it's past twelve, he should be home. I'm not supposed to be out at all, and I'm going to get an earful if Charmaine gets home from Asda and finds that I've gone AWOL (never mind that I left her a note). I've been on lockdown since the Emerson incident. Part of me wonders whether that's for everyone else's safety or my own sanity. Right now, I don't care.

I select a few rounded pebbles off his front drive and aim my throws carefully so that they hit the top right front window, where Dayan's room is. The *tink!* noise echoes all the way down the street.

I freeze. Then continue. This is for my fam. I'll take the rap.

After eight pebbles, approximately ten seconds apart, the window opens and the curtain ruffles as a shadow appears behind it.

Dredging up a humorous tone, I take my chance. 'Oh roadman, roadman, wherefore art thou, roadman?'

Silence.

I swallow and drop the rest of the pebbles. Maybe this wasn't such a good idea. Maybe he's not ready.

'That's wrong.' Up above, the curtain presses against the window and I glimpse a brown hand. 'I'm sure it's Juliet who says "where farteth thou, Romeo?".'

'Nah, fam. There's no farting in that scene. Not even in the Leo DiCaprio version.'

'You mean to tell me my revision notes are all wrong?' he asks dryly.

'Yep.' This isn't right. How is he coming at me with the same sarcasm as always, when days ago he was in a dangerous place?

My heart pounds, anxiety churning up all the questions I want to ask but know I shouldn't. The silence between us seems to dry out my throat and finally I manage to croak, 'You haven't been answering my DMs and I got really worried, you know? I just came to see how you are.'

Again, he answers with silence.

I rub the inside of my arm where I used to run Emerson's blade. 'I know how you feel.'

The curtain flaps slightly. Looks like he's moving away.

'I'm sorry,' I say to the living room window. 'I don't . . . know what to think anymore. Everything's so confusing. I don't blame you for not reaching out to anyone.'

'It's not your fault.' His voice is so quiet I can barely hear him, but he's there, somewhere behind the curtain.

'Yeah, but . . .' I trail off, remembering the day when Josh taunted him. I said something, but I said it too late. I saw those Snaps and I didn't tell anyone, not even his mum. Doesn't that make me one of the guilty parties?

'You want to come in, don't you?' Dayan asks.

I shrug. 'No. I shouldn't even be here, really.'

'That's everybody's cop-out, bruh.'

'The boys have been by—'

'Don't try making excuses for them.' He sounds tired, as if he's heard about them one too many times. I open my mouth to try and backtrack, to defend the boys who defended him even when it was too late, but the curtain flaps and Dayan is gone again.

Guess that's that.

But then a minute later the front door opens a crack and Dayan slips out in his socks, wrapped up in a puffer jacket, his hood and obligatory snapback – New York Yankees today – pulled so far over his face that most of his features are cast in shadow. He sits down on the front step and looks up at me, and in that second I see the blotches of purple around his eyes and jaw. They're fading, but still bad enough to make me grit my teeth in anger. To think there was a time when I thought Josh would make a good boyfriend.

I wedge myself on the other half of the doorstep, trying to contain my inner heartbreak at the state of Dayan's face. It's one thing for one of them to betray someone like me who they've hardly known – but for them to fail to support someone who's been a long-term friend – and yeah, their back story's a bit weird, but Dayan is a friend – is just appalling. It fills my eyes with genuine angry tears.

'I'm sorry,' I mumble.

Dayan pulls his hood further over his face. 'Is it true you got excluded?'

Ugh. Here we go. 'Yeah.'

'Tough times.'

'Uh-huh.' You don't say.

'Are you moving?'

I glance at him; he's staring at the fake rip in his jeans. 'No. I need my friends.'

His shoulders jerk at that. Whether surprise or frustration I don't know. 'I don't know who mine are anymore.'

It's not a question, but oddly enough the statement feels directed at me. We sit in silence for a few moments. When he speaks he blinks hard, obviously trying to keep his cool. 'I'm just proper scared still,' he says eventually, staring at his feet. 'No one was there when I needed backup, time after time after time – isn't that what friends are for? Like, that day I was running and running and hoping maybe someone would stick their neck out for me. I can't even tell you how many kids just watched us go by and didn't do jack about it, even when I was on the floor being kicked. Tch. People are stupid. Everything's stupid.' He pauses. 'What I did was stupid.'

'It wasn't stupid,' I say without thinking.

'It was. They chased me into a park and took my phone. If I hadn't bumped into that lady and told her . . . Yeah, it was.'

'It was,' I agree, 'but—'

'The reasons weren't,' we say together.

'I was scared,' he admits, after a moment. 'I'm still scared.' He exhales sharply. 'I don't even know who's on my side anymore.' Finally, he looks at me and his eyes are welling up in a way that really shakes me.

I nudge my elbow into his side gently. 'I'm on your side.'

He leans closer and lets me put my arms around him.

'And if the mandem aren't already on your side, I'll make them be.'

Dayan groans a little. 'You can't make them see.'

'I can lead a horse to water.'

He moves back, composes himself, and wipes his eyes. 'Yeah. I guess people do change occasionally.'

This surprises me. 'You speaking of someone we know?'

'Yeah.' He gives me a wobbly smile. 'I never thought Shadavia would be jumping in my DMs again. She really backed me up about Josh and that. Their story was that I took Ellis's tie so that's why they chased me. Which is a lie, because I only got hold of Ellis's tie when he started on me. So yeah, respect to Shadavia for having the guts to snitch.'

A flush of anger goes through my body at the memory of that morning, the way one thing led to another. I feel my screw-face coming on.

He adds quickly, 'Nothing is going on. For real.'

'What kind of nothing?'

'The kind where we just straighten things out between us so we're just cool.'

Just cool.

It would be nice if we could be 'just cool'.

'Maybe you two should talk about stuff as well,' he suggests.

I shake my head and laugh. 'Yeah, because Shadavia and I are really on "deep talk" level at the moment.'

'Give it some thought.'

I flip the conversation back at him. 'What about the mandem?'

Dayan stares ahead and says nothing. I wait twenty seconds and he doesn't say a word. Maybe he's not ready to think about them.

'I'll talk to them when I'm ready,' he mutters.

'I promise you,' I say softly, 'they honestly did stick up for you that day. The last time I saw them they were going to

357

chase down Aidan and the rest to ask them what they were doing with your phone. And apparently after that a scrap broke out. I didn't see it, but it went on Snapchat.'

Dayan huffs a little. 'Huh. I must've missed that.'

We sit there for a little longer, listening to the faint buzz of life around us. Our shoulders are touching a little and I wonder if it makes his heart jumpy. Part of my brain is very conscious of it and is spewing butterflies into my stomach. The other part is just enjoying it, because friends can enjoy sitting shoulder to shoulder without saying anything.

Eventually, Dayan stands. 'Thanks for coming to see me,' he mumbles.

I nod. 'You can count on me for that.'

A smile flickers across his face, disappearing as quickly as it comes. He takes a breath. 'I just wish . . . I wish . . .' He trails off.

'I spend a lot of time saying the same.' I shrug.

Dayan turns to his front door and slips inside. 'Guess I'll see you around.'

'Do I get a goodbye hug or something?' I ask his back, but the door's already closing.

'Roadmen don't do cuddles,' he whispers. And then the door clicks shut.

THIRTY-ONE

I'm not supposed to be anywhere near the school. Exclusion rules. It's the weekend so it doesn't really matter, but I still feel my naughty streak flaring as I roll past King's Manor College on my hoverboard.

They suspended me for two weeks up to the court trial and after that – when they let me go with a community order, a curfew, and a referral for anger management therapy – they made the final decision. Apparently they needed a 'final decision' because somebody told them about the trolls. I didn't expect to get any support, but after the creator of the fake Goldilocks account was mysteriously discovered, suddenly loads of people were jumping on this anti-bullying thing. Word is that Kelly was the culprit. She must've got done for something, because she was excluded for two weeks as well – along with Ellis, Josh and Aidan. Dayan somehow managed to upload a shaky video of them chasing him before school, and also one of them was stupid enough to post a snippet of a video of the three-on-one beating.

Junior says I'm still on the register, but they're already talking about moving me to the next nearest school and I've been stuck studying at home until things get straightened out. Charmaine did her best with that battle for the sake of maintaining my friendships, but with Emerson in the picture, she was never going to win.

I'd like to say I don't care. But I can't help slowing down to stare at the school that used to be mine, and wishing things could've gone differently. A new school is the last place I want to be now, and even if I deserve it I'm still scared, deep down, that this is just the start of another cycle.

I reach the circle of shops a few blocks down from the school exactly on the hour, just like I planned. Six hours' on-and-off sleep is an improvement on the usual three to four, but progress is going to be slow.

'Alright?' Tia materialises at my shoulder. I teeter too far to one side, sending my hoverboard into a spin, and fall off. She watches me, smirking slightly, and adds, 'Haven't seen you for some time.'

'Yeah, you could say that.' I'm not sure how to act. Before I got kicked out, she was just like all the rest. Neutral around me, laughing behind my back. As of three weeks ago, she and Junior started a #baitoutthebullies thing on Snapchat, for anyone that didn't hear the rumours about how it went down. She messages me sometimes as well, as if we're old friends who drifted apart. She's a bit like Shadavia. Still confusing me.

'Where do you go to school now?' Tia asks.

I eye her cautiously. 'No one's told you?'

She tuts. 'I was just asking.'

So she's not messing me around. 'That girls' school couple miles west,' I tell her, a little more nicely. 'I mean, I think I'm starting there soon.'

'So you're not coming back.'

'Dunno. Kelly's mum doesn't wanna see some knife-wielder in the same school as her precious innocent daughter.' I shrug. 'It's cool. I just keep my head down. Don't get involved in anyone's business.'

Tia smiles and looks at the floor. She starts texting but lingers by my side. People have been doing that a lot lately. It's like I've become a celebrity due to being kicked out, or maybe because of 'Crazy'. Suddenly I'm Goldilocks again, not the girl being laughed at 24/7. I'm not sure why people think that this means I'm instant best friends with everyone.

'Why you loitering?' I demand.

'Calm yourself,' Tia says airily. 'Michael asked me to come to the video shoot. He said you'd be okay with it.' She peers at me for confirmation. 'I messaged you as well, but you obviously never check your DMs.'

I narrow my eyes. 'I've been working hard, you know. I don't have time for people who aren't sure whose side they're on.'

'So we're cool?' she asks pointedly.

'Are you asking permission?'

She folds her arms. 'Are you always this difficult?'

'I'm picky, yeah. In case you haven't noticed, I haven't exactly been the most popular person around these days.'

Tia sucks her teeth. Yep, I've annoyed her by skirting round her question. She must be for real.

I eye up her trainers. Some nice Jordans, matching her tracksuit – looks like she keeps them in tip-top condition, which seems about right. Tia's always been pristine at school, right from her polished pumps up to her slicked edges and mascara. I mean, in school even her blazer looks pristine.

'Hey, where do you get your creps?' I ask.

'Mostly JD Sport,' Tia says without looking up from Snapchat. 'My sister gets a staff discount. But these are from the States.'

'They're fresh still, you know.'

She wiggles one foot. 'Thanks.' She checks my face to make sure I'm serious and relaxes.

I get back on my hoverboard and practise keeping it in one place. I still haven't got the hang of it yet, so it jerks back and forth as if I have no control.

A crowd of kids appears around the corner, chattering and laughing loudly. I turn, ready to greet them – Junior promised they'd be here by now – but it dies on my tongue. It's the Kelly clique, and they're too close for comfort.

Tia peers around me and sucks her teeth. I try to distract myself by looking the other way for Junior's familiar blue hat, but even from my peripheral there's no missing the screw-face Kelly throws me as the group passes. She's doing her best to

362

look on-point, but no amount of makeup is going to hide the healing scar across her face.

I tighten my jaw and glare right back.

'Thought you were in the sin bin,' Kelly says lightly.

I look her dead in the eye. A snotty response is about to roll off my tongue like normal – after all, some things never change – but Tia deepens her scowl and points a perfect nail down the road. 'Beat it, before I get the squad on you.'

Raquel laughs. 'What squad? You don't even like her.'

'Oi, stop it.' Shadavia waves the argument away with one hand. 'Just move on.'

Kelly rolls her eyes. 'Yeah, let's not waste our time.'

She starts to walk away. Raquel and Eisha follow, but Shadavia lingers. Kelly spins around, hands spread. 'Aren't you coming?'

Shadavia looks at the floor. She hasn't looked anyone in the eye much since the incident. 'I told you. I'm linking AMD for a video shoot.'

'So you're ditching us.'

Shadavia shrugs.

Kelly looks like she's about to blow a fuse. Her lip curls. 'You're a little snake!'

'Hisssss,' Shadavia says sarcastically.

Kelly sighs. 'Fine. Do what you want. I don't care.' She spits on the floor by my hoverboard.

Shadavia's head jerks up, eyes narrowed. 'If you spit at Kadie one more time—'

'What?' Kelly challenges. 'What are you gonna do?'

Shadavia shuts her mouth.

That familiar heat opens up inside me again. I step off my hoverboard, fists at the ready. I'm not taking this. Not for a second time.

Tia puts her arm out to stop me and I grab her, ready to push her off, but she holds her own just long enough for me to notice that she's looking past me, down the road. 'I think that's our ride.'

So it is.

The Hummer pulls up to the curb, engine purring, and a second later the back door pops open and Reuben and Junior get out, the sound of music and chatter following them from inside. Neither of them seem to notice Kelly, whose face is about melting off with surprise and possibly envy. Even Eisha is studying the door as if she'd rather be inside.

'My girrrl,' Junior drawls, giving me and Tia both a high five. 'You ready for this?'

Reuben looks between Shadavia and me. 'You sure you're okay with her coming?'

I nod. It takes all my willpower not to throw Kelly another screw-face. 'We're cool.'

'Good. Let's go.'

He clambers back into the Hummer. Shadavia and Tia squeeze in after him.

Junior glances left and right. 'Where's Lips?'

'Lips?' I peek inside the Hummer. 'I thought he was with you.'

'He said he was meeting us here.'

There is a moment of silence.

'I hope he's okay, you know.' Junior rubs his face. 'He hasn't been the same.'

No duh. He's been in contact with the boys, apparently, but no amount of coaxing would make him let them into the house, even after I told him I'd explained the Snapchat deal to them. I'd even showed them some of the unopened Snaps, when they came to get his phone to take it back to him. They were really vexed after that and I could see it was genuine, but Dayan was still sceptical.

He still *is* sceptical.

'I wouldn't be surprised if he hates me.' Junior traces his toe along the curb. 'Wouldn't blame him either. It was like he said. I didn't have his back when it really mattered.'

'Took you long to realise, huh?'

Junior play-punches me.

'He doesn't hate you,' I say.

'How do you know?'

'I've been there. It takes a lot to really hate someone.' I'm looking at Kelly as I say this. She's finally got the idea and is storming off with Raquel and Eisha, who both keep glancing back. 'Hate is a strong word.' It's usually the right word – I hate bullies, hate rejection, hate being moved – but somehow it takes a lot for me to put it in front of a name.

'I kind of hoped this would be the start of making it up.' Junior gestures to the Hummer. 'He always said he wanted to do a fancy video, you know.'

I spin in wobbly circles on my hoverboard. 'Bruv, a Hummer isn't gonna make up for what you did or didn't do.'

'You think the song will?'

'I don't know if he even listened to it.' I'd sent him the link – the song, 'Sunny', is all produced and just waiting on today's video shoot to be released. Michael found it one day while we were brainstorming ways to cheer him up. The boys had recorded Lips' verse and the chorus ages ago and then it got forgotten, so we thought it would be an appropriate riddim to resurrect. The chorus is something like:

We gon ride when it's sunny
Swag from head to toe
We put on a show
We gon ride with the honeys
Only my team around
Listen to our sound
We been making that money
Don't throw shade it ain't funny
You know she like my hair all tufty
Got my chain and I'm looking all cunning
But it's true I only ride when it's sunny

We'd thought he'd be chuffed to hear that we were bringing back an unfinished project. But I haven't heard

366

anything back from him. Reuben had told me that the song was like a declaration of friendship, but then it never got finished – which was, as I pointed out, slightly symbolic in an unfortunate manner. Junior had pretended to kick my bum then.

'What did he say when you called him?' Junior asks.

'Not much. Just that he'd be here.'

The driver of the Hummer kills the engine, leaving us in relative silence. I hold my phone tight, but it stays quiet and still. Junior stares at the ground.

I count two minutes and forty-seven seconds before Dayan comes around the corner on his hoverboard. He rolls up with his special air of nonchalance, stepping off when he gets near and plodding up to us with that familiar roadman-cross-toddler gait. To look at him, you'd think nothing has changed. The snapback's perched sideways today. Jeans on point – a little bit low with the wonky belt and a giant Superman buckle.

'Alright, my man?' Junior lifts a fist to bump.

Dayan ignores the fist and shoves him hard. 'Wasteman.'

'Bruv—' Junior protests, but Dayan's already greeting me. 'Alright, Goldilocks?'

I nod, not sure if I want to hug him or thump him for nearly standing us up.

Dayan catches sight of Shadavia through the open back door of the Hummer. 'Who invited Kelly's minion?'

'I did.' I cross my arms. 'I thought you and her were cool now.'

'We are.' He wiggles his eyebrows. 'I was just checking your reaction. I knew she was coming.'

'Wait. You two have been talking?' I start getting in his face. 'But you've been airing me.'

Dayan looks sheepish. 'I was waiting for the ideal moment.'

'The ideal moment for what? To apologise?'

'Apologise?'

'For scaring me out of my mind!'

Michael pokes his head out of the Hummer. 'Goldilocks, if we're gonna get into this apologies thing, you owe me two. One for getting kicked out of school and one for all that dead-end flirting.'

'Bruv, you're irrelevant.'

The driver of the Hummer pokes his head out of the window. 'You're all going to be irrelevant if you don't get in soon.'

Junior turns to get in the Hummer. 'Just kiss and make up already, you two.'

Dayan waits until Junior has disappeared into the car. Then he pulls something out of his back pocket. Something red and brown and small.

'I remembered about the death of Homo Sapiens Rubber Butt,' he says. It hadn't taken him two days to notice when said Rubber Butt disappeared off my school bag, but I never told him that the cause of this was murder. Nonetheless, he's holding out a new one in his palm. 'So I made you another one.'

He hands the rubber band person to me. It is almost identical to Homo Sapiens Rubber Butt, apart from the brown strands of hair sticking out from the head.

'Eve Rubber Butt,' Dayan announces, adjusting his snapback, 'meet Adam Rubber Butt. Totally original.' He produces another Rubber Butt (also complete with brown hair which sticks straight up in the air), adding regrettably, 'I didn't know how to make Eve's hair curly. There is no making an Afro with a rubber band.'

There's a smile spreading across my face. I fight it.

'You can stop acting now,' Dayan says, running Adam Rubber Butt along my shoulder and into my ear. 'We both know you want to cry.'

'Who's acting? You're the one who was moving like it was all okay.'

He arches one eyebrow. 'So were you. I knew there was more to that knife than you said.'

'Have a gold star.'

'Thank you.'

'You're welcome.'

'You gonna get in the car?'

'No.'

'Why not?'

'You owe me an apology.'

He lolls his head. 'You're too stubborn.'

'Me, stubborn? You're stubborn.'

'Okay.' He inches into my personal space. 'How about a truce? No more heart attacks, no more acting, no more lying. From you or me.'

'If you two don't get in here now, we're leaving without you!' Junior yells.

Dayan sticks out his pinky finger. 'Promise me.'

I link my little finger around his and tug.

He pulls me close, harder than necessary, and wraps his other arm around me so that we're pressed together tight, his lips in my freshly-slicked hair and my face in his chest. Today he smells like half a bottle of aftershave and brand-new jumper.

'No more madness, yeah?' he whispers.

'No more madness. I promise.'

'I promise.' We move apart, but he's still so close that his breath is tickling my nose and lips.

'What are you doing?' I ask.

'I don't know. Just . . .' He screws up his face for a moment. 'I wanted a hug. A friends' hug.' He studies my face. 'We're friends, right?'

I rest my head back on his chest and breathe in his too-strong aftershave. 'Yeah.'

'Friends can hug each other?'

'Friends can hug each other.' I hold him tight.

'But there is a Zone Two, right?' Dayan asks hopefully.

'Zone Two?'

'As in, outside the friend zone. Or maybe inside.'

I laugh and push him away gently. 'Yeah, obviously. Just not right now.'

'Oh. Poop.'

'There is this thing called *future*,' I remind him.

He makes a perplexed eyebrow-arch. 'I thought you didn't believe in that stuff.'

I touch my lips with the tip of one finger. 'I don't. But I have a good imagination.'

Dayan's smile stretches into a grin. He watches me adjust my clothes and says, 'That can be our secret.'

'Cool. I'm good at keeping secrets.'

'Oi!' Junior pokes his head out of the Hummer. 'When I said kiss and make up, I didn't mean literally!'

Dayan pulls another Rubber Butt out of his pocket and tosses it to him. 'Chill, man. We're coming.'

Junior looks at the Rubber Butt. 'Is this what you were working on during the Maths test yesterday?'

'Yes. It's a peace offering.' Dayan scrambles into the Hummer and wedges himself between me and Tia. He glances at Michael. 'What was that you said about me not having any girls?' Then he sits there looking smug until his smile sets off laughter.

The driver revs the engine of the Hummer and I feel it vibrate through my feet, in my skin. The eight of us are tightly packed into the back, our legs pressing into each other, the ceiling low and the lighting almost lower. Somebody's phone starts to ring – something Ed Sheeran – and Michael and Tia start singing.

Across from me, Shadavia is watching my knee do its perpetual jiggle, while my fingers tap-tap on my other knee. I catch her eye and grin and she sticks her tongue out. Reuben's taking bare snaps on his phone and Lips is posing. The vibe's so clear of negativity that it feels as if a boulder has been lifted off my chest. I mean, the lies and the anger are definitely still there, deep down. So is the craving for Emerson. He hasn't been replaced but is now a story that everyone who needs to know is aware of. Those sorts of things don't just disappear; the scars are proof of that. The scars are proof that all of us are human. But the thing is, some of them are healing. The older ones are now just mars in the skin, a reminder that I had a way to deal, that it failed – but that I'm going to get through it because there's always a better way.

As always, the same words are going through my mind, like a reflex.

Follow the rules.

No one gets hurt.

Head says the rules are still there.

Heart says we don't need them.